Feathered Serpent Press

Filth Eater

Tlazolteotl

Filth Eater

Filth Eater

is

Printed in Palatino Linotype

ISBN 978-1-7345949-8-0

Printed in the United States of America

ABOUT THE AUTHOR

Stan Struble is a graduate of the famed Father Flanagan's Boys' Home, Boys Town, Nebraska, and holds an M.S. in Anthropology from Kansas State University, where he taught Social Anthropology and North American Indian courses. He is presently an Adjunct Professor of Social Sciences at Metropolitan College in Omaha, Nebraska. In addition to teaching anthropology and sociology courses at Metropolitan Community College, he manages a successful freelance writing career and is an occasional guest speaker on a variety of topics.

Stan has published five mystery-suspense novels, including *Filth Eater*, *Xibalba: In Search of the Lost Mayan Texts*, *Gospel of the Feathered Serpent, and In the Time of the Feathered Serpent*. *Xibalba* was published by Nowtilus of Madrid, Spain and was translated into several languages, including English, Spanish and Czech. All books received praise from print media and notable individuals, including Lew Hunter, Chairman Emeritus of the UCLA Screenwriting

School. All Stan's books are now available in English and Spanish.

Stan is a former three-time President of the Nebraska Writers Guild, Nebraska's oldest and most prestigious writers group. As a member of **MENSA**, the International High IQ Society, he was elected and served two terms as president of the local Mensa group.

Stan's unusual background and employment experiences include working offshore in the Gulf of Mexico, and living and working in the Sierra Madres of Jalisco and the coastal lowlands of Sinaloa on the Gulf of Baja. He is married, has three children and lives in Omaha, Nebraska.

Praise for Filth Eater

"This sure and exciting melodrama with archaeological thrills rivals Indiana Jones in entertainment and Dr. Leakey in information. Highest kudos for the entire family to read the *Filth Eater*."

Dr. Lew Hunter—UCLA Screenwriting Chair

"A skillful blend of anthropology and intrigue, *Filth Eater* is a real page-turner!"

Dr. Harriet Ottenheimer—Kansas State University

"In an intriguing blend of archeology, sexual titillation, and high-level political chicanery in Mexico in the 1980's, Stanley Struble presents a fast-paced scenario that will engage a spectrum of readers whose interest in Mexican culture may range from intense to non-existent."

Jim Tuck—Guadalajara Reporter

"A tale of brutality and murder for the sake of securing priceless artifacts, *Filth Eater* exposes sins of greed and gluttony aimed at procuring vast riches at any cost....sic...possess a vivid insight into the pitfalls of modern social structure."

Cheryl Golden—Omaha Reader

"An intriguing look at the Mexico of just a few years ago as well as a glimpse of the Spanish conquest and the problems it brought."

Sally Fellows—The Whole Truth Review

"A book of the first order – the use of Filth Eater's dialogue is innovative and effective." "Good parallels between the ancient Filth Eater and modern religious beliefs of sin and redemption."

Sierra Foothills Women's Club

Very Special Recognition

For Valerie, the encouraging midwife,
whose
sighs of frustration and sharp pencil led
to the birth of this book.

Thank You

To Father Flanagan's Boys' Home, Boys Town, Nebraska for helping me turn my life around. Words fail me when I think of what might have happened.

Very Special Acknowledgment

Without the patience, charity, and friendship of the Gonzalez-Corso family of Mexico City, Guadalajara, and San Cristobal de Las Casas this book and its sequels would never have been written. The significance of their contribution and the depth of their friendship cannot be expressed. Gracias and vaya con Dios, amigos.

Special Acknowledgment

Special thanks to anthropology Professors Harriet and Martin Ottenheimer of Kansas State University, who have gifted several generations of students with lenses through which they can view man's esoteric and seemingly bizarre behavior and make sense of it.

Filth Eater

by

Stanley L. Struble

Feathered Serpent Press

PROLOGUE

La Noche Triste (The Sad Night)

July 10, 1520 Tenochtitlan, Mexico

"Heathen bastard died when I needed him most," said Captain Cortez, standing within the Aztec temple. "Damn him anyway. He'll roast in hell for sure."

The captain glanced at Malinche, then back down at the dead god-king, Moctezuma. The monarch lay prone on a straw mattress, dressed in full regalia of quetzal feathers, turquoise, and gold ornaments. Death tinged his skin with its waxen, yellow pallor. A pervading, foul odor of blood and feces emanated from the body.

Malinche, Cortez's traitorous Indian guide, appeared terror stricken at the king's death. She reverently reached to retrieve a gold statuette of a woman giving birth that lay beside him. Earlier a filthy priest, stinking of dried blood and tobacco, had left it next to his dying king.

"What is it?" The captain's beard did little to hide a disapproving frown.

"It's Tlazolteotl," she said fervently. "It's the Filth Eater. She eats the sins and the filth of one's life. She gives absolution to the dying, so that they may enter the Paradise of the Sun."

"Pagan, heathenish nonsense!" Cortez tore it from her grasp and threw it onto a nearby pile of gold vessels, ornaments, and jewelry stolen from the Aztec Treasury. "It's an abomination. We'll give it to the King and Queen of Spain. They'll know what to do with it. They'll make good Spanish pieces-of-eight with it, they will." He turned abruptly and walked toward his horse, then stopped and turned to Malinche.

"You're a Christian now, remember?" His eyes burned with the fire of a zealot. "Only one God gives absolution from sin and it ain't any Filth Eater."

The Conquistadors numbered but a few hundred. Outside the temple in the blustering rain, stood Jaguar and Eagle knights at the head of armies numbering in the thousands, all bent on the Conquistador's complete destruction.

Cortez had allowed the Aztec king to believe that he, Cortez, was a god incarnate—the legendary Toltec king Quetzalcoatl—returning to claim the kingdom he had abandoned one thousand years earlier when he had dishonored himself with drunkenness and disappeared into the east. Thus Moctezuma had welcomed Cortez and his army into Tenochtitlan, the Aztec capitol city.

In the clear light of the afternoon Cortez had forced the Aztec king to the rooftop of the temple to encourage peace and to quell the anger of the Aztec's. But the people ignored their god-king and responded with darts, stones, and arrows, leaving Moctezuma mortally wounded. The Aztec king had died, and with him Cortez's one hope of escaping the island city. The Aztec army, huge and renowned for their savagery, believed that their king behaved as a fool and wanted to destroy the bearded, bleached faces from the east. The setting sun had brought Cortez, a great battlefield strategist, no solution to extricate his forces from their own trap. He was unprepared to reap the consequences of his lies, and knew that lingering in the temple would bring certain death. If caught, he and his men would be sacrificed to the voracious Humming-Bird-On-The-Left, the Aztec war god. If they were to live, the Conquistadors must take the gold and leave - now. Success or failure would be measured in one way—escape or death.

Each night, fearful of revenge from those whom they had conquered and demanded constant sacrifices, the Aztecs dutifully removed access to their city. Cortez had ordered makeshift bridge constructed of strong beams and planks to be to be transported and placed in position by the Conquistador's Indian allies. It would replace the missing section of viaduct on the causeway leading to the mainland and Tacuba. The bridge remained their only hope of escape, and Cortez knew that this would be a bloody night. Outside the storm raged unabated. Rain blew in relentless waves, pounding the walls and doors, daring him to sally forth and pay for his deceit.

After a quick prayer, he cursed silently and mounted his horse. With all nearly ready, he gave the order to load King Ferdinand's gold first, as one-fifth of all treasure belonged to the Crown. His band of usurpers and their traitorous Indian allies stuffed their pockets and loaded their horses with the remaining four-fifths of the Aztec Treasury. Unwilling to leave the fruits of their treachery behind, the soldiers filled every

15

available space within their armor with precious metal. Many were so heavily laden that they walked clumsily, encumbered by their wealth. Greed and disaster are sisters.

Fear soaked the air and permeated the nostrils of the horses. They stomped nervously and chomped on their iron bridles. Most suffered from open wounds incurred in battles of the last few days and some stood lame, favoring a leg, but all were heavily loaded.

Cortez ordered the bridge go first. A vanguard of 400 Indians and 150 soldiers were dispatched to carry it nearly a half a mile and place into position. They would guard the passage until the captain and his entourage could pass over and escape. With Cortez and his lieutenants in the lead, the Conquistadors left the shelter of the looted temple.

Throughout the city Jaguar and Eagle Knights harangued growing throngs, inciting them to attack the Spaniard army, accusing them of killing the king. "We are the Mexica!" they cried.

Suddenly the spark of rumor caught like tinder coaxed into flame: Cortez and his army were fleeing the island! An Eagle knight blew a call to arms on a conch shell, sounding a blast of warning throughout the canals and streets of the city. Others joined in, trumpeting the alarm to rouse the enemies of the Conquistadors and prevent their escape. Hundreds more grabbed obsidian-edged swords, spears, and clubs, then boarded canoes to cut off Cortez's escape on the causeway. If they caught him at the bridge before reaching the mainland, victory would be theirs.

The captain and his army met little resistance until they approached the movable bridge. As they engaged the Aztec warriors already in place, the battle began.

16

Cortez's heart pounded and his breath came in gasps. His arm grew weary from the weight of his steel sword as he charged forward into the melee, only to retreat from a sea of furious Aztecs dressed in feathered regalia and the hides of jaguars. Their obsidian bladed swords flashed and glinted in light reflected from the lake's water. Ahead, down the causeway, his army of Tlaxcalan Indians had been slaughtered and cast aside into Lake Texcoco, trying to defend the makeshift bridge. The heavens thundered with fury and rain fell in huge drops. Driven by powerful gusts of wind, the torment swept the causeway with stinging curtains, blinding the captain and his army. He couldn't see to strike and his sword grip slipped, slick from the rain. Fear pierced him like a spear of light when he again heard the trumpet of conch shells. As if by magic, canoes illuminated with thousands of torches lit up the lake on both sides of the causeway and the Aztecs began to sing while rowing toward the captain and his small army.

Cortez felt a surge of battle rage loosen the fear gripping his chest. 'It's now or die,' he told himself, then screamed, "Santiago!" at the top of his voice, rallying his men as he brandished his sword in the air for all to see. Urging his mount forward into the battle for the bridge, he heard echoing screams of "Santiago!" and the pounding of hooves from the rear.

Cortez and ten mounted men hit the bridge at full gallop, scattering and hurling Aztecs and his own men into the lake to be speared like fish in a barrel by canoes of Indians. The conquistador and his ten rode on. The tide of the battle stood momentarily in balance, then the Aztecs surged inward from both sides of the lake and onto the causeway, casting the bridge into Lake Texcoco.

17

Again the Aztecs burst into song as torch-lit canoes vied to reach Cortez's trapped army. Everywhere, bodies and horses fell into the chasm left by the missing bridge. Soldiers fought hand to hand on both sides of the gap. The Conquistadors, heavy with treasure, became easy prey and were swept into the lake to be killed. Hundreds divested them- selves of booty by hurling it into the lake, trying to save their lives, but for many death came before wisdom. The few remaining Conquistadors stood trapped on the causeway, surrounded by colorful banners and warriors of every level who came to avenge the death of their king. As the Indians sang, they slew Cortez's army and the lust of battle filled the Aztecs with joy.

The slaughter continued, and the space of the missing bridge was choked with abandoned baggage, gold, bodies of horses, and dead soldiers. This allowed a few desperate soldiers to slip and slide over a nightmare of rain, mud, and wounded and dead, clawing their way to the causeway road leading to Tacuba, a small city on the shore of the lake. They followed Cortez and his ten, staggering into Tacuba empty-handed, a day ahead of the Aztecs.

Shortly after midnight, his army destroyed and his Indian allies dispersed, Cortez sat and sobbed beneath an ahuehuete tree adding his tears to the soaked earth, bemoaning his fate and lost army. A brown-robed friar placed himself in front of the captain. With hands on hips, the priest berated the Cortez for abandoning the fight and his army to the Aztecs. He threatened him with hell-fire and damnation and threatened to withhold the sacraments if the captain did not take his lieutenants and engage the filthy pagans in battle at once! The friar screamed and harangued until Cortez remounted his bloodied horse and rode back down the causeway into the black, tempestuous night looking for survivors. He met only fleeing stragglers, and as he rode, Cortez swore the Aztecs would pay dearly for this Noche Triste, this sad night.

Cholo Skins His Knuckles

June 1, 1983, Mexico City's Famed Zona Rosa

Cholo Rodriguez, ex-Colombian sicario (drug soldier), sat behind the wheel of a rusty, white taxi in Mexico City's Zona Rosa. Most of the revelers had gone home. The taxi reeked of unwashed bodies and sour pulque, a viscous, fermented sap of the agave plant. His three hired zopilotes (vultures) slouched uncomfortably in the back seat. The zopilotes were recruited from a pulqueria in a neighboring barrio. They waited impatiently for the young archeologist, Juan Degas, and his girlfriend to appear. With Cholo calling the shots, they would give the young man a beating he would never forget.

Cholo's wristwatch said 3:00 a.m., the early morning hours before dawn. A lifelong thug and retired Medellin sicario, Cholo frowned and shifted his weight restlessly, unhappy with having to do this job. But his pesos were few and his needs great, and this sordid business brought a small bonus in addition to a monthly stipend. El Toro, his patron whom he had never met, had left explicit instructions taped to the underside of the seat in the church confessional. This was where Cholo usually received his instructions, and he knew it didn't matter why El Toro wanted the job done. Cholo was a good soldier and soldiers do as they are instructed. So he stole a taxi and left its owner dead in a pool of blood, one bullet hole in the back of his head

He squinted through thick-lensed, wire-rimmed glasses and pulled himself upright and stretched when his leg began to cramp. His bile rose and burned his throat as the effects of two prescription Tagamets and a joint of marijuana began to wear thin.

Where was the pinche bastard? Would he spend the whole night drinking and dancing? Frustrated, he popped an antacid into his mouth and shifted forward, leaning onto the steering wheel.

Then they appeared! The couple paused to embrace, then walked hand-in-hand in the direction opposite their parked car, away from Cholo and his henchmen. Degas and his girlfriend moved unsteadily, laughing and conversing as they walked toward El Parque Violeta where several groups of sequined mariachis serenaded starry-eyed lovers.

The Colombian's thoughts raced. It was doable. He looked at the distant park and its occupants, then surveyed the empty streets for wit- nesses. Satisfied, he shushed the zopilotes, started the taxi, and while he pulled slowly from the curb, told them of the new plan.

He drove two blocks past the couple and turned right. Here the zopilotes exited the taxi and stood ready and out of sight behind the building. Cholo backed to the corner and parked between the young lovers and the park.

The unsuspecting couple walked, his arm around her slender waist, to their rendezvous with disaster. The young man said something that brought easy laughter and a swat from the girl. They took no notice of the parked taxi cab, a common sight in the Zona Rosa. The distant sounds of the mariachis grew louder with each step.

Cholo opened his door and approached the young man when they reached the corner. "Taxi, señor? For you and the señorita?"

"No, gracias" came the unsteady reply, and the young archeologist moved to walk around Cholo.

The Colombian kicked the unsuspecting archaeologist in the groin, then rammed a ham-handed fist into his stomach. The zopilotes rounded the corner and the girl screamed.

The young man rose to defend himself, showing himself to be a game fighter, but finally succumbed to the beating, no match for the terrorist and his thugs. Leaving him bleeding and unconscious, they turned to the screaming girl. A quick fist to the stomach stopped the screaming and put her to her knees. The zopilotes kicked her senseless, slamming their thick boots into her head and body.

"Enough!" ordered Cholo, pulling a frenzied thug from the bodies, "we don't want to kill them! Get into the car, cabrones!"

This is the last one, he told himself bitterly, watching the zopilotes crawl into the back seat. Cholo hated working with unprofessional rabble and low-life's. He preferred assassination and bombs and only felt safe when working alone. But since leaving Colombia, he had been reduced to a barely middle-class existence. Money was short and he could no longer refuse jobs, regardless of how distasteful.

He punched the accelerator to the floor and recklessly steered the taxi six blocks to a Metro Entrada where he paid and deposited the zopilotes. "Espuma," (scum) he muttered with silent malice, pulling away. He drove another mile before

22

parking the taxi and hailing another to take him home. Lupe, his live-in woman, waited for him. She would be distraught and anxious and they would argue. He licked the blood from his knuckles in anticipation. Tonight he welcomed a fight.

***

Three hours later, Captain Luis Alvarado, homicide detective, was driving east on Madero in his white, '55 Mercury convertible when he spotted the stolen taxi across the street. "Sitio 28" was clearly painted in small black letters on the fender. He checked his mirrors, glanced at the taxi, then did a U-turn and pulled in behind. He unholstered his .45 automatic and approached the car cautiously. It appeared abandoned. The doors opened freely. He saw no visible signs of foul play; only a pack of Rolaids in the seat and the sour smell of pulque.

Four hours earlier the dead cab driver had been found with his wallet and gold pocket watch intact. Since robbery hadn't been the motive, what had? Luis puzzled over this dilemma momentarily, then looked at his watch—5:00 a.m. The day had begun early and badly. Too late to go home and too early to go to the precinct house. He returned to his car and silently debated his options. Finally, his stomach suggested the nearest restaurant for eggs and chorizo. He could work on the taxi later. There was no hurry, he reasoned. The taxi driver was dead and the vehicle recovered. A half day's work done, he assured himself, driving toward Denny's restaurant. He must remember to take his time or they would expect him to be conscientious all the time.

***

Dr. David Wolf, American expatriate and Professor of Anthropology at the National University in Mexico City, sat at his kitchen table sipping hot tea and chewing a fibrous mango while reading the morning paper. His kitchen clock showed 7:00 a.m. when the ring of the telephone broke his concentration. The front page story on mutilated cattle and goats would have to wait.

"Bueno."

"David...it's me, Marco."

"It's awful early...can't it wait until..."

"Professor...Juan and Linda were beat up...they're in the hospital.

The policía are here asking questions."

"What happened?" a dull, leaden feeling enveloped the archaeologist.

"Some guys jumped them in Zona Rosa last night. Linda's in bad shape."

"Jesus!" said David. "I was afraid of this. I warned him about that museum project. Where are they?"

Muted background conversation trailed over the line. "**El Hospital Jesus**."

"Tell the policía I'll be there within the hour...and Marco..."

"Yes?"

"You and I know who probably did this, but keep your mouth shut until we're sure. Got it?"

A long pause, then, "If you say so, professor, but..."

"No but's, boy. They're in the hospital now. They'll be in a pine box if you mention the wrong person's name. Keep a cool head. Their lives depend on it."

"Okay, but we need to talk..."

"See you there, Marco."

The professor cradled the phone, thinking of his student, a young man fighting the good fight and nearly losing his life.

24

"Awww, Mexico…" he groaned with disgust, burying his face in his hands.

Unresolved Issues

Wednesday, June 11, 1984 Mexico City, One Year Later

David sat in a leather overstuffed chair in the study of his modest, six-room apartment in Colonial del Prado. His eyebrows furrowed in concentration, revealing dark eyes and crows-feet wrinkles, a result of the sun and countless hours in the field as a "dirt archeologist". Smile lines tugged at his lower face, identifying him as a man of quick wit and cheerful disposition.

As midnight approached, an inevitable fatigue found him. At fifty-two he had difficulty maintaining the frenetic pace of youth—to bed at 12:00 each night and up at 5:00 every morning. God had gifted him a keen mind and boundless energy, and his father had instilled an uncompromising work ethic. The professor required little sleep.

A lamp focused a narrow beam of light on the desk's materials. Now weary from exacting concentration, he sat hunched over a stack of artifact inventories, the compilation of many years of excavating the metropolitan subway system.

The lists were nearly complete, as the excavations and construction were winding down. A major discovery notwithstanding, this job would soon be over—a mixed blessing at best. His large thick-fingered hands effortlessly shuffled the pages, searching and collating, seeking the elusive page he sought.

If Raul Cordoba, the museum director, would submit his reports on the Tacuba excavation, David could finish his own work. Raúl, erratic at best, remained a constant source of frustration, and David found it irritating to work with someone so unprofessional and unscrupulous. But politics were ever present at every level in Mexico, and Raúl's position as Director of The National Museum of Anthropology ensured that they must work together, mix in public, occasionally suffer awkward circumstances and, in general, endure a mutual disdain and distrust. Raúl was a political appointee and the professor a scientist. Their values and the worlds in which they operated were light years apart.

Deep in thought, David stroked his mustache and pondered the lists while an incipient idea struggled upward from the recesses of his mind. Still nebulous, it hid stubbornly and refused to make its appearance. Over thirty years in academia had created a man of patterns and habits and he knew the sentiment would present itself when ready.

His cup of yerbabuena had cooled. He took a sip and frowned, then decided to have a brandy. It helped him sleep and he enjoyed a small glass each night before bed. He extracted a bottle of El Presidente from the bottom desk drawer and poured two fingers into the remains of the tea. He smiled, remembering his wife, Alicia's, inevitable frown when observing him do this. She considered it a tactless breach of etiquette and accused him of being too lazy to find a clean

27

glass. In truth, while his cluttered mind left him too forgetful to keep glasses in the study, he actually preferred the mix. He sipped, then slowly coated the inside of his mouth, savoring its sweet bite. Delicious. He took another, then gently swirled the liquid in the cup.

Memory — that was the lost strand, he realized, an elusive but challenging subject. A person could have eidetic memory, yet forget the same thing day after day. Were memory and habit somehow linked? Which had come first during man's evolutionary journey? Did memory serve as the catalyst to revelation? Or, did habit lead to memory, memory to awareness, and awareness to cognition? Was inspiration the result of cognitive flexibility? Awareness, of course, was humankind's great gift (or accident) that separated him from the animal world. It was also his greatest frailty – understanding how fragile his situation was, knowing that he didn't and couldn't know the ultimate spiritual causation that created the human mind. Awareness also created fear and futility as well as inspiration and achievement through cultural invention. He chewed his lower lip and pondered the dilemma. As usual resolution lay just beyond the periphery of his consciousness, playing a waiting game, tantalizing him. *Enough!* he thought, shaking his head. If he slipped into hypothesizing this late at night, he would never get to sleep. Life, he assured himself, was a riddle. But as an archaeologist they were the basis of his profession. Like all things important, he pursued them with a passion.

His large hand dwarfing the cup, David walked to the balcony and breathed deeply the tangy night air to pull his mind from work. Leaning onto the balcony rail, he allowed the sounds and smells of the city to assail him. A timbre of vibrancy resonated in the night sky. Mexico City pulsed with life, never sleeping, in some ways behaving like a living organism. It had structure, patterns of repetition and replication, as well as its own sustaining energy system. Like a stubborn child it resisted sleep at night, then appeared robust and wide awake at daybreak. The redolent odor of car exhaust, rotting trash, cooking oils, and diesel permeated the polluted night mist, each an individual odor, but all part of the whole. A glow of red-orange luminescence shrouded the city under a haze of smog while the Milky Way, offended but resolute, attempted to pierce the particle-laden atmosphere. Complete darkness was a stranger to the Mexico City skyline.

Even here in David's secluded suburb, the distant rattle of cars was heard. Calle Insurgentes, the city's main thoroughfare, flowed bumper to bumper all day and night, the traffic never diminishing. And at this moment twenty million people were making love, eating, sleeping, crying, praying, or fighting. How many millions lay awake with worry gnawing at their sense of well-being? How many lived in squalor and poverty? Ten or fifteen million? The numbers were staggering.

As he watched the occasional jet with blinking lights land and depart to parts unknown from the airport, an incipient melancholy gripped him and he wondered to where the years had fled. Alicia, his wife, dead thirteen years now. Gone, but remembered. An attractive and vigorous man, he had courted several widows, and even allowed a female graduate student or colleague into his bed during infrequent bouts of loneliness. But all his affairs ended in disappointment. And it was Alicia's fault. She was the perfect soul-mate and wife—no woman since had measured up. Strong-willed, yet compliant in her feminine way, he had admired her intelligence and depended on her intuition. A trouper in the field, she had

29

dutifully accompanied him for twenty years, packing and unpacking from Quintana Roo to Costa Rica. She had worked under many guises; camp counselor, doctor, organizer, cook, sage, and even clairvoyant at times. Most importantly, she had been his best friend.

Tragedy struck unexpectedly in 1972. Killed in Oaxaca by a careening tourist bus headed down the mountain from the Monte Alban ruin, Alicia had been swept over an 800-foot cliff in their Volkswagen van and crushed to death. The gravel-pocked road wound narrow and steep and had no side rail for protection. The bus' brakes failed and had managed only to stop when the driver deliberately crashed into the mountain side, killing himself and six passengers.

Unresolved anger at the gods of fate had left no room for catharsis. He reluctantly came to grips with her death, but harbored a sullen bitterness. After twenty years of dirt archeology he found himself unable to stay in the field without her. Three colleges in the U.S.A. had offered him faculty positions but he declined, preferring the tradition and familiarity of Mexico to the hustle and hurry of the United States. He only had a few relatives in the states with whom he rarely visited and a fifteen-year absence from the Land of Liberty inspired no longing to return. When offered a tenured position with the National University in Mexico City, he accepted. By working and publishing prolifically over the years, he became widely respected as an archaeologist and theoretician. Gradually, because of his work and the university social scene, he acclimated himself to urban life and attempted a new beginning, never once regretting his decision to abandon the stable, material-rich culture to the north. His mother and father were both deceased and he had never felt close to their extended relatives.

David became the mentor of a new generation of archaeologists and social anthropologists. A talented researcher, he managed to be a contributor or co-author on at least three publications a year, while overseeing the progress of concurrent excavations. His quick mind and attention to detail had combined with considerable field experience to make him an extraordinary teacher and lecturer.

The 70's and 80's brought an explosion of new technologies into the laboratory and field. New dating techniques were developed. The Maya glyphs were deciphered and, most importantly, an accurate chronology of pre-Colombian societies had emerged. Extensive excavations in the southern Mayan jungles resulted in Latin America's "New Ethnography;" an extensive history of highly complex societies, complete with rich and elaborate cultural traditions. Columbus was not a hero and Latin America could no longer be viewed as "lost" or "inferior" to European civilizations.

David peered into the darkness, searching for the outline of distant mountains that enclosed the highland valley. Dark cumulus formations struggled to cross the peaks and slide into the valley. Veined lightning danced in the east, illuminating gray-black thunderheads that threatened to capture the city. Gusts of moisture-laden air greeted the smog entrenched valley. Though late this year, the rainy season had arrived, bringing cleansing and renewal. He yawned, breathed deeply once more, then returned to his apartment to ready himself for sleep.

Sitting heavily onto his bed, his shoulders slumped, his eyes strayed to a tablet on his lamp stand. Lists of unfinished tasks were scribbled within, reminding him of a former student hiding out in the Jalisco highlands. Juan and his girlfriend were attacked and nearly killed last year. Upon recovering, they fled the city for the anonymity of the countryside. David had written Juan regularly and now, after a year, he hoped his former student would return and accept a job as his assistant. Time healed wounds, and the antipathies the boy had created at the National Museum by creating up-to-date inventories of endless storerooms could be averted this time by simply avoiding the museum and minding his own business. Besides, if the boy was to make any professional progress he must reengage his pursuit of archaeology again. If Juan returned, David planned to place him in an adjacent office at the university where he could view his activities and monitor his interactions vicariously to ensure he didn't stir up old antipathies. The young archaeologist had been one of his best students, and the professor anticipated having him back on staff.

Things had cooled off since Juan's self-induced fiasco at the museum. His antagonists, the Museum Director, Raúl Cordoba, and the Minister of Natural Resources, Hector Vicario, would have to be kept away from Juan. They had proven themselves to be a dangerous pack of thieves who were above the law in Mexico. Their greed and theft of antiquities were, as yet, an unknown scandal waiting to burst into headlines.

He reached for a pen and wrote on the tablet; cat food, Juan Degas' office, and lunch with Baltazar. He hesitated, frowned, then wrote— *Suspicions—Raúl Cordoba*. **_Go to Tacuba_**! He underlined the last entry with a dark line.

The museum director, as usual, had not submitted his report on the Tacuba excavation. Why did he withhold it? Had he discovered something? If anyone but Raúl, the professor wouldn't worry. But Cordoba, unsavory character that he was, might be involved in unscrupulous or illegal activity and be purposefully withholding his report.

32

David stroked his white Persian cat and murmured endearments. Exhausted, he turned out the lamp. Five minutes later, his breath came slow and shallow. The cat yawned, indifferent, then crawled to lay on top of her master's legs.

Juan Degas Fights A Scorpion

Thursday, June 12, 1984 - 7:00 P.M. Tapalpa, Jalisco - One Year After the Beating

Juan Degas relaxed on the front stoop of his cabin at Ojo Zarco (gray eye) ranch, high in the Sierra Madres of Jalisco State. Inside, the lilting melodies of Mozart played to an empty house. He took a drag from the cigarette, flicked the ash, then sipped a brandy and rested his shirtless, broad back against the white stuccoed wall. The lean muscles of his chest and shoulders rippled with each movement. His face and upper torso were a dark testimony to Mexico's punishing sun. His hands were callused from years of archeological field work and, more recently, planting seed and harvesting the produce of Ojo Zarco in the highlands. But a hard days' work and the brandy did little to dispel the gloom of this morning's fight with Linda. The argument left him painfully aware of unresolved, simmering issues in their relationship and the fear that she would tire of him and leave.

34

While he brooded he watched the progress of a yellow scorpion crawling toward the steps of his cabin. Well into the bottle, he saw the animal as an opportunity for diversion. Choosing a small stick, he began to tease the arachnid. Deeply offended, the scorpion postured and struck back repeatedly. Its poisoned barb flailed at the enemy, striking often, but the stick seemed to be everywhere and the scorpion had no memory of this type of animal. It twisted and turned, striking again and again, then stopped, bewildered, and attempted to leave the gaming area. The stick impeded escape, blocking all avenues of retreat until the scorpion, confused and unwilling to press the attack, sat motionless and waited.

Tired of the game, Juan used the stick to toss the scorpion aside. It righted itself, paused for bearing, then moved resolutely toward the dirt road that fronted the cabin, its barb poised and ready. The young archaeologist took a final drag off the cigarette and flicked it at the retreating arachnid. A last sip from the glass and he rose to go inside. Linda Maria had returned to school in Guadalajara and her absence left a void in the house. He didn't want to spend the night alone, so he decided to drive into Tapalpa, a small colonial town tucked away in the wooded sierras, and check his mail. Grabbing a woolen sweater from the garment stand, he exited the cabana.

The grille of his bright red `65 Mustang smiled as he approached. The chrome pony emblem on the hood was pitted and had lost its luster, and closer inspection revealed small dings and dents from fifteen years of highway gravel, tree limbs, and people setting objects on it. A companion since turning sixteen, it had carried him from one archaeological site to another for ten years.

When he reached for the door handle, something tapped his boot. He glanced down, yelped and jumped away from the scorpion he had earlier tortured. Cursing, he stomped the creature and felt a satisfying crunch. He lifted his boot for a look, then kicked the remains aside.

Sliding behind the wheel and starting the engine, he slowly navigated the ranch's washboard dirt road, moving past dilapidated cedar plank cabins with corrugated roofs, and then onto an asphalt road lined with shady canopies of hemlock. With the sun hanging low in the sky, he leaned back into the seat and propelled the car into shadowed curves, passing cathedral-tall pines that stood erect and austere near roadside. He swerved to avoid pot holes and fallen rocks, carefully navigating the familiar road another 10 kilometers to the highland town of Tapalpa.

He braked upon seeing a small herd of cattle blocking the road. An Indian boy shooed them along with a leafy branch, swatting and prodding their protruding ribs, coaxing them across the road, worried that harm might befall his charges. Juan moved by cautiously, waving at the youth as he passed. Picking up speed, he topped the hill, then backed off the accelerator and coasted.

As the Mustang devoured the asphalt, he thought of his most recent letter from Professor Wolf. David had nearly completed his duties as head of the Division Archaeologica de Recobrar Antiguidades for the excavation of the Mexico City Subway System. The excavations, begun twelve years previous, had revealed marvelous discoveries and captured the imagination of the Mexican people. But Juan felt only discontent and bitterness. He had been out of the loop for over a year – away from the excavations, academia, and nightlife of the city. But the professor's newest correspondence held an offer of employment and might be an opportunity to renew his short-circuited career as a pre-Columbian archeologist. Juan had met the professor 10 years ago as an undergraduate and quickly become attached to the smiling, knowledgeable archaeologist. The man had become a second father to him, looking out for his interests and providing unsolicited advice, while demanding that he take his studies seriously. He loved the man, and respected him above all others in his field, and wanted to please him, if possible. But return to Mexico City? Maybe not. Maybe it was still too dangerous.

He slowed for a sharp curve on the periphery of town. The Pemex, the only gas stations in Mexico, was fueling three Dinas heavily laden with fruit who were bound for Aguas Calientes. The truck's slatted ribs bulged with mango and potatoes. The drivers stood motionless, no one in a hurry, no one willing to begin the tortuous twenty-kilometer trip down the mountains. While they leaned against their trucks and chatted, a shoeless dusky-skinned waif hawked chicle gum to anyone who would suffer his presence.

Tapalpa, beautiful, but remote and traditional, had begun to wear on the nerves. Maybe David's offer was the remedy? Juan recalled the events that had brought him here. Two years ago he had been selected to work as Raúl Cordoba's assistant—primarily because the museum director involved himself as little as possible with the day-to-day operation. Nine months later, and without Raúl's permission, Juan had initiated a comprehensive inventory of the museum's considerable holdings, only to discover a complete mess. Years of apathy and poor organization had resulted in chaos. Artifacts - hundreds of important pieces - were missing. Worse, the staff appeared indifferent and didn't care. While many were visibly resentful of his efforts, others were evasive or secretive when questioned.

The trail of mismanagement and deceit led back to the museum director. Cordoba should have cared, should have helped, but didn't. This, of course, led Degas to understand the problem. The majority of the missing artifacts were quite probably sold to private collectors, some of whom were the most powerful people in Mexico. Cordoba, Hector Vicario, a powerful government minister, and other powerful politicians had stolen the artifacts with the aid of Cordoba. The closer the young archaeologist came to the truth, the more dangerous his task became.

The harassment began with notes left on his desk. Then came punctured tires, wine in his radiator (the mechanic had been amused), and the theft of his own two-thousand-year-old artifacts from his first excavation on his uncle's Michoacan ranch. Then disaster struck. After a night of partying with Linda in the Zona Rosa, four men, reeking of pulque, had attacked them. Juan's jaw was broken, Linda was knocked unconscious and kicked repeatedly while on the ground. Hospitalized with injuries to her head and back, her kidneys had failed and left her near death. She recovered, but both still carried emotional scars. It had been enough.

Professor Wolf was helpless to intervene, so Juan felt he had no option but to leave – before it happened again or before he was murdered. This was Mexico. It happened all the time; powerful people unrestricted by law, doing as they wished whenever they wished, sometimes with the blessing of their superiors, who were probably feathering their own nests. But before resigning, Degas wrote a ten-page report detailing the conclusions of his investigation, naming people, places, and missing artifacts. He tossed it on Cordoba's desk, leaving the museum for the last time, knowing it would never see the light of day. The narration clearly stated that there were other copies in the hands of people who would act if he was attacked again.

Linda had moved to Guadalajara and Juan had taken a job with Pafritas in the sierra highlands as a grower of certified seed potatoes from Holland. It paid the bills, but left him unfulfilled. He wanted to be in the middle of an excavation somewhere, anywhere; the Yucatan or south to Chiapas. Most of all he wanted to be with Linda, but she lived in the big city seventy kilometers north along twisting mountain roads.

The asphalt became uneven cobblestone as he entered Tapalpa. Depressions and holes pocked the roads and he slowed to a crawl. Groups of townspeople loitered in the streets and on the sidewalks, gossiping and joking. A gray burro, its bowed back supporting two metal containers of raw milk, stood patiently on the sidewalk. Black and mattered, the burro's eyes stared vacantly while his tattered, filthy tail moved in rhythm, worrying a horde of flies intent on biting and laying eggs in his flesh.

He drove slowly toward the zocalo, the town's center, and parked in front of the dirty, white, stuccoed Post Office and walked inside. The Postmaster eyed him, hungry for news or gossip. Juan knew the Postmaster had already read all the postcards in the office. He saw himself as a great purveyor of knowledge in the small village and a central figure in the local government. In fact, his indiscreet whisperings and intrusions had angered many, and after living in this small town his whole life, he could count his friends on one hand. Juan checked his mail nearly every day and knew immediately when a letter from Linda had arrived by the knowing looks of the Postmaster's ever-present friends.

Juan collected his mail, tipped his hat to the loiterers, and exited. As an outsider, he held an ambiguous status in this

39

conservative community. In a town where twenty percent of the men were unemployed, no one wanted to get on the bad side of a Pafritas representative, the community's major employer on the Ojo Zarco ranch. Thus, his cosmopolitan demeanor and scandalous relationship with Linda Maria must be overlooked. They were essentially outside the system. Tongues wagged, but most remained careful of what they said.

He walked diagonally across the square to the Fiesta Mexicana where his friend Marco worked. 7:30 p.m. approached and the dinner crowd would begin to arrive. He paused a moment, looked around the flower-filled courtyard, then seated himself on a wrought-iron bench skirted with potted cannas and diffenbachia. He opened the letter from Professor Wolf and began to read.

Marco Wants to Leave

Thursday, June 12, 1984 - 7:30 P.M. Tapalpa, Jalisco

Marco Gonzalez, age 29, and friend to Juan Degas, stood eight meters back from the balcony railing under a doorway. He was not visible from outside. A late afternoon visitor by the name of Rodrigo Torres had come to see him. Rodrigo had brought his friends: a scarred, chrome .32 revolver which he pressed to Marco's forehead, and a large, sharp knife pointed at his genitals. As Rodrigo talked, he emphasized his words by lifting the knife and applying pressure to Marco's groin.

"I'm glad we had this conversation, Sr. Gonzalez. I think you understand my feelings on the matter." Rodrigo pressed the point of the blade upward.

"I never touched her, Rodrigo! I swear it!" pleaded Marco, paralyzed with fear. "Ask her...it's the truth. I respect her too much for that."

"Cabron! You playboys come to town and take advantage of our daughters...then leave. None of the local boys will talk to them when you're done."

"Rodrigo...please!" begged Marco.

"Her mother is home checking to see if she has had sex with you. I'll send your blessed cojones to your uncle in a jar if she's not a virgin. Understand?" he pressed the knife into tender flesh, holding it firmly in Marco's crotch.

Fear hung on him like a silent scream. He hadn't touched Lucinda.

Well...almost...just a few kisses. But what had she told her friends? "Rodrigo, you're making a big mistake. I never touched her!" he repeated.

The stocky, sunburned father ignored his protests. "I don't want to talk of this again. Can I trust you to do the right thing and leave my Lucinda alone?"

"Yes...yes!"

"Better yet, cabron, maybe you should leave Tapalpa...eh? This gun belonged to my great-grandfather. He fought with Morelos. He taught me the importance of making a point. Am I making my point?" he pressed the gun harder to Marco's forehead.

"Yes! For God's sake...yes, Rodrigo!"

"Good! I hope I don't need to mention your hard dick and bad manners to the other fathers in Tapalpa. They won't be so forgiving." He stepped back, lowering the gun, then sheathed the knife.

"Adios, cabron." With his thumb and index finger shaped like a pistol, he pointed it at Marcos and said, "bang!" With one last glance at the wide-eyed young man, Rodrigo retrieved his cowboy hat from the table top and turned and slipped down the stairs. His shadow danced briefly on the stairwell wall, then disappeared into the dark.

Marco collapsed on a stool at the bar, his gut quivering and heart thudding dully. Adrenaline coursed through his veins, signaling his brain to fight or run. Taut with fear, relief was slow to come. He sat unmoving, his head resting on the bar, and considered his situation.

God! What had the pinche virgin told everyone? He barely knew her. Marco knew that calling the policía was out of the question. They would almost certainly side with Rodrigo or any other complaining parent. He was afraid something like this might happen, and if not Rodrigo, it would have been someone else's father, he realized sourly.

The townspeople were conservative and suspicious, much like they were in all small Mexican towns. They talked and joked with him—but warned their daughters to stay away. Nonetheless, he had found a few prospects, young girls mostly, who liked to flirt. They behaved like Lucinda; wanting it but not wanting it, afraid but flirtatious, insinuatingly close yet distant. Latin America's parodic version of the Dating Game.

He sometimes received dinner invitations, which broke the monotony of tending bar, drinking brandy, and useless talk of winning the National Lotteria. On separate occasions two young widows had arranged to meet him in Guadalajara and bed him away from the prying eyes of the townspeople. They had taken a big risk, and if anyone discovered their indiscretions they would be ostracized and the frequent target of gossip. It would hurt their chances of finding another husband. Reputations were made quickly and permanently in small Mexican towns.

With shaking hands, he lit a cigarette and walked behind the bar to retrieve a cold beer. Three long pulls on the bottle and several deep inhalations on the cigarette steadied him. He looked around the second-floor restaurant and considered his next move.

A clean town with breathtaking colonial architecture, Tapalpa's remote location in the Sierra Madres of Jalisco removed it from the mainstream of commerce. Other than an occasional rodeo or national celebration, Tapalpa remained uneventful and uninvolved with the world. It survived as an anachronism, even in a third world country such as Mexico. A young, educated man raised in the city where action was available all hours of the day and night needed more than this sleepy town could offer.

La Fiesta Mexicana boasted a vaulted ceiling, hardwood floors, and aromatic cedar walls. Long-stemmed ceiling fans hung from the rafters, turning leisurely so as not to disturb the dust. Sallow rays of sunlight from a late afternoon sun illuminated the balcony dining area, casting stark shadows and exposing floating dust motes. A Tecate clock above the bar said 7:30 p.m. Everything was made ready for the dinner hour.

For the last year he had tended bar for his uncle Max, earning thirty dollars a week for his efforts. Always ready for a new adventure, Marco had followed Juan south into the highlands. Degas was a good friend, but Marco had his own life, and he was considering returning to the city to find serious work. Nostalgia for the city and university life had become a constant companion, and he reminisced and daydreamed of long-haired, firm-limbed freshman girls with white shiny teeth.

The incident today sealed his decision to leave. He felt better now. The threat of Rodrigo Torres faded with the evening light. Marco walked to the balcony railing and flicked his cigarette butt into the street. There sitting on a bench in the

44

zocalo, he spotted Juan Degas. His friend held a letter and appeared to be staring vacantly at nothing.

"Que pasa loco?" Marco called.

Juan looked around, then up to the second floor balcony. "Who're you calling crazy?"

"You, amigo. You're crazy to stay in this provincial waste land. Me? I'm leaving. Rodrigo Torres says so, and I think I agree. Come up and have a beer," he motioned. "We need to talk."

***

Juan shoved the letter into his back jean pocket and crossed the cobblestone road. He climbed two flights of stairs, entered the restaurant, and walked past the bar.

"Out here," called Marco, setting a second bottle of beer on the table. His friend's brooding expression invited a question. "What's up? You have that look in your eyes like the time we ate magic mushrooms at Palenque." But Marco's attempt at humor failed.

Juan pulled up a chair and plopped himself down, fatigued from a long day of work. He reached for the Negra Modelo. "If I remember correctly…you're the one that O.D.'d." He took a long pull from the bottle, pursed his lips, then sighed. "Got lost and stumbled off into the jungle chasing a bird." He caught Marcos' eyes. "You ate about a dozen of those things," he added, taking another swig from the bottle beaded with moisture.

"Hey…that Lacandon shaman said you had to eat at least six to fly like a hawk, I wanted to fly like an eagle."

"Yeah…right," said Juan indifferently, distracted.

"That's not the point," sniffed Marco, attempting a straight face. "I did it out of professional curiosity and a desire to

45

experience the same spiritual and religious ecstasy as that of the Mayan ritual."

"You just wanted to get high," accused Juan, smiling in spite of himself. "Anyway...it isn't possible unless you're a native believer and have a vested interest in the ritual."

"Why's that?"

"Well...for example, the Maya and Aztec believed that blood nourished the gods, so they sacrificed captives from their wars. Blood served as tribute, food, or sustenance to nurture the gods and ensure their blessing and approval. When captives were unavailable, they stood atop the pyramids and pierced their penis foreskins with prickly pear cactus thorns, or obsidian blades. The blood was collected on paper and burnt in offering."

"I know all that...what's the point?"

"The point is...do you think you could whip out your penis and cut it in front of everyone without being a true believer? Even if you had eaten a bag of magic mushrooms? Unless you're already loco, it can't be done - except maybe if you're lit up on psilocybin and in a state of religious ecstasy."

"I get the point," conceded Marco, reaching protectively for his genitals while visualizing self-mutilation, recalling Rodrigo's large knife pressing into his groin. "However...you enjoyed the mushrooms, too."

"Not so much...and I don't go out of my way to get them. Take care that the federales don't catch you and put you in El Bote."

"Quit your preaching. I'm careful...I just need a little entertainment sometimes. Marco changed the subject. "Listen..." he glanced over the railing and down into the zocalo, then again at Juan. "I've been thinking...maybe it's time to blow this place and return to civilization. Rodrigo

Torres just pulled a gun on me and threatened to cut off my cojones. I need some action, but if f I don't leave town before long, I might start acting like a Maya shaman one of these nights."

"Fool! I warned you about these small town girls. You're lucky he didn't shoot first and ask questions later." Juan thumped his bottle on the table. "I know it's tough being up here—especially for you. I've got Linda, but even that's not working." He stared at the table top. "We fight a lot and I know she's thinking of breaking up. Her in Guadalajara and me here is making me crazy."

Degas slumped in his chair and began peeling the label from his bottle. "I'm thinking of leaving, too. Dr. Wolf still writes and lets me know what's going on in Mexico City. I got a letter today." He patted his pocket. "He's offered me a job with the excavations and restorations of the metro artifacts. He's also researching some old Spanish documents and believes there's a possibility we could hit it big."

"Such as?"

"Don't know…but he says big…something about the old roads, the Aztec causeways into Tenochtitlan during the Conquest. He also says he'll never find it without help…too busy with other projects."

"That's kind of indefinite, don't you think?" Marco began peeling his label also. "No other clues?"

"No, but if David says big, he's not just talking potsherds, right?"

"The major Aztec temple was discovered eight years ago. What could be bigger than that? The metro's nearly completed and half the track is above ground. The excavations are winding down."

"What else you got going?" insisted Juan. "Had any offers lately other than Rodrigo's? David knows you do good work. I could get you on, if you want to come along."

Marco chewed his lip and stared at his empty bottle.

Hearing no protest, Juan pressed the attack. "Look, I'm going to Guadalajara to talk to Linda. I've been hiding out ever since the mess in Mexico City…"

"You had to," interrupted Marco.

"I know, but it's time to get back to work, even if it means running into Cordoba and Vicario again. David will be in charge. I'll just follow orders and do as he says. He can handle the politics and the crooks.

"And Linda?"

Juan faltered, chewed his lip. "The problem will be convincing her to leave that second-rate art school and clammy-handed professor of hers."

"Do I detect a note of jealousy?"

"It wouldn't hurt you to fall for a girl…eh…Casanova? It would solve the problem of your chronic erection. Love isn't a debilitating disease. You'll end up dead or a eunuch if Rodrigo or some other father gets tired of you chasing their daughters."

Marco choked off a retort. "Yeah…maybe," he conceded, "and that would be permanently debilitating." He hefted his empty bottle, then looked at Juan. "Already thinking about it. Nothing holding me here now. When do we leave?"

***

The sun, a puffy magenta orb, lolled low in the sky, spilling an orange glow over the horizon, slowly burnishing the red tile roof of the old cathedral. It stole the evening like a thief and hid beyond the horizon while the two young archaeologists laughed and joked, reminiscing familiar stories that became better with each retelling. The past spread before them as they feasted on yesterday's memories, relishing an event, savoring a shared moment, and toasting their friendship. Their camaraderie was tinged with the excitement of the coming adventure; the knowledge that once again they would become time-travelers, and scientists. The possibility of pre-history emerging from beneath the rubble of centuries fired their imaginations.

Tentative plans were made. They would meet when Juan returned from Guadalajara on Sunday. They parted with spirits soaring—Juan to his cabana in the pines of Ojo Zarco and Marco to the bar to greet the incoming Munoz brothers, ready for their nightly meal.

With a spring in his walk, Juan crossed the zocalo. A full moon illuminated a star-speckled sky and the night air felt crisp and cool, promising to caress and protect. The lilting laughter of young couples entering the zocalo for an evening of courtship under the watchful eyes of the town drifted on the breeze. A troop of four mariachis tuned their instruments and talked to gaily clad young girls who flirted and laughed, waiting expectantly for the romantic refrains of their music.

Juan drove through town, careful not to punish his old car on the cobblestones, then pressed the Mustang into the curves leading to Ojo Zarco. As he drove, he mentally composed a letter to his mentor, Professor Wolf. Tonight's decision and the assurance of a new beginning would keep him awake tonight. But one item remained. One thing could go wrong. He would call and make arrangements to meet Linda in Guadalajara. She must agree to return with him to Mexico City. He thought of what he would say to her, and a plan took shape as he maneuvered Mustang along the narrow mountain road. He would be home in minutes.

Filth Eater

I am safe in the darkness. I wait patiently for Quetzalcoatl, the Feathered Serpent. It is my divine duty. Buried and forgotten for five-hundred years, I have lain in the silt of this ancient lake bed, hidden from the eyes of men these many years. It was the white bearded men who took me from my temple, then destroyed it in an irrational fury. They are ignorant and greedy and have no respect for the gods of The One Universe. Perhaps they committed their outrageous acts in stupidity or ignorance. Perhaps they are the worst of men, those without souls or conscience, and those with no empathy. That, I cannot understand. Those sins are too difficult to eat.

I am Filth Eater, Tlazolteotl to the people of The One Universe. I eat the sins and transgressions of man. I give absolution to the dying. It is an awesome responsibility, and I have eaten the sins of thousands in The One Universe. At this moment their spirits reside in peace and they will continue forever in The Paradise of theSun.

Seventy years prior to the arrival of the bearded, bleached faces I served as Filth Eater to Moctezuma, and before him, Axayacatl. Axayacatl was a great leader. He sent thousands of grateful souls to The Paradise of the Sun by sacrificing them at the great Sun Pyramid. His son Moctezuma was a fool, but a pious fool. His yearning for the Feathered Serpent and his desire to bring on the Millennium, to merge heaven and earth, was the greatest disaster any leader ever brought on his people. I ate this filth. In the final days he knew of Cortez's deceptions and greed. Impious and void of conscience, I believe their filth beyond my capacity to eat. Who could consume such corruption? Their filth enslaved the pious of The One World and the bones and blood of the people lie not only here, but everywhere.

Today they are close. I can sense their presence above and feel the vibrations of their bleached feet as they draw near. They have returned for Moctezuma's filth! This must not happen. His filth has lain buried, here beneath me these five-hundred years. I must prepare. I must ensure that Moctezuma's filth does not enrich the bleached faces again. The Plumed Serpent may still come. If so, the filth of the bleached ones will be consumed in holocaust with the filth of Moctezuma and all the pious who have gone before him and transformed into a penance for the survivors of The One Universe. In the meantime, I wait.

Hector Wants The Tlazolteotl

Friday, June 13, 1984 7:00 P.M. Mexico City One Year After The Beating

Hector Alfonso Vicario-Sanchez walked onto the patio of his resplendent Coyohuacan home. He glanced around, cataloging the riches. Six marble columns rimmed the periphery of a red-tiled roof which covered the house. The patio floor, a mirror of beautiful white terrazzo, had been imported from Italy. Entry doors on each side led into the colonial-style mansion. The courtyard opened to the sky and was graced with numerous trees. An avocado, a tamarindo, and two lime trees stood well-groomed and heavily laden with fruit. The opulent home, tastefully decorated, sat at the end of a long, circular drive. One did not move into Coyohuacan simply because of wealth; living in the exclusive suburb required power and name recognition. The area directory read like Who's Who in Mexico. Hector was just one of many famous people—politicians, writers, artists, and businessmen who resided in the ancient Toltec suburb of Mexico City.

The Vicario-Sanchez mansion, however, was different than most since it contained the world's largest collection of illegally obtained pre-Colombian artifacts; statues, pots, mosaics, gold and silver jewelry, jade and more. Maya, Olmec, Toltec, Zapotec, Tarascan, Aztec; Hector Vicario had it all. Some pieces had never been classified and many were completely unknown in the scientific community. A few had briefly seen the light of day only to be relegated to obscurity in this collection, to be fawned over by Hector. Many were stolen from the National Museum of Anthropology.

Hector Vicario had two compulsions—power and pre-Colombian art. Persistent and acquisitive, he obsessively collected both. An obsession must be fed or it preys on the host. Hector fed his well. As Mexico's Minister of Natural Resources and a lifetime member of the ruling PRI party, he had reached the zenith of a superlative political career under Presidente Lopez Portillo. Hector had secured his position in typical PRI manner—graft, theft, and sweetheart deals. Two supertankers laden with Campeche crude oil were diverted to Spain, the contents downloaded and the money from the sale deposited in a special account for El Presidente. Hector, at the behest of his boss, arranged the whole affair.

The few who had knowledge of the multi-million dollar theft, though envious, knew better than to speak up. This, after all, was business as usual in Mexico. It began during The Conquest and continued until today. Although names and administrations change, they are all familiar. Five hundred years of tradition had created a corrupt, but stable system that everyone but the poor understood.

Word of the scandal had leaked to an overzealous reporter at the *Veracruz Voz*. He, in turn, had attempted to turn the story into cash by printing it. Alas, local PRI officials learned of his poor judgment and intervened. Today the man walks with a limp and drives a cab in Coxocoalcos.

Vicario, a big man, stood almost two meters and weighed a hundred kilos. A lined forehead and sagging jowls dominated his face and at sixty-one the vigor of youth had succumbed to gray hair and a substantial girth. Today he wore tan polyester slacks, white shoes, and a white guayabera shirt open above his stomach, exposing a hairy chest and drooping pectorals. A gold Mayan bracelet clasped the forearm of the hand that held a glass of brandy while the other pressed a telephone to his ear. As he spoke to Raúl Cordoba, the director of the National Museum of Anthropology, the glass stabbed the air, punctuating his conversation.

"So...when do I get it?" asked Hector.

"I don't know...there are problems with security and I've got to be careful. The old professor is like a mother protecting her children. He takes notes of everything and has his nose in everyone's business. He's a pest. He could be dangerous."

"Buy him!" insisted Hector, exasperated.

"He can't be bought, he's an academic. I think his values are warped, myself. Surely you know that money means nothing to people like him."

"Nonsense! Everyone has a price - you were an academic once."

"Be patient!" pleaded the museum director. "We don't want anyone to know. It's lain there five hundred years...surely a week or a month more is insignificant. If we're careful and follow our plan..."

"Raúl...you fuck this up, I'll have your cojones! I want that statue! Hear me? I know you...you have your methods...your own people...use them!" Vicario's knuckles turned white as he squeezed the phone, imagining it to be Raúl's neck. "I want

Filth Eater in my collection within the month! Too many people know of it already."

"Not true. Only a bulldozer driver and a few campesinos saw it, and they could care less. None of them know anything of archaeology. Nobody knows we have Tlazolteotl. It's hidden until we're ready. I'll wait for the right time, then I'll bring it to you."

"And the gringo?"

"Who?"

"That gringo professor."

"Leave Professor Wolf to me."

"He's a friend of that bastard son of Malinche, Juan Degas! We should've killed him and dropped his body into a volcano," groused Hector. "He almost took everyone down."

"Be patient!" pleaded Raúl, "I'm more concerned about snooping reporters than David Wolf and his clan of academic fools. The newspapers are full of excavation stories and are hungry for more. If word gets out…even you could have problems you can't handle."

Hector became silent for several heartbeats. His neck bulged and twitched. His jaw clenched at the veiled threat.

"Cordoba," his voice rang like steel, "you're up to your neck in shit like the rest of us. If anyone finds out, I'll give your cojones and manhood to the Mexican people. Even Malinche will be considered a candidate for canonization when the newspapers discover that you've stolen from their precious museum."

"We're in this together!" came the shrill reply.

"I'm in it for the art, you're in it for the money." Hector forced himself to relax. "Calm yourself, my friend. I'm just reminding you of the stakes. I'm not asking for the Aztec Sun Dial…only a small statue of Filth Eater. It's a rare find and I must have it. I want daily reports. Call me every night. In an emergency, leave a message." He slammed the receiver into its cradle.

"Fool!" spat Hector. Cordoba was a liability to everyone. He thought like an old woman: fretful and cautious. He knew too much and could use it to hurt Hector. So far the museum director's influence at the Metro excavation had been invaluable. Hopefully the sneak would still produce the Tlazolteotl or something even better. The minister frowned. It would be impossible to know everything the rat had dug up, and Raúl would be the last to tell. But the Filth Eater would be one of the crown jewels of Hector's collection. He would just have to play the effeminate fool along until he outlived his usefulness, then, who knows? Perhaps the time had come to replace him with someone more compliant and appreciative of his patron.

Hector drained the cocktail glass and ended with a grimace. He rattled the ice, then set the glass down, satisfied and refreshed. As an afterthought he extracted a lime wedge from the glass' lip, and sucked and chewed until the sourness and pulp were depleted. He cast about for a trash can to discard the rind, but saw nothing. Irritated, he spat the rind onto the floor and wiped his hands on his pants.

The Interior Minister went to his bedroom to open a wall safe and extract a key. Upon returning to the courtyard he noticed that the rind had disappeared, and smiled with approval. He walked to the other side and opened the lock to his private vault. He allowed no one inside unless accompanied by him. The servants had never been inside, and his wife and daughter only a few times. This is where he hid the priceless pieces, the illegally-gotten booty and those favorites too dear or too fragile to display as home decor. A lifetime of accumulated treasure lay within.

He basked in a feeling of smug self-importance. Someday he planned to reveal his incredible collection to the world. It would enhance his reputation, he believed, and ensure that historians saw him as a savior of the Mexican Heritage, a man worthy to be placed in the annals of Mexican history.

He toured the room, looking at the displays and collections, reminiscing the acquisition of each piece. As he walked, his chest swelled and a smile lifted his jowls. He stopped, slowly looked around, then saw it: the perfect place to display the Filth Eater. Yes. Perfect. His eyes did a quick inventory, then he re-locked the door and replaced the key in the wall safe.

Hector glanced at his watch and frowned. The museum director's call had upset him and he'd lost track of time. He returned to his bedroom, quickly undressed and stepped into his shower. He had a rendezvous with a young lady and didn't want to be late. He knew that she would wait, she didn't have a choice, she was his mistress, but he wasn't sure that he could.

Hector had discovered Amparo Ocampo at a friend's grandson's baptismal party. Hector normally avoided such boring gatherings and saw them as a waste of time. The invitation, however, had come from his good friend the Minister of Transportation, an art collector also, and Hector was unable to refuse a request to attend such an important event from a political colleague. So he went with his daughter, albeit reluctantly. Amparo had drawn his attention immediately, and so he had asked his daughter to introduce them. Amparo's raven-like hair and oriental-Indian mixture produced a stunning prettiness. Exotic, leggy, and a fashionable dresser, she had a manner of posturing and gesturing that invited attention. She oozed sex.

She came from an old political family and her dead father had been a minor PRI functionary of sorts. She had married once, but had no children. What she did have was the morals of a Zona Rosa puta and a little heroin problem. She claimed only to sniff it, which might be true, but Hector didn't like it. Drugs weren't his style. But she was beautiful, and he had been drawn to her like a bear to honey. He promised her the world, bedded her, then procured her a job at the National Museum working for Raúl.

Lately, though, she had become demanding and her dope habit was difficult to satisfy. He constantly found himself having to lean on that Colombian butcher, Cholo, to keep her in heroin. Although Cholo was kept on retainer, Hector loathed using him unless he must. Like Raúl, the bitch was becoming a liability.

He soaped himself all over, visualizing Amparo naked and laughing drunkenly with one leg drawn up, her back to the headboard of a canopied bed, her breasts jiggling each time she gestured with a champagne glass. An intense sexual longing stirred his loins, and he soaped himself until he grew erect. The fantasy begged to play itself out, but he rinsed and toweled himself vigorously.

Dressing quickly, he left instructions for his daughter. He backed his silver Mercedes 500 sl through the wrought iron entry gate of the tall, stuccoed wall surrounding his home. Broken glass shards embedded in the top of the wall flashed in the evening sun, sending an iridescent warning to anyone daring to scale its vertical plane.

Gripped with a sense of urgency, his mind filled with sexual fantasies, he headed for the university district. He imagined that he could feel her long legs wrapped around his back, urging him on, his manhood gripped softly in her warm, moist core. He stared unfocused through the windshield. One short stop at the church to pick up Cholo's heroin delivery and he would be between those legs.

Raúl Cordoba Is Afraid

Friday, June 13, 1984, 7:30 P.M., Mexico City

His hands trembling, the museum director hung up the telephone. He wanted to run. He wanted out. What should he do? My God! You couldn't reason with Hector. His greed would get them all thrown in jail. And the threats, what of the infernal threats? One had to take Vicario seriously. Dangerous and practically untouchable in Mexico, the minister lived his life immune to the law.

"I should never have started with him," he whispered to no one. He must be very careful. He must plan ahead.

Raúl sat in his office at the National Museum of Anthropology in Chapultepec Park, staring impassively at large, colorful pictures of the metro excavation lining his walls. An unprepossessing man, he was slight in stature with a pale and plain face. A few acne scars and a black mole set off a weak chin. The hair on his bald head grew in the pattern of a toilet seat and his hands were soft and uncallused. Inactivity had invited a paunch, and his belly strained against polyester pants. His eyes moved about furtively while his narrow fingers nervously tapped the desk's surface. Except for the occasional sound of a mop bucket being dragged across the white terrazzo floors, a sullen silence had descended. The staff had long since gone home and the night watchman stood outside, serving and protecting.

He peered at his watch; 7:30 p.m. No wonder he felt tired. A bachelor, he kept irregular hours, coming and going as he pleased from his mother's home, living the life of a middle-aged, mediocre bureaucrat. The cigar in his ashtray had grown cold, so he relit and pondered his worsening situation. As he puffed, he sought out the photographs of the Metro excavation. His eyes rested on one in particular, a color photo of a shiny jade mask. Thin and delicate, its pieces were connected with gold wire strands. The mask, a grotesque face displayed in typical Aztec fashion, appeared to be wearing the flayed skin of another human. It had been identified as Xipe Totec, The Flayed One, who wore the face of a skinned virgin girl during the spring renewal rites, an important and popular Aztec ritual.

His attention wandered to other pictures, but inevitably returned to Hector—the immediate problem. He took a final puff and ground-out the cigar. It provided no respite, and his gut began to clench. Piercing intestinal cramps contorted his face and his bowels felt liquid. His anus threatened to open of its own accord. Stooped and grimacing, he hurried to the office bathroom and perched on the stool, Hector's unrelenting mental image pursuing him. As Raúl relieved himself, he considered his options. What should he do? The minister had single-handedly robbed the museum of some of its finest pieces. Everything he saw, he wanted. Why didn't he just come to the museum like everyone else? Somehow he had to be

61

stopped. His obsessions had become a danger for everyone. Couldn't he see that?

Look what he'd had done to Juan Degas and his pretty girl friend last year. Hector had wanted to kill them, but Raúl had convinced him of the peril in doing so. Vicario had no boundaries, for God's sake! Raúl hated the young archaeologist, also. Degas had made his life miserable, but murder? "And now he's threatening me," he mumbled, shivering. He knew that he had been appointed as the museum director with the expectation that he must do whatever Hector asked of him — and Raúl had. He'd given the grasping bastard everything he wanted. But it had to stop. He groaned and slumped forward, his bowels continuing to spasm.

Hector was right about one thing, reflected Raúl. The museum director was up to his neck in shit and would be choking soon. Others were becoming aware of his unholy alliance. Juan Degas, for sure, knew enough to ruin them all, and had once nearly done so with his inventory project. Who did he think he was, the Cisco Kid? Zapata? A Penitent priest from the Conquest wishing to atone his guilt? Bah! How could anyone be so politically immature and foolish?

Raúl had read Juan's report, his alarm increasing with each page. One could get away with much in Mexico if you were well-connected. But after reading the report, the prospect of being sent to Lecumberri penitentiary and taking it in the ass for many years no longer seemed remote. Jesus! How had the boy discovered so much? He even knew in whose houses the pieces lay! Where had he gotten the information? Degas had discovered things that even Raúl didn't know.

The museum director hadn't told Hector of the report. If he had, Juan Degas would have died. Vicario would have seen to it. Degas had not understood that Raúl merely wished to protect him, to save him from his own stupidity. How could one become an adult and not understand how things were in Mexico? Nothing could be done about it. Cordoba couldn't control greedy, entitled bastards like Vicario and the country bred them like rabbits. Hell, they ran the country! The boy was lucky to have left town or Hector would have put him three meters under.

Unfortunately it now appeared that Raúl might leave in the same manner. He felt strongly that Hector was thinking of dumping him, and experience suggested that it would cost Raúl his life. This, of course, lent no reason to give Hector the Filth Eater statue—he would just want something else tomorrow. Thus Raúl must move on Hector before the minister took the initiative. Shit.

He sat motionless, bowels evacuated, calmer now that the intestinal spasms had ceased. Where should he begin? He must do something drastic—his life depended on it. He sat perfectly still and thought. Suddenly an idea crystallized. The beginning of a plan crawled over the barrier and sashayed through the corridors of his cerebral cortex. He became agitated—it might work! Now where had he seen that name? He quickly finished the paper work, pulled up his pants, and hurried towards his office to search for a file.

Raúl would be home late tonight and would miss work tomorrow. He had much to do and would get only a few hours' sleep before driving to Puebla. Deep in thought, he turned and went to make coffee. As he poured his first cup, he remembered the file's location. Fumbling through a cabinet of research articles, he retrieved a file entitled *The War of the Witches*. He returned to his desk to read and plan. His dilemma could only be solved in one way. Hector Vicario needed a good killing and Raúl knew the name of a witch in Puebla who could help.

Linda Maria Takes A Shower

Friday, June 13, 1984, Guadalajara Jalisco

Linda pulled two wooden combs from her dark brown hair. A gift from Juan, they were very old and unique, crafted 1500 years ago by an unknown Maya artisan. A quick flick of her head loosened the coils, allowing her hair to cascade below a slim waist.

From the mirror, a pretty face with green eyes and a classic Maya nose looked askance. She frowned and stared, trying to find fault with even the smallest detail. Juan swore that he desired her more than any woman he had ever seen. He lied, she knew, but maybe she wasn't too bad? Her eyes moved to a half-circle scar above her left eye. It appeared pouty and more prominent than usual. She stroked it lightly with her fingertips—a permanent reminder of the worst incident of her life.

She closed her eyes and the pain of memory surged like a storm-driven wave onto the beach, leaving its ugly detritus exposed. She could still recall the smell of the night air and the stink of her attackers as if yesterday. Four men, thugs hired to

65

hurt and maim, had attacked and beaten them in the Zona Rosa. The weeks that followed were filled with pain, invasive tubes, and saline solutions. An involuntary shiver wracked her, and her shoulders slumped.

The event had left her permanently changed. The concerns of her friends and family had become petty and frivolous and she had withdrawn into a cocoon of morbid despair. Her family tried to shelter and smother her after the attack. But when her father blamed Juan for the trouble and insisted that she shun him, Linda rebelled and sided with her boyfriend. Her mother claimed not to recognize her anymore. Instead of enjoying the protection and love of her family, Linda sought out Juan. Only he knew how she truly felt. What's more, they both knew it could happen again—and the next time might be fatal. They were driven to leave, to get out of Mexico City and the imminent danger lurking in every shadow.

Linda, always devout, found some solace in her religion. But it wasn't enough. Bitterness and fear clung to her like a leech, so she left her family and barrio for another city— Guadalajara—causing a storm of disbelief and outrage in her home. Mexican women do not leave the nest until they are married, regardless of age. Filial devotion is valued just below wealth. When she left home against the wishes of her parents, she cast aside the innocence of childhood and the support of her family. Her decision was a betrayal and her parents mourned her as lost. She had become a fallen woman.

She turned to the mirror again and drew close, searching for the insidious beginnings of a wrinkle. She touched the scar, then lightly traced her fingertips over a high cheekbone, resting them briefly on the arc of a smile line.

"Twenty-seven," she told the image, "and still unmarried."

Almost a disgrace, and surely a scandal in her parents' eyes. And maybe they were right? After three years with Juan there was no engagement ring—only implied promises and vague pledges of a better future. Each meeting last year had become an unrehearsed fight, each argument a slow dying in their relationship. Their future was contingent on his career, which had disappeared since his resignation at the National Museum. How much longer could a girl wait? The future presaged nothing but more of the same: a weak-spirited, vacillating lover always planning but never executing. Again the thought occurred that she should end their relationship and start looking around. How many years did she have before the signs of middle age were visible, four or five? How much longer could she wait for promises to be fulfilled?

Her robe fell to the floor and she stepped into the shower, adjusting the knobs until the water sprayed hot and stinging. Relief was instantaneous. Her body absorbed the pounding and a calming mist enveloped her within a protective, foggy haze. She stood unmoving and allowed the stinging needles to massage and wash away the smell of the city. Refreshed, she lightly soaped her naked body, then rinsed streams of soap bubbles from her svelte frame.

Her skin heavily beaded with water, she stepped from the shower and reached for a white cotton towel to wrap around her waist. The mirror beckoned again and so she moved to view her breasts and upper torso. She cocked her head to each side, then interlocked her hands above her head and spun around. Not bad for an old lady, she decided. She stared at her image, then did a slower pirouette, pausing to look over her shoulder into the mirror.

The intrusive ring of the telephone interrupted her flirtation. She quickly donned a robe and ran to the living room, snatching the phone from its cradle.

"Bueno?"

"It's me, Linda."

"Juan!" she exclaimed, catching her breath. She hesitated. Was this the time to tell him their relationship was over? Should she pour out long suppressed feelings and say the difficult words that would lead to their breakup? Or did she really want that? Oh…God, she thought.

She stuttered "I…I think we need to talk about some things and…"

"Before you start…just listen…okay? Don't argue. Something great has happened, but I want to tell you in person. I'm coming up tomorrow. We'll have dinner…listen to mariachis or something, okay?"

"Wait…what's going on?" she stuttered, confused. "You can't afford it and I need to study. Besides, the neighbors are still talking about your last visit. They all think I'm a puta."

"They're jealous. You knew people would gossip if you moved in by yourself. What difference does it make now?"

"Juan…you're the one arguing…and you're not listening again. I said…we need…to…talk!" she cried.

"Look…I want to see you…be with you," he pleaded. "What do you say? Besides, I'll cut out my heart and roll myself down the stairs at the Temple of the Sun if you say no."

An involuntary smile tugged at the corners of her mouth. "Pervert," she chuckled. "Like the kinky stuff, do you?"

"No…just the esoteric and erotic. Does that mean yes?"

"Ah…well…I guess so," she capitulated. She shoved wet hair aside from her face. "I'll have to call Professor Hernandez and tell him I can't work the exposition."

"That old lecher just wants to grope your grapes."

"Juan! He's a dear old man and he's really taught me a lot. Besides…I need him as a reference for my portfolio."

"Okay," he conceded. "Call me later." "How's 9 o'clock sound?"

"Great…I'm holding my breath, so don't be late. Te amo, Linda."

"Te amo, Juan." She replaced the phone with a smile, then frowned, realizing that she had botched it again.

"Stupid," she whispered. How could she break up with him if she kept saying she loved him, kept sleeping with him? Stupid. She slumped onto the couch and rested her head in her hands. Now what? He sounded so urgent— almost excited—but she should have told him. It wasn't right to lead him on anymore. She just didn't think they had a future.

Dispirited at her failure, a gray brooding melancholy descended, cloaking her mood and depressing her spirit. She unconsciously stroked the scar on her forehead, glanced at a crucifix of Jesus on the wall, then stared blankly at her bare feet. Why are beginnings preceded by an ending, she wondered, miserably. Why do people have to hurt before they can feel good again? Why?

Juan Brushes Linda's Hair

Saturday, June 14, 1984, Guadalajara, Jalisco

A full moon parked high above the star-studded sky far above the Guadalajara Plateau. It cast a pale translucent light over the city, leaking a subdued fluorescence through the windows, illuminating two lovers in the gray shadows.

Their meeting had begun with a quarrel, much like the previous ten. Both had rehearsed what they wanted to say, each aware of the stakes and both wanting to control the momentum of the meeting. But Linda had quickly capitulated and listened, immediately recognizing that Juan seemed different. Holding both her hands, he had talked with passion and told her about his new job offer in Mexico City with Professor Wolf.

Finished, he said, "So…Linda, what do you think? It can work don't you think?"

She sighed and began, confessing how unhappy she was and that she had thought that maybe they should break off their relationship.

But it didn't sound real to him. "No!" he had said, then took her hands again and professed his love. He explained why it

70

was wrong and how much better tomorrow would be. Kind but firm, loving but persistent, he won her over, stealing resolution from an abyss of disappointment. Now, in celebration of renewed passion, they engaged in the ancient and intimate ceremony of lovers.

Linda closed her eyes and concentrated on the rhythmic strokes of the hair brush. The gentle pull and occasional static pop lulled her into a near somnolent state. She lay in repose, clad in a white lace chemise and satin outer robe, her head comfortably extended and her neck resting on a pillow.

Juan pulled the ebony-handled brush through her hair and breathed deeply of her perfume. Never breaking rhythm he continued to stroke, pausing only to lean forward and glaze her neck with his lips. This she enjoyed, he knew, and brushing her long beautiful locks brought them both joy. They had done this often in the beginning of their relationship. It had been a year now since leaving Mexico City and they had for- gotten how wonderfully erotic it was to use the hair-brushing ritual to arouse their passions. As he pulled the brush through her hair, her shoulders sagged and her head lolled backward. While he worked the brush, he would occasionally kiss her the top of her head and slowly work his way down to the sides and back of her neck. When she turned to face him, he kissed her eyes and whispered endearments. She responded with a barely audible moan and placed her arms around his neck. They began a long, passionate kiss.

Tingles of erotic energy streamed into their loins. She purred when he cupped a breast, then lifted the chemise and gazed at the perfect ovals and marveled at their symmetry. He buried his head in her chest, trembling with pent-up desire. Their sexual tension rose, then soared to a crescendo. They stood to embrace, but Juan, mad with desire, tugged at her

71

lace straps and panties. The satin robe fell to the floor and he slid the white lace panties over her hips and they fell to her ankles, revealing a dark triangular fleece. With a fluid movement the chemise came off over her head and she fell backwards onto the couch, legs splayed, pulling him to her as she reclined. They paused momentarily, then with a long passionate kiss he mounted her. Moving gently at first, then urgently, until the gap closed. They began the primal pleasure grist slowly, not wanting to break the magic spell. They moved in unison, but then patience succumbed to compelling passion, and nature's own cataclysm seized and shook them.

Spent, their bodies interlaced just as their destinies were entwined, they slept as only sated lovers can. They would return to Mexico City and confront their personal demons. Linda would reconcile with her family and Juan must find a way back into archaeology without appearing as a threat to the people who had hurt them.

Upon awakening, they chatted late into the night, joined their bodies again, then talked more of their plan. A naive sense of excitement cloaked them from the daunting reality of their task, but when morning found them, they still lay curled together and deeply in love.

Professor Wolf Cleans His Old Office

Monday, June 16, 1984, Mexico City

Professor Wolf perused a Mexico City map and the yellow lines he had drawn with a magic marker to indicate the proposed routes of the Metropolitan Subway System. The map, old and worn, was now obsolete. The majority of the metro system was completed and in operation, already transporting millions of people daily. Only a few areas on the periphery remained under construction.

The office in which he stood near the Zocalo had become rather useless. The museum director and he had shared the space during the excavation of the Aztec Major Temple and David had planned for over a year to return and pick up the remainder of his belongings. Since Raúl had been withholding his reports, David had begun to suspect that the museum director might use the office to stash unreported artifacts. Thus he came to see for himself, and he felt relieved to see that everything remained much as he remembered. Immediately upon opening the door, it also occurred to him that this would be an ideal place for Juan and Marco to have their office. Out of sight, out of mind. Out of trouble, too, he hoped.

He returned to the map. The professor loved maps and never missed an opportunity to stop and examine one. A cursory glance at this one showed the zocalo to include the Palacio National and the Cathedral.

Its boundaries were Avenida Suarez, 16 de Septiembre, Guatemala, and 5 de Febrero. Yellow lines radiated to the four corners of the metropolitan area; from Universidad to Politecnico and El Rosario to Zaragoza. Numerous barrios were located asymmetrically around the periphery of the city with more were being built as he stood.

The oldest city in the Americas had begun with a plan identical to that found throughout the Iberian Peninsula; a central square, or zocalo, surrounded by churches, businesses, and barrios. But Mexico City had outgrown its central planners two hundred years ago. Numerous revolutions and several rulers later, the city continued to grow out of control. The population swelled daily, eating land mass at a pace impossible to calculate.

His eyes focused on the area of the recently discovered Aztec Major Temple near the zocalo and, in actuality, only a few feet from this office. The glimmer of a long suppressed idea waffled momentarily, then held firm. Would it be possible to discover the old causeway roads leading to and from Tenochtitlan, the Aztec capitol city? It was all beneath his feet at this moment. With luck it could be done, he told himself. Some transparencies, magic markers, the old maps in this office and the books at the museum by Fray Sahagun and Bernal Diaz would be needed for the task. Maybe by cross-referencing the maps and comparing them to narratives from the Conquest he could get a general idea of their location. He knew it was a stretch, but if he redrew the old maps on transparencies, then overlaid them on the city map, it might work.

The problem was drawing them to proper scale. It would require much experimentation, and chances were one in a million that anything would come of it. The old Conquest maps were notoriously disproportioned—some almost unrecognizable. Perhaps the narrative accounts of the friars and the old maps by Juan Gomez de Transmonte would help? He would have to try several scale models before beginning the overlays, but who knows? Perhaps more clues would present themselves as he progressed. Pulling a pocket tablet from his shirt, he began to list the needed items. As he scribbled, he remembered that he must leave for the university no later than 1:00 o'clock if he wished to start the project today. He would pack and go quickly, he decided.

A cacophony of noise and accompanying vibration from outside permeated the building. The raucous sounds of Mexico City's zocalo arrived unbidden, leaking through the cracks and vibrating the walls. He surveyed the room. Upon arriving and seeing the large quantity of items to be removed, he saw that too much remained to be transported at once. Next time he would bring help. Better yet, he would have the boys do it for him.

The walls were papered with maps; topographic, stratigraphic, contour, street, utility, and more. Rows of shelves were strewn with rocks, an occasional potsherd, and a few items of which he couldn't be sure—most left by Raúl Cordoba. All of the important artifacts were taken to the University for cleaning, identification, and study. Some would stay at the

University, but most would go on display at the National Museum of Anthropology or into storage. If possible, he hoped for a traveling exposition to show off the Mexican marvels to the world. But that would be Cordoba's job. His, he thought ruefully, would be to find the artifacts, study them, and try to keep them from disappearing.

This thought prompted another and he reached for his notebook and turned to the page he had written the night before. "Raúl Cordoba? Check on suspicions!" it said. Cordoba behaved erratically at best, and had missed several important meetings. He didn't return the professor's phone calls and kept irregular hours at the excavation. His artifact inventory sheets were late, too.

David would wager that the museum director was entangled in another scheme. He personally couldn't stand to be around him. The professor knew him to be shallow, vain, and dishonest. Everyone was aware that Raúl came to the position well connected to the country's top ministers—and therefore to P.R.I.—the political party which ran the country. A political hack turned bureaucrat, the museum director had a limited knowledge of anthropology and was not considered a serious scholar. Juan Degas claimed to have evidence that Raúl had stolen from the National Museum and David had no reason to doubt it. He suspected the museum director of much worse than stealing.

Raúl's primary job beyond his responsibilities at the museum appeared to be attending cocktail parties in and around Coyohuacan where he stroked the egos of his patrons. Juan hated the museum director and swore that he had fingered him to Hector Vicario, who in turn had nearly killed the boy and his girlfriend. David had no reason to believe

Vicario innocent, either. Juan had taken his job too seriously and the young man's zeal had ended in tragedy.

David knew the illicit market for pre-Colombian artifacts very well. In the old days pieces had been openly sold and traded. Many of the finest artifacts lay in private collections here in Mexico, the U.S.A., and Europe. During The Conquest, the Spaniards had thrown away or burned anything that didn't look like gold and melted down everything that was.

Ah…well, his thoughts returned to the notebook and his decision to return Juan to Mexico City. The boys would arrive in a couple of days and final arrangements must be completed for their office and work itinerary. David must get organized. What's more, he must ensure that Juan stayed out of trouble, which entailed keeping Cordoba and Vicario away from him. The boy would have to keep his head low and mouth shut to transition himself back into the mainstream. In the meantime, David still must plan for his upcoming field trip to the Olmec sites of San Lorenzo and La Venta where two of his graduate students pursued investigations.

Would Marco really come along? That boy, too, had potential as an archaeologist, but wasted his focus on the glands between his legs; and the professor suspected that he took drugs. What attracted these kids to marijuana and mushrooms? David had tried it once and earned a sore throat for his efforts. He'd take a glass of brandy any day. When David had put the question to Juan, the boy had mumbled something about recreating the shamanistic experience. With Juan he might believe it. With Marco, who knows? He'd have to keep his eye on that one.

He tucked a few maps under his arm and started for the door, but his mind remained fixed on the Juan-Raúl problem. What had drawn his suspicions to the museum director? When did he first suspect something? Had he found and not reported something? If so, who would know?

He resolved to spend some time with the shovel men and heavy equipment operators at the excavation. The old town of Tacuba, now part of the metropolitan area, lay adjacent to the area in which he intended to test his new theory regarding the location of the old Aztec causeways. This might be his last chance to discover one of the old roads into Tenochtitlan. He had noticed several new faces at the Tacuba site, and it had been weeks since he had checked on Raúl's excavations. Maybe he should go today? But then he remembered his lunch with Baltazar.

Damn! Always something. He was planning too much again. David started to leave, thought better of it, then went to a chalk board still containing last year's old notes and scribble. If time allowed, he would return for the remainder of his things tomorrow or the next day. He would write himself a reminder. He quickly erased, then wrote a note to himself in bold letters: **GO TO TACUBA**. He grabbed the Seismic Isopak and threw it over his shoulder, placed his black leather tobacco pouch and pipe in his jacket pocket, and closed the door behind him.

High above the valley a hazy yellow orb struggled to pierce the polluted air of the city. He walked the periphery of Tenochtitlan's excavated Templo Mayor. The ancient city literally lay beneath his feet, buried under meters of silt and rubble. He looked west toward Tacuba and speculated on the location of the causeway. He knew one of the Aztec roads went west from the old city. Cortez and his army had chosen it the night of La Noche Triste and ended up in Tacuba with much of his army missing.

78

He paused at the fence and looked down into the excavated area. Workmen and researchers still arrived daily to measure, photograph, and ponder unsolved mysteries. David returned a wave from someone he didn't recognize, then hoisted his load and headed across the zocalo. The heart of the city, the Palacio Nacional, Mexico's seat of government, and many of the accompanying ministries and bureaus were located here. The City Hall, the Palacio De Artes Finos, the Latin American Tower, and the National Cathedral were all situated in or on the periphery of the zocalo. Many of the older buildings, including the National Cathedral, have foundations constructed from stone taken from the Aztec temple. The zocalo, an awesome spectacle, is one of the singularly most impressive areas of Mexico City. Unfortunately, the Aztec city of Tenochtitlan is buried beneath it.

The attempt to build an underground subway system had been considered folly. Millions of tons of stone and concrete buildings rested upon a notoriously unstable prehistoric lake bed. But so far the engineers had backed up their promises with deeds. A huge, shallow lake had once covered the valley floor during pre-historic times. The heavily populated cities at the time of the Conquest—Tenochtitlan, Coyohuacan, Tlateloco, and Texcoco—were built on naturally uplifted areas in or on the periphery of the lake. In order to enlarge or enhance existing land, sections were drained and filled in with rock transported from the surrounding mountains and used as a base on which to build.

Tenochtitlan had been the Venice of the ancient world. At the time of the Conquest, it sat completely surrounded in the placid waters of Lake Texcoco, interlaced with canals, palaces, and pyramids. Exquisite white and pink marble was quarried at nearby Xaltocan and used by the ruling and merchant

79

classes to construct decorous, ornate homes. Tenochtitlan had boasted plazas and markets to rival anything in the world. In fact, the contemporary cities of Europe—London, Paris, Seville and Constantinople were filthy eyesores. Smaller and vermin ridden, they were drab dismal in comparison.

By all written accounts, the Aztec city was clean and well-ordered with homes dressed in brocades of bougainvillea, colored banners, and various tropical plants. Spectacular feathers from the beautiful Quetzal and multi-colored red parrots of the southern jungles were used to adorn clothing and bodies. The city was painted in polychrome colors— turquoise, red, yellow and green. Its monarch possessed more wealth than any king in Europe and surrounded himself with aviaries, plazas, gardens and a menagerie.

Immediately following the Conquest the Aztec city had been systematically razed, stone by stone, until the remnants of its former splendor (and pagan beliefs) were erased from man's memory. After five hundred years its exact location remained unknown, although records placed it somewhere near or under the present day zocalo.

David Wolf walked toward Avenida Guatemala and on to his car. Raúl could wait. The professor would stop by Tacuba tomorrow or the next day. He probably would discover nothing, but he knew someone would inform the museum director that David had made inquiries. This, of course, is exactly what he wanted to have happen.

Filth Eater

Malinche, Cortez's guide, was an abomination—an odious, detestable woman. Ask anyone. Ask Humming-Bird-On-The-Left, or Tonatiu, the Sun god. Ask me, I ate her filth. She overreached, and in doing so, destroyed The One Universe.

The people were not perfect—far from it. In their effort to cherish, nurture, and honor the gods the Aztecs conquered many thousands in their Flowery Wars to sacrifice to Humming-Bird-On-The-Left, Tonatiu, and Xipe Totec, The Flayed One. This, of course, is how you nourish the gods. All people in The One Universe know this. The blood of the people sustain The One Universe. The end of the world comes every fifty-two years and it is imperative to sacrifice to ensure its continuation. In this, they acted correctly.

Unfortunately, there were those along my people who were lazy and greedy, much like the bleached faces, and they succumbed to the practice of slavery. Slavery is filth. Malinche was a slave when Cortez found her. But she believed the lies of the bearded ones, that the Aztecs were the cause of slavery. She began working for him with a fervor, imbued with the hope of changing her world, crusading to help free the slaves of The One Universe. To do so, she thought it important to help defeat the hated Aztecs.

The Liar, Cortez, took advantage of Malinche. He said that he understood her and that his God did not permit slavery. He fawned over her and courted her shamelessly. He bedded her and impregnated her and promised to free the slaves. In the end, of course, he betrayed her.

Malinche gave herself willingly to this bleached purveyor of deception. Cortez was evil incarnate; a charlatan and a pretender to the throne of Quetzalcoatl. This filth I cannot eat! This obscenity is too great. Who would ingest such foul matter? Perhaps his "Redeemer" is able. If so, his God is truly a vessel of enormous capacity to contain the filth of such an obscene and odious people.

Malinche died a tormented wretch. She lived to witness the people of The One Universe placed under the yoke of slavery. She lived to see the end of the world. The filth of millions lie in her grave, uneaten and unabsolved. A civilization of incomparable complexity and splendor was destroyed through her ignorance and foolishness. Today and forever she is cursed and reviled—an eternal symbol to the Mexican people of a craven, traitorous woman. She is a bitch, but I forgive her this filth.

Hector Cuts A Deal

Tuesday, June 17, 1984, Mexico City

Hector couldn't concentrate. Earlier he had felt like a raging bull and had planned to put it to her until she begged him to stop. But he should have waited to give her the small envelope of brown powder until after their lovemaking. Zip! Zip! Two quick lines up her nose and the edge was gone. Now she wanted to talk of their relationship. Their relationship? Are you fucking kidding me? Get serious! He promised to talk later, right now he wanted to get laid. Somewhere in between her sniffing the lines and wanting to talk, his sense of urgency fled, leaving him naked on the bed and uninspired. Worse, Raúl Cordoba and the Filth Eater statue had captured his attention, leaving him flaccid and unable to perform.

He tried again to focus on the naked, long legged, dark-haired woman at the end of the bed. He could feel her rough tongue and the tickle of long hair as she licked and sucked; first one toe, then the other. Her warm wet mouth continued to massage him, stroking and probing until he felt cool air caress his toes because of the dampness left by her mouth.

Resolved to put Raúl on the back burner, he willed himself to concentrate. Hector relaxed, his head lolled to the side, and he began to fantasize.

***

Amparo moved upward between his legs, nuzzling and stroking him until he became erect. Within minutes he was twitching and ready to convulse. She paused and swept her hair aside, looking to see the progress of her ministrations. His glazed eyes told her all she needed to know. He might be rich, but she controlled the sex, and that was how she had planned it. Moments later he writhed on the bed and begged her to finish, but she stopped and withdrew her mouth, wanting to maintain control. Beads of sweat layered his forehead and he looked distraught. Amparo despised oral sex and felt no concern for him. But she had to end the ordeal, and so she played him like a musical instrument and brought the song to a crescendo. His head jerked from side to side and sweat rivulets were thrown from his face. He stiffened as his reality shifted into a surreal, out of body experience. She sent him soaring, and then he convulsed and erupted. His toes curled and his face transformed from one of ecstasy to a enameled, mute expression of delight. Then he went limp and lay unmoving, his legs splayed grotesquely, arms fully extended. She smiled grimly, glad the deed was done. She had exhausted him and hoped that he might sleep now.

The bedroom smelled of sweat and musk. Naked, she left the bed to rinse her mouth with the remaining champagne, gone flat from the wait. She sloshed the sweet wine in her mouth, then gulped the remainder. She turned to look at her Sugar Daddy, taking care not to betray that his body and personality repelled her.

He was a macho, demanding pig; always taking, always grasping, and hurtful without regard for anyone's feelings. Twice he had raped her. Once, after too much of the brown powder, she had made the mistake of not paying attention to him. This lapse, and his anger at being ignored, had cost her dearly. She had beaten her severely and had developed hearing problems.

Amparo would give anything to get out of the relationship, but didn't know how. She had learned to control the sex, but otherwise he treated her like a slave, ruthlessly ordering her whole life. She was afraid to do anything without asking. He controlled her with drugs and money. The heroin made everything easier but he rarely brought it anymore. The money, credit cards, and clothes helped insulate her from his brutish reality, but she had become trapped in another dead-end relationship. Why did she keep making the same mistakes with men, she wondered?

Amparo was terrible at ending relationships. She became anxious and near hysteria. Though unhappy and depressed, it was easier to vacillate and do nothing. She didn't want to know where Hector would lead her next. She just wanted something now, anything that allowed her to forget the vacant melancholy of her life. Amparo had become an empty vessel; an amoral, hedonistic, pretty face totally devoid of a young woman's dreams or humanity. She had learned to despise men, but didn't allow her disdain to get in the way of her needs. Recently, though, her want had grown in proportion to her emptiness and only the brown powder could satisfy her need and fill the void. Heroin quelled the anxieties so that she didn't lose control. She could crawl inside her mind and lock out the world. The narcotic anesthetized her and quieted the shrill, inner voices that demanded she pay homage and come visit them in their aberrant, tortured world.

It hadn't always been so. Her mother, a tall languorous beauty from Coahuila, had died of cholera two days after Amparo's tenth birthday. Her father, a drunk and PRI underling, had never been allowed to be anything except a gofor for the better-connected, richer families. Bitter and unfulfilled, he turned to strong drink. His frustration became anger and he became a spoiler and a bent man, privately directing his bitterness at those who loved him the most, his two daughters.

By age ten, Amparo was the second incest victim in her home. Her older sister was the first. Her father molested her until age sixteen, and the guilt and horror of her actions festered like a boil. In a deeply parochial country like Mexico, no one would ever question whether or not to keep such a terrible secret. The victim would be expected to maintain her silence. Thus she grew up without personal boundaries and practiced a morality based on wants and how to satisfy them.

She was diagnosed as a borderline personality at age fourteen, three years after reaching puberty. This resulted in three in-patient stays in mental health institutions over a ten year period. She still occasionally displayed schizophrenic behavior, but no one knew the cause. When pressed into service by her father, she wilted like a flower and withdrew into her own fantasy realm. Her secret world had once been a safe place where people didn't hurt one another, but as the festering chancre of guilt consumed her innocence it became a place of horrors filled with rapacious, hungry images; a personal hell she could visit at will.

Amparo began sniffing cocaine as an eighteen-year-old debutante while attending the National University. She had tried several prescription drugs for her depressions and dalliances with madness, but they were all ineffective or unsatisfactory. Most left her listless and feeling stupid, one or two steps behind everything that happened around her. Narcotics, however, calmed her and allow her to navigate in polite society. Just a little took the edge off her anxiety and frustrations. A lot would quell the demons.

During the years that followed she had numerous failed relationships and a childless marriage that ended tragically. She had mysteriously left Chihuahua in a hurry after a particularly bad period of mental health and returned to Mexico City to escape an uncertain past. Here she met Hector. He used and abused her, but kept her habits fed. He allowed her some semblance of respectability by finding her a secretarial job at the National Museum of Anthropology.

Consequently she spied on Raúl Cordoba for Hector and apprised him of anything unusual at the museum. But like everything else in her life the job had done little to enhance her self-esteem, and lately she had begun to despise the people with whom she worked, especially Raúl.

***

Hector heaved his mass to the side of the canopied bed and sat up. His aging, sagging flesh shifted with each move and one could see the remnants of a once-robust physique gone soft from inactivity and soft living.

"The best ever!" he exclaimed, smiling appreciatively.

"I'm glad," she replied without passion, taking a sip from the glass.

"Where did you learn such a thing?"

She flicked her long hair over a shoulder and turned away. "You don't want to know."

87

He studied her. "You're definitely one of a kind. Sometimes I think I'm tired of you, but then you always come up with a surprise."

She reacted immediately and spun to face him. "You're a bastard to think of leaving me!" she cried, slamming and nearly breaking the glass on the table.

"I won't have to…you'll chase any hard dick with an opium farm in Sinaloa."

"Why are you saying these things? I'm devoted to you…I'll do anything for you!" she pleaded.

"You'll do anything for money or drugs, you're nothing but a puta! I don't want devotion, I want your loyalty, bitch." He stared, unblinking, a threatening misshapen hulk.

"I do as you ask. What is it you want? Do you want to do it again? I'd be happy…"

"Not now," he reclined on the bed, "I couldn't live through it twice in one night. You forget my age."

"Hah! You're like a bull, always ready," she flattered him. "With the right woman you're better than a young man," she added insincerely.

"Bring me a cigarette," he ordered, sitting up again.

She reached for her robe, but he said "Leave it, I like you without clothes, maybe I'll get inspired again."

Amparo dropped the robe, pulled two cigarettes from a pack and fired them. She walked provocatively toward him with both cigarettes in her mouth. He eyed her approach, appraising her as one would an animal at an auction. He took the offered cigarette and patted the bed to indicate he wanted her there. He took two drags from the cigarette, then looked at it indifferently as smoke shot from his nostrils. A sigh escaped and he pondered his next move.

"The sex was great," he said, without passion.

"I like to give you pleasure," she lied, flicking her long locks aside, then took a drag of the cigarette. "You're my benefactor, I'll do anything for you. Tell me what you want."

"A small thing," he paused, extending a fleshy hand to stroke her hair, then let it trail down the small of her back. "I need you to keep an eye on Raúl Cordoba."

"I always do…" she began, but he cut her off with a wave.

"This is different. Pay special attention to his coming and going. Go through his desk and files. Tell me anything and everything you see that crosses his desk. If he acts out of the ordinary, or becomes worried or preoccupied, I want to know."

She shrugged a naked shoulder. "He's rarely there anymore, Hector. He's always downtown at the excavation. He arrives early, stays until noon, then leaves. Sometimes he comes after everyone's gone home. I know because he makes coffee and leaves the mess until morning, and sometimes the toilet seat is up instead of down. He's the only man in our work area."

Impressed, Hector gave her a wry smile. She really was a smart little puta to notice such small things. Putting her in the museum had paid off a dozen times already. He knew that Cordoba suspected, and probably even expected, a spy in the office. A sneak and a coward, Raúl would surely recognize others like himself.

The Interior Minister watched all his employees to ensure he remained in control of his own affairs. He had to know what they did, how they lived, and what they said before it affected him directly. One didn't become a cabinet level politician by doing a good job. The world was full of well-meaning, competent bureaucrats. You had to control people and manipulate them to your purpose. You must make

89

powerful friends and incur the debt of others so that you could perform difficult jobs when necessary. You must be decisive and ruthless. Nothing else worked.

Cordoba, he decided, had out-stayed his usefulness. He must replace him with someone new, but first he wanted the Filth Eater and the sneak had decided to withhold it for some reason. Why did he delay? What was he planning?

With an uncharacteristic flourish of affection, Hector smiled and took her hand. "You do a good job…I'm happy with you. I'd like to do something special for you…something out of the ordinary." He kissed her hand. "But first you help me, eh? I'm out of town through the weekend and I'm worried about Raúl." He took a drag off the cigarette. "He promised me a Tlazolteotl statue, but keeps making excuses not to deliver it. He's up to something. Bring me information about what he's doing and I'll take you to Denver to see the snow."

She spun around, her hair swirling and face smiling. "Oh…please, Hector…you know I'd do anything for such a trip! But what do I look for? What do you want?"

"You'll know when you see it. Bring me any and all information. Everything is important. You have a good nose for these things and Raúl is a fool. He'll show us what he's up to."

Amparo positively glowed. "Can we ski? Will you buy me some new jewelry?" she asked in rapid succession.

He chuckled and reached for her, "Bring me what I want and I'll buy you Macy's. He cupped a breast and fondled it roughly. "Put that thing out…I want you to show this old dog some new tricks."

Amparo stubbed the cigarette and reached for him.

"I'm going to need some help…" he began, but she put her hand across his mouth, smiled, then pushed him back onto the bed.

90

"I know your needs, Hector. Remember that, I know what you want," and she bent her head and went to work again.

Amparo Steals A Report

Wednesday, June 18, 1984, 7:00 A.M., Mexico City

Amparo walked the shady sidewalk of Molino Del Rey in Chapultepec Park. She came early almost every day to enjoy the cathedral-tall pines and dense green carpets of grass that spread in every direction. A quiet day, the morning fog had fled with the first rays of sunlight, leaving only wisps and thin tresses of gray mist hovering near the ground. The air felt thick with humidity and the sour odor of the lake wafted in on a light breeze.

She trod thirty more paces, then turned east towards Maximillian's Castle. She skirted the periphery of the forbidding structure, an imposing, austere fortress on a lonely hill. It stood as a stark reminder to the European countries who had tried to impose a monarchy and dictate the affairs of the Mexican people from half a world away. Spain and France had both learned the hard way to mind their own affairs.

She walked onward, approaching the National Zoo, her purse in hand, head down and unseeing, intent on her

92

thoughts. In a city of twenty million people she was but one of a handful in the park this morning. She appeared pensive and taciturn, the result of sleeping poorly, and lately she always seemed to be tired. Between Hector and the heroin, she was wrung out in the morning. The days were either filled with melancholy, or moments of excruciating eternity. Nothing brought her joy or had any real meaning to her.

Two quick lines from a quickly diminishing supply of heroin had put her in the right frame of mind to come to work this morning, to be pleasant and smile. She would need a quick pick up around noon to make it through the day, but nowadays her want had grown disproportionately, and Amparo knew that she had arrived at the early stages of a heroin addiction.

Hector used his man, Cholo, to buy it in the Zona Rosa. But thank God he didn't bring the stuff every day! She feared losing control again, even though the old demons were trying to talk to her. They wanted her to come and visit, but Amparo knew she must resist and be strong under pressure. But always she wanted what scared her—the heroin—and this insight she found devastating. She had played with drugs for years; always self-assured, smug in her belief that she remained in control. But was losing ground and knew that she would have to start saying no.

Upon approaching the zoo, she heard the roar of restless, hungry lions demanding their breakfast. She stopped in a grove of towering hemlock to listen to their grumbles of protest and listen to the early morning sounds of the waking zoo. The piercing cries of parrots and macaws broke the stillness when shrieking monkeys threatened may- hem. She glanced behind her, then continued on the shady path.

Her mind returned to Hector. He behaved like a beast with a festering rancor. His personality was like a disease; a chronic, unshakable affliction. He spread darkness like cancer, rotting and destroying everything beautiful and whole. He subverted the charm and order of life with his greed and hatred. Yet the misogyny he projected actually seemed to draw her closer to him, as if she wanted to be hurt. She had never been around anyone quite like him before, except for her father. He acted so much like her father, she realized. This comparison further weakened and depressed her spirit. The Virgin save her! What would she do?

She understood that Hector was terrible for her. The warning signs were clear and ominous. If she continued her relationship with him, she flirted with a personal cataclysm that would dwarf previous disasters. She must decide soon. How could she get away from him? Where would she find the strength to say no to the money? The heroin? If she had a plan, would she have the courage to pull it off?

She sat on a stone bench midway between the zoo and the lake to consider her deteriorating situation. The look inward prevented her from enjoying the beauty of the park. As far as the eye could see, ancient pines stretched to touch the clouds and broad stately oaks shaded expanses of green velvet that rolled out of sight. The lake lay serene and placid, its shallows choked with green algae. Regal swans slowly and purposefully glided one direction, then another, searching for an unwary meal. The Aztecs had called Chapultepec "The Hill of the Grasshopper," and it was deemed sacred by them. The foot of the hill contained carved images of numerous Aztec rulers as well as a stone-lined pocket, known today as the Bath of Moctezuma.

Always a source of delight and solace, today the park brought no respite. Finally, with no solution in sight, she closed herself to the nagging questions and remembered her purpose in arriving so early. She stood and straightened her dress, looked around quickly, then strode toward the National Museum of Anthropology across the street from the zoo. She crossed Paseo De La Reforma, walked north fifty paces, then turned west, facing the entry to the museum. To the right of the doors stood a massive basalt head of the Olmec god Tlaloc. It stared at her intently, its jaguar-veiled eyes hard and threatening. Uncaring, she walked on, intent on her mission but with a growing apprehension.

"Buenos dias, señora!" said the ever-present guard, reaching for his keys.

"Buenos dias, Renaldo" she replied with an encouraging smile.

"Bien...bien, y usted?" he offered graciously. "You're early this morning, señora."

"Yes...I've much to do and señor Cordoba depends on me greatly," she lied, dropping her boss's name.

Renaldo opened the door and she threw him a big smile as she passed. The white terrazzo floor of a spacious atrium greeted her. She moved to the stairs and began to ascend, her anxiety growing with each step and an inchoate panic beginning to rise. Then her heart began to pound and she thought of running and returning to the comfort of the park. But no, she knew she must proceed according to plan. Hector would call tonight and she must have something, anything, to tell or give him. She swallowed, took a deep breath and climbed resolutely to the second floor.

Sixty seconds later she knew that her boss had been there all night. She surveyed the chaos on his desk and surmised

95

that he was in a big hurry when he left. The coffee pot sat half full, and clutter covered his desk. At first, she thought he might still be here. She quickly looked around, then waited a couple of minutes in case he had gone to the bathroom. When he didn't appear, she began her search.

She preferred order. It was easier to put things back neatly than to remember their placement in a jumbled mound. On the desk top lay several texts; a book by Bernal Diaz from The Conquest and several volumes from Friar Bernardino de Sahagun's "*General History of the Things of New Spain.*"

"Must be doing research," she muttered. Amparo thought this curious. Raúl rarely involved himself with academia. As the director, he spent most of what little time he allocated to the museum in administrative or bureaucratic functions. What had he been doing? She reached for the book, then stopped. Had she heard something?

She ran to the office door and looked down the hall. Shit! She was imagining things. Get a grip, she told herself. Leaving the door ajar so that she would hear anyone climbing the stairs, she returned to the office. Half way across the room she saw it. There! It practically screamed for attention—a yellow manila folder on the floor beneath his desk. After stooping to retrieve it, she opened the file to read the cover page of a report: "*Conclusions Regarding the Continuing Disappearance and Obvious Theft of Antiquities From the National Museum of Anthropology.*" It had been authored by Juan Degas. A involuntary shudder jerked her. Juan Degas—public enemy number one at the museum, a prima donna who refused to get on the team. Why hadn't she seen this before? Had Raúl taken to hiding files from her?

Amparo recalled that she liked Juan and his friend, Marco. They were friendly and amusing and had never done anything to hurt her. Marco would hit on her for a date every time he came by, and if not for Hector, she probably would accept. He looked hot, unlike that limp, wrinkled shit Hector.

She turned the page and saw the date: June 12th of last year. She read on: *"be advised that the conclusions reached herein are all documented. Evidence exists which cannot be refuted by the actions or word of others. This report has a dual purpose:*

To expose the graft, theft, and treachery regarding the National Museum's artifacts by some of the leading citizens of the country.

To protect myself by warning the reader that two additional copies of this report exist. One is in my possession and the other in the hands of someone known only to me; to be revealed in the event of any harm to me or my loved ones."

Blackmail! she thought, her mouth gaping with surprise. Or protection—maybe he did it for protection. It didn't matter. What incredible luck! Her hands shook at the enormity of the find. She recalled the series of events leading to Juan's departure from the museum. It had been a scandalous mess with noisy confrontations, shouting, cursing, and threats. It ended with Juan angrily stomping from the office and the museum director beside himself with worry.

Less than a week later Juan and his girlfriend were attacked in the Zona Rosa. The girl had a two week stay in the hospital and had nearly died. Everyone at the museum knew it had something to do with Degas' arguments with the museum director. Amparo liked them, but she had to stand firm in her boss's corner. Everyone in the office had seen it coming. It's what happened to people in Mexico who didn't mind their own business.

She didn't hesitate, this is what Hector wanted. She didn't have a clue about Raúl and the Filth Eater statue, but this report could be worth a trip to Denver. This is what she had hoped to find. She switched on the copy machine and began making a duplicate. Her nerves were frayed from the worry of being caught, but so far she was holding up under the strain. She checked her watch: it said 7:25. People would begin arriving soon.

While she made copies, Amparo thought of Hector and his promise. Shopping and skiing in Denver. Yes! Que buena suerte! (What good luck!)

Maybe Hector would buy her a new wardrobe, or some jewelry? She began to fantasize about Denver. Would he rent a mountain cabin with a fireplace? Amparo didn't know how to ski, but it looked like fun on T.V. Hector probably wouldn't want to learn; he looked too old, but maybe he would drink brandy by the fire while she took lessons from a handsome ski instructor. They did have snow in Colorado this time of the year, didn't they? She tried to visualize snowcapped-mountains and stately pines, but her memory would only conjure a picture from Life magazine with photos of the Winter Olympics.

She had no qualms about betraying Raúl. Remorse didn't exist in her repertoire of emotions. Although Hector and Raúl were both bosses, Hector paid the bills and kept her in dope. If there was one thing she knew for sure, it was that you had to accommodate the boss.

Even though she didn't know all the events surrounding the report, or the implications for Hector and Raúl, she felt confident that Hector would reward her for this day's work. He was a creep, but he wasn't dumb, and if he told you to do something you had better do it—the bastard.

Sometimes she thought she had too many bosses. Even Raúl refused to keep his hands off her. He used every opportunity to harass her to go to bed with him. Hector

ViVID

98

would kill him if he knew what the museum director wanted. Raúl behaved like an asshole too, but now he could make amends without knowing it. This report would settle his debt to her.

She checked her wristwatch again. Time had gone swiftly, so she returned the report to its folder and repositioned it under her boss's desk. She thought to leave, but stopped to survey the messy desk top one last time. Her attention was drawn to several pages of paper protruding from beneath his desk calendar. Carefully lifting it up, she retrieved the papers. These, too, looked like a report, and the title page read, *"Witchcraft Beliefs and Violent Death Among the Nahuatl Indians of Puebla State, An Investigator's Research and Interviews With Survivors of The War of the Witches,"* by Armando Antonio Marcello-Sapullo. She shivered, the spasm shaking her whole body. Her hands clenched the report, creasing the pages. Witchcraft! She crossed herself involuntarily for protection and dropped the report like a red hot chili.

Why did Raúl read stuff like that? She knew that the Indians still believed in witches and that most villages had a shaman who brought offerings to the old gods. They performed cures and served as an intermediary between the gods and the people. The witches claimed to be Catholic and worshipped Jesus and the Saints, while having taken on the duties and characteristics of the pre-Conquest priests. Amparo didn't know for sure herself. She didn't understand any of it, but the title of the report vexed her greatly and she felt a twinge of fear.

Enough! she warned herself, inserting the report under the calendar. Perhaps she could use this later. She folded Degas' report and stuffed it into her purse. Mission accomplished. She felt like a burglar, and took a deep breath, exhausted but elated. Her underwear, damp and sticky, clung to her skin. She trembled slightly, but felt relieved. The deed was done. She needed a quick pick-up, just a little one, deciding she deserved it after all this shit. She grabbed her purse and entered the office bathroom. She locked the door behind her and approached the sink. Her hands shook as she prepared a line of heroin on the broken compact mirror. Not too much, she reminded herself, chopping the brown dirt into ever finer pieces with a single-edged razor blade. Someone might become suspicious if she sniffed too much.

She hated her co-workers. The women in the office gossiped about her mercilessly; her marriage and no children, living by herself, and an occasional boyfriend in the office were widely discussed behind her back. She had no desire to give them something else to talk about.

Her long, auburn hair hung like willow branches as she bent over the mirror. Holding one nostril closed with her index finger, and using her other hand to hold a short straw to her nose, she sniffed. She repeated the procedure for the other nostril, then re-packed the razor and makeup kit. She looked into the mirror above the sink to check her appearance. Relief came immediately and a sense of well-being cloaked her, creating a buffer between her and the world. She straightened her clothes, checked her makeup, then returned to the work area to await the rumor-mongers. She could handle anything now that a boost of confidence percolated in her blood. Today, the silly bitches wouldn't bother her; Amparo had checked out.

Marco Meets Amparo

Wednesday, June 18, 1984, 10:00 A.M. Mexico City

Marco coughed nervously, then took a quick glance at his fingernails. He had been given his first assignment since returning to Mexico City—trip to the museum—and he needed to stay on track to make a good impression with the professor. He had hoped for a week off upon returning, but the professor was adamant, so Marco had readily agreed. After all, how long can you argue with the boss? He had sworn never to return to this place, but the books were needed and Juan's coming was out of the question. David had warned that working with Raúl Cordoba and serving as an intermediary for Juan would be one of Marco's major responsibilities. It made sense. His buddy sometimes talked as if he would kill Raúl given the chance. To say that Juan hated the museum director and his friends understated the obvious; Juan wished them all dead—or worse, if possible.

Flicking his cigarette butt into the street, he turned left and followed a shady concrete path to the National Museum. Broad-limbed oaks lined both sides of the street, creating an umbrella to block the bright June sunshine.

He turned to walk towards the museum. A huge head of Tlaloc, the Olmec Rain god with jaguar eyes and Negroid features, stared poignantly into the distance through veiled eyes. As he passed the giant head, he recalled the sensation surrounding its discovery in Veracruz. Tlaloc had been on the front page of every newspaper in the country. Ironically, it had rained for ten days during the period of discovery and transport to its new and permanent resting site here at the museum.

The reporters had made much of the rain, promoting it as a super- natural occurrence when in fact it wasn't. But stranger things than this happened routinely in Mexico. One couldn't explain away everything, and Marco would just as soon believe the story as discount it. It had a certain romance, and it gave the Mexican people a reason to be proud. They could talk and speculate endlessly about the miracle of rain and the finding of the Rain god. The professor described it and other miracles, as "unnatural events that occur naturally." But the newspapers had feasted on the wondrous events, their headlines reading; "Rain God Tlaloc Inundates Mexico City," and, "Tlaloc Shows Displeasure With Ten Days of Rain." The Olmec god had been the topic of conversation for weeks afterward.

He climbed the steps to the second floor and considered what he would say to Raúl. He would be polite, he decided. Raúl knew him from previous encounters and they had never argued. Unspoken mistrust was a barrier, but he doubted if Raúl wanted a fight today, either. Marco would just get the books and be on his way. Hands in his pockets, he walked casually into the office and saw immediately that the pretty, dark-haired girl still commanded the front desk. Her name plate helped him begin.

Amparo sat at her desk doing nothing, anxious for the day to end so that she could go home. Since exchanging insincere greetings with the other women in the office, they hadn't spoken again. A loud voice startled her.

"Buenos dias, Señorita Ocampo!" boomed a vaguely familiar voice.

Amparo, floating along in a heroin induced reverie, acted unsurprised at seeing Marco. She corrected him with a smile, "Señora, if you please," then added, "but you may call me Amparo." Señorita was a title for virgins and other liars and Amparo hadn't been a virgin since she was ten.

The effects of the narcotic were diminishing and she was more alert. The fact that she had thought of Juan Degas and his friends earlier that morning while burglarizing Raúl's desk, bothered her not at all. The reality of finding Marco standing in front of her, she found very intriguing and difficult to resist.

"Remember me?" he coaxed, placing both hands on her desk and leaning toward her.

"Of course...Sr. Gonzalez, isn't it?" she tossed her hair behind her shoulder, her interest evident. She held his eyes and returned his smile, thinking that he hadn't changed much—still a flirt. Raúl looked like a pot-bellied, bald-headed burro, and it was refreshing to see a good looking man in the office, even if this one ogled her like the museum director. Marco's stare never wavered and she felt the warmth of a blush, something that rarely happened anymore.

"Okay, Sr. Marco," she panned, "is there anything I can do for you? No, wait...I phrased that wrong." She leaned back into her chair and languorously crossed her legs. "What is it you require?" Again she flicked her hair to the side and cocked a shoulder, knowing the insinuation would not pass unnoticed.

Sure enough, his eyes dipped to her legs, then back to her face. It worked every time. She watched him hesitate, as if doing a quick analysis of her behavior.

"Uh...Professor Wolf at the National University requested that I borrow a few books from the museum library. But now that I'm here, I see a beautiful woman that I'd like to take to lunch." He winked. "Would you, Amparo?" he showed her his pearly white teeth.

Very smooth, she thought, but then she had invited his attention. Amparo recovered quickly, not wanting to appear a blushing virgin. She hesitated. This, after all, seemed a familiar situation to her and she moved immediately to regain control.

"Well," she replied, her voice all business, "we don't really know each other very well, do we? I'm not hungry. What did you have in mind for this lunch?"

"I prefer open air and the shade of a tall tree to stimulate the appetite. Don't you agree? After I pick up the books, why don't I buy some quesadillas and a licuado at the zoo. We can get to know each other better by the lake."

Amparo couldn't think of a reason why not. He stood tall and attractive, a plum waiting to be plucked. She had done nothing all day, and though boredom invited temptation, Hector and Raúl would never know. But she shouldn't say yes too quickly.

"What books do you want?"

"Huh?" he said, put off track. "What books?"

"Uh, let's see, *The Discovery and Conquest of Mexico* by Bernal Diaz, and *The Conquest of Mexico and Peru* by...uh...I can't remember. If you'll let me see, I can figure it out for myself."

104

He stepped back from the desk, his eagerness gone, his face a blank.

"Follow me," she ordered, and strode away as if expecting him to trail her like a dog. He paused briefly to follow the movement of her hips, then followed.

She walked into a small room and motioned him to accompany her down. She pointed, "What you're looking for is probably in this area." She smiled to reassure him, then left him standing with a quizzical expression. When he reappeared with the books, Amparo was just exiting the bathroom and tucking her makeup mirror into her purse. She walked toward him with the bag under her arm, her face an impish mask. She rubbed her nose and sniffed loudly, rubbed her nose again, then with a look that revealed all said, "I'm ready when you are." The pupils of her eyes seemed to gleam and spread into shiny, obsidian plates.

Marco stared, fascinated, and said "Great! My appetite just came back. Do you need to check out or anything?"

"Not today. Raúl's gone and I'm my own boss when he isn't here. Can I trust you to be a gentleman?" she flirted.

"Not always," he leered. "Let's see how well we get to know each other over lunch."

Amparo looked him straight in the eye. "I think I'm getting hungrier all the time."

Hector Reads The Report

Thursday Evening June 19, 1984, Mexico City

A light breeze buffeted hanging mobiles of tinkling sea shells on Amparo's balcony. It parted her curtains, allowing a mote-filled beam of sunlight into the apartment which illuminated and exposed the shadow of long curvaceous legs in her sheer, satin evening wear. She stooped over an end table to retrieve a broken makeup mirror and rolled-up $1,000 peso note through which she had earlier snorted heroin, her third and last line of the day. The bag lay empty, but she appeared unconcerned; she felt great. She tucked the paraphernalia into her purse, then walked to the balcony and looked beyond the billowing curtains toward the National University. You couldn't buy a better view.

The huge, colorful mosaics of Juan O' Gorman stood in full display, clearly visible on two sides of the library. One, a marvelous creation scene, the other a series of images; suns, moons, and eclipses. But she didn't care, didn't even notice. A familiar sense of self and well-being rippled from her center to the tips of her extremities. She stood barefoot, leaning against the door with one leg cocked, slowly moving it to and fro, playing with long strands of her hair while enjoying the delectable, rising tide of ambrosia sweeping through her. She had felt even better five minutes ago, but that bastard Hector had called to say he was on his way. He had been away two days, but had returned, and now she felt anxious.

The heroin did much to assuage the pangs of guilt after enjoying herself with Marco. He treated her like a lady, and she wanted to see him again, soon. But she must be careful. If Hector discovered that she was seeing a younger man, he'd beat the crap out of her and dump her.

She had thought out a partial, and maybe permanent solution to the Hector problem, but first she would see if he followed through on his promise to take her to Colorado. He promised a lot, but didn't always deliver. Although she usually had money, the credit cards only had a six-hundred-dollar a month limit, and for some reason she always found herself broke. She never really had enough income to do as she wanted. It took more than an apartment and a fist full of pesos to meet her needs. Hector had become just another disappointment—the miser, and an even greater problem. She must get away from him somehow.

The last few months at the museum had been crazy. Raúl Cordoba was still pressuring her to have sex. The cretin. How much longer could she forestall his demands? Twice last month he had insisted that Amparo meet him after work on the pretext of working. He had taken her to the Tacuba site while she watched him load the Museum's small pickup truck. She had broken the heel on a new pair of pumps, snagged her hose, and gotten mud under her finger nails. Disgusting, but necessary, she supposed. The crap a woman had to put up with! The last two weeks he rarely came to work at all, which she thought just fine. She felt trapped into a balancing act between two men and knew what would happen if she didn't find a life preserver soon.

If this were not problem enough, yet another man wanted her. But something about Marco made her think he might be different from the others. Oh sure, he wanted to get in her pants—they all wanted sex—but he talked about interesting subjects and he did such intriguing things. He was a real archaeologist, not a bureaucrat like Raúl who spent his free time digging in ice buckets and measuring gin shots for his mixer.

Marco treated her well—unlike others who knew too much of her past—and he wasn't a disapproving, macho-man insecure about his masculinity. He also had a rebellious, anti-social streak just like herself. She wondered if he got high. He had alluded to it, but she had let it pass and not encouraged his questions. In a way, she hoped he didn't. When she dated men who got high, the relationships turned ugly quicker.

She glanced out the balcony doors and saw Hector approach in his Mercedes. He stopped at the red light, waited for the change, and drove his sleek silver machine into the parking lot. She stepped away and shut the sliding door and pulled the curtain. Hector sometimes acted paranoid and didn't like to be watched. A twinge of anxiety stabbed her vitals, but she suppressed it, determined to maintain control of the situation.

Moments later his key rattled in the door, then his big body filled the doorway and he stepped into the dimly lit room. His jowls, red and sagging, framed a drunken smirk. He stood unsteady, his shoulders sagging, and a bottle of Rojo's champagne clutched under his arm.

Shit! He's been drinking. An involuntary shiver shook her. She felt repulsed, but said, "Hector…you're here! I've been missing you all day," she lied. "You don't spend enough time with me and I get so lonely by myself in this apartment."

Hector plunked the bottle on the table and turned to look at her pouty face. "You know I'm a busy man. Be patient. I can't stand it when you complain!"

"I'm not complaining," she returned smartly. "I just want you to know that I miss you. Besides…I think I have something you want."

"You always have something I want," he slurred, innuendo dripping from his tongue.

"Hector! You've been drinking!"

"What's it to you, bitch?" he gave her a hard look. "Someone who sniffs heroin is in no position judge others!"

A warning bell rang in her head. *Shut up, stupid!* she warned herself. She held out her arms and walked to him. "Let's not fight," she cooed. "Here, let me make you feel comfortable. I know you have so many demands on you. I just want to give you the pleasure you deserve."

Placing her arms around his waist and her head on his chest, she whispered soothingly, coaxing and snuggling against him, trying to blunt his bad humor. She felt his tenseness dissipate, then fail him. He took a deep breath and sagged perceptively.

"It's good to get away from everything," he said. "I'm called at all hours of the night. Sometimes I don't remember leaving work or going home," he complained. "The country is plagued by fools who can't make decisions and idiots who shouldn't be."

He hesitated, then returned her embrace, putting his face in her hair and breathing deeply. He reached for a firm, round buttock to squeeze. She accepted his rough handling and intrusive pawing, then pulled away when she sensed his rising ardor, timing it to precede his arousal by seconds. "Aiee! you're like a horny stud bull," she flattered him. "Open the champagne and I'll massage your feet while you have a drink?"

"Sure," he said grudgingly, missing the curvy softness of her body. "You have a surprise? Is it about the statue? I hope it's good…you know how I hate to be disappointed." He looked expectantly. "So, surprise me, bitch. What's the worm doing? What did you find?"

She pointed to the chair, "Come on…sit down. First things first, Hector." She knelt submissively and began to massage his feet, first one then the other, thinking about her plan and playing for time. She wanted him to recognize her contribution and the risk she had taken. Most of all, she wanted him to remember his promise of a reward.

"What would you say, if I brought you something that would prove Raúl was withholding information that could damage your reputation and have you put in jail?"

"He wouldn't dare!"

"I don't know," she replied wistfully, "you'll have to judge for yourself. He must be crazy to keep this from you."

"What! What is it? No more games, Amparo!" He jerked his legs from the hassock and leaned forward.

"No games, Hector. I've got it, but first you must promise to protect me."

"Protect you? From what?"

"If Raúl knew what I'd done, he'd fire me."

"If what you say is true I'll cut off Raúl's cojones and have him sent to Lecumberri. I'll make sure he takes it in the ass the rest of his life."

"Hector…don't be so crude," she chastised.

"Enough…no more games! If you have something let's see it!"

"Oh…hold your pee," she huffed. "I just wanted you to know that I took a big risk for you." She rose from her kneeling position and walked into the bedroom to retrieve the report.

***

Hector gulped his champagne, grimaced, then slumped back into his reclining chair. What in the hell was she talking about? The museum director was a sneak and needed to be watched—but a major double cross, a plot against Hector? Not likely. Cordoba was a rabbit. Hector vowed that if what Amparo said had any truth, Raúl would be looking for a job by week's end—if he was still alive.

Amparo returned waving a sheaf of papers in the air. "Hec…tor," she drawled, "remember your promise to take me shopping to see the snow?"

"Yes…I remember," he growled sourly. "Give it to me already! Is this about the Filth Eater?" He snatched the papers from her hand and glanced at the front page. "What the hell?" he muttered, reading the title page *"Conclusions Regarding the Continuing Disappearance and Obvious Theft of Antiquities From the National Museum of Anthropology"* by Juan Degas."

His heart thudded, then begin to fibrillate, making him cough. He jerked upright in his chair. My God! It couldn't be! Agitated, his facial muscles twitched and he suddenly felt ill. "Fill my glass, Amparo!" he commanded, turning the page.

Phrases and words leapt from the manuscript, piercing him like a sword: *"evidence exists"*, *"cannot be refuted"*, *"to expose graft, theft, and treachery"*, and *"leading citizens of the country"*. He read on, disbelieving and incredulous and with a growing cholera verging on cold fury; *"warn you"*, and *"to be revealed in case of*

111

harm". Vicario sat and read the report in its entirety, sometimes grunting or making a face in recognition of a statement. His hands trembled. With barely concealed anger and his face a mask of steel, he looked directly into Amparo's eyes.

"Where did you find this?" "Hector, I ..."

"Think! I need to know everything, from the beginning, bitch!" he threw the papers next to the chair. "I want to know when, how, and at what time...everything."

Amparo took a step backward and hugged herself, surprised and frightened. She had never seen him scared before, and she made her face a blank mask. She must be careful not to show any enjoyment of his discomfort.

He watched as she extended a long, thin arm for the bottle, then turned to face him. "Calm down," she said in a pleading voice, then narrated the events leading to the discovery of the report, omitting a few minor details she thought of no interest.

He collapsed into the chair—destroyed—betrayed and double-crossed by Cordoba. The rabbit had become a fox! But why? Juan Degas had them by the balls and Cordoba was pretending it wasn't so. Degas could ruin their lives, maybe have them put in El Bote. Hector should have killed him!

He had no illusions, his authority and power went only so far. He would receive no help from anyone above and if someone leaked this report, his position as the Minister of the Interior would be in serious jeopardy. The damage to his reputation would be irreparable. What should he do? Why hadn't Cordoba shared this confidence with him? What was the snake doing? Why hadn't he delivered the Filth Eater? Was there something special about the statue that Raúl hadn't told him? Damn him to hell, anyway! It just didn't make sense.

Rising from his chair, he began to pace. Amparo, meanwhile, refilled his glass and handed it to him in mid-

112

stride. She opened her mouth to say something, but a malevolent look shut her up. He continued to pace, sipping from the glass and planning his next move. Tension hung in the air like dusty, slumping spider webs. The air felt oppressive and difficult to breathe, Amparo though how nice a quick toot would be.

Finally, he spoke. "You did well Amparo, but I need time to think about this. Continue as you are, watch everything that Cordoba does. He's a rat and a snake. Next weekend you can fly to the United States. No…don't interrupt! You're flying to Denver, or wherever. I don't care because I can't go along. I'll arrange it with Raúl."

"But, Hector…"

"Shut up and listen!" he hissed. "You decide where to go…it doesn't matter. I'll put five thousand dollars in your account tomorrow. Shop your brains out, I don't care. I want you back within a week because I'll have more work." He whacked the sheaf of papers against his leg, "After I've decided what to do about this report, Raúl Cordoba is done, fini!" he whispered with a clenched fist.

"What about Juan Degas?" said Amparo, almost as an afterthought.

"Huh?" he replied, startled at her question. Then with a voice dripping with malice, he said, "Degas is no longer a problem. I have plans for him and his little puta." Hector tossed the remainder of his glass down, then turned and stared at her.

***

Amparo shivered even though the evening temperature hovered near eighty. Hector gave her the creeps. It was scary when he acted like this and she worried that he might turn his anger on her. She looked again and saw that he watched her; strangely calm, almost subdued, thinking and planning his next move.

His voice startled her. "Amparo I want you to go to Cholo's house again."

"Ohhh, Hector…I hate…"

"Shut up and listen," he repeated.

She cringed at his tone and his menacing expression. Still hugging herself, she turned away, but listened closely.

"Give him a note to meet me at the church next Tuesday at 3:00."

"What church, Hector?"

"He'll know. Get me my shoes. I have things to do and places to go," he replied gruffly.

"But Hector…"

"Hush, and do as I say!"

Amparo knelt to tie his shoes while her mind reeled with possibilities. Confusion reigned. She couldn't go to Colorado by herself, could she? What should she do?

"You only made one mistake, Amparo," he said, peering down at her. "You should have taken the report, not just copied it. Tomorrow, when you go back to the museum, I want the original, okay?"

"Sure, anything you say darling," she lied, knowing she had no intention of retrieving the original. Her neck remained secured, her job intact, and Hector, though angry, appeared to be happy with her. It was better this way. Tomorrow promised a shit-storm, and she had no intention of being around when the sewer backed up. "I wish you could stay," she lied again.

"Read a book…listen to music…do something! I'm busy and can't be entertaining you all the time. It might be a couple of days before I call. Make plans to leave soon if that's what you want. Goodbye and quit calling me at home! It disturbs my daughter." He turned and strode through the doorway, moved heavily down the stairwell, and out to his car.

Amparo, peeking around the curtain, watched his silver Mercedes approach the intersection, then deliberately run the red light. God! Finally gone—and maybe for a week! She always felt exhausted after he left, and tonight was no exception. You walked on egg shells when he was around. Anything could set him off.

Slumping into the recliner, she considered the possibilities of the proposed trip. Who would come with her? She didn't have any friends, and didn't want to go by herself, that was out of the question. Besides, she didn't speak English and one didn't go on a trip like this alone, anyway. She must share it with someone special. Gripped with indecision, she stared at the balcony curtain, immersed in her dilemma. Unexpectedly, the telephone rang. After two rings, she picked it up.

"Bueno?"

Her expression went from one of irritation to a smile that told all. "Marco, you devil! I told you never to call me this time of day!" She listened, her joy evident, then without hesitating she said, "Sure…Shakey's Pizza…one hour."

She hung up and sat down to consider what she had done. This could be dangerous and Hector might find out, but she didn't care anymore. She wanted to have some fun and Marco could be the ticket. He would help her in more ways than one, and Hector could pay for it.

Filled with anticipation, she picked out her sexiest outfit and held it beneath her chin to preen in front of the mirror. Perfect, she decided, then checked her make up and put on the colored print dress. She returned to the mirror to make sure that it clung to her curves and accentuated her figure.

115

A bold plan had come together, but she must be persuasive tonight. Amparo, wily and skillful when manipulating men, felt confident that Marco would cooperate. He wanted what all men wanted from her — and she would give it to him. But in order to collect, he must accompany her to the United States for a short, romantic vacation. There were plane tickets to buy and clothes to pack. She must be at her best tonight, but she had seen his frank, appraising looks at her body.

Child's play, she assured herself. Euphoric with anticipation and enthralled in romantic fantasy, she left her apartment, taking the stairs two at a time. She jumped into her VW Beetle.

"Goodbye Hector, goodbye Raúl," she whispered, then smiled with glee. She turned west into the orange haze of the sunset and drove toward Shakey's Pizza. As she drove and sorted the details of her new plan, she forgot to worry that the last of the heroin had gone up her nose an hour earlier.

Filth Eater

Human sacrifice is a spiritually up-lifting ritual as old as the jade in the mountains of The One Universe. The first great ones, the Olmec, recognized the need for blood sacrifice. Later, the Toltec, the Maya, and finally the Aztec continued the practice and brought it to its zenith. Thankfully, old beliefs die hard. Today in The One Universe the few remaining Huhuetes (shamans) make due by sacrificing animals to the old gods and spirits.

Now one can walk the forgotten roads of The One Universe and see shrines built to the old gods. But the names have changed. St. Anthony, St. Mark, etc. are the new purveyors of spiritual blessings to humanity. My people bring gifts of liquor and tobacco to these spirits. This is filth—to forget the names of the Immortal Ones. It is wrong to substitute mundane products for the most precious substance in the world, blood.

The Christian Filth Eater died to ensure the passage of the bleached faces into the great void. In The One Universe people were willingly sacrificed to ensure the continuation of the gods and The Paradise of the Sun. This was necessary because the world ended and began every fifty-two years.

The Aztecs were a pious people. They understood the duality of existence, the significance of life and death. They realized that one was temporal and the other a spiritual realization of life's major goal — to ascend into The Paradise of the Sun. The dim-witted and unlearned bleached souls were woefully ignorant of the complexity and mysticism of the Aztec belief system. They saw the world through the pale void of bleached eyes instead of the rich, red fullness of their bloody hearts. The filthy ones allowed their eyes to interpret what only their spiritual body could understand. When they encountered human sacrifice, the bleached ones screamed in terror and crossed themselves. They cursed and reviled the Aztec priests, then destroyed hallowed places and built churches on top of holy sites throughout The One Universe. The National Cathedral in the zocalo of Mexico City was begun in this way, using rock taken from the great Aztec pyramid, El Templo Mayor.

What the bleached skins interpreted as cruelty and violence was actually compassion and virtue. The Aztecs fought their Flowery Wars to provide the ultimate gift, blood, to Tonatiu and Humming-Bird-On-The-Left. In the Aztec language, nahuatl, flower and blood are nearly synonymous. If one understands the semantics of the concept, then the duality of life and death as well as the spiritual purpose of the Aztecs are readily divined.

Although they won't admit it, the bleached ones have a long history of blood sacrifice. Indeed, they celebrate the blood sacrifice of their "Redeemer" in ritual masses thousands of times a day throughout The One Universe. Their priests ritually drink blood and eat the body of their Filth Eater, Jesus!

True to their shallow character, they have found a way to drink the same victim's blood and eat his body over and over again. Filth! Sacrilege! Abomination! The bleached faces are spiritual miscreants compared to the Aztecs. Their ritual enactment falls far short of the real thing. Can a god be satiated with a facsimile? Will the Mightiest Ones be satisfied with pretend, with simulation, with a lie?

Juan Proposes To Linda Maria

Saturday, June 21, 1984 Teotihuacan, Mexico (Thirty miles north of Mexico City)

Standing on top of the great Sun pyramid at Teotihuacan, Juan pressed his hand to the pain in his side and gasped for breath. His heart pounded painfully from the strenuous run up the pyramid's stairs. Linda, trailing behind, now sat slumped and panting in the middle of the platform. She hugged her legs. Entranced by the scene, hands on hips, Juan looked into the distant gloom and let a familiar sense of awe grow within as his body recovered from the climb. He began to walk the periphery of the pyramid's apex and gaze into the nightscape. Standing on its pinnacle, he could clearly see the top third, but the remainder hid, occluded in the early morning darkness. It would soon be light, and the pyramid's majesty revealed to all. Lightheaded from the exertion, his spirits soared and he turned his attention to the sequined travelers journeying slowly across the sky. Twinkling brightly, the stars boasted of their splendor against a dark satin background, their eternal trek unimpeded by mortal concerns, indifferent to the two young lovers atop the 2,000 year old pyramid.

On this morning the group of stars known as the Pleiades reached its zenith directly over the great Sun pyramid just as it always did on the 21st of June. As the dimness and mist dissipated in the pre-dawn and the Milky Way slowly faded, and where the sky joined earth, a glow waxed in the east. Summer Solstice, the longest day of the year, had arrived. The Sun god had yet again won its nightly battle with the demons of the underworld. No sound came from the two adventurers; each lost in their own thoughts. They had come to witness the constellation Pleiades rise to its highest point and confirm that the heavens held their order. This momentous event, now largely ignored and hence unimportant, was mostly forgotten. The Toltec temple had originally been built as an observatory for this purpose, but now no one used it. The city had been abandoned for nearly a thousand years.

Juan sat next to Linda and her head lolled onto his shoulder. They sat unmoving, listening to the quiet. He watched the eastern glow of the horizon while his imagination began to reconstruct the city and its inhabitants.

Below lay the Avenue of the Dead. Smaller pyramids lined either side of the street and at the far north end sat a smaller pyramid, the Temple of the Moon. His mind's eye imagined wooden structures with palm-leaf roofs atop each pyramid. Beautiful flowers adorned the homes and streets and colorful banners waved in the wind. Rows of white-washed houses lined the periphery of the city. Children played in the streets while neighbors stood and gossiped of the most recent events.

With his imagination free-falling into the past, he looked two miles to the south where the markets were in full swing. Thousands of people gawked, shopped, and talked. A mile

121

further, lay the Citadel and the Temple of Quetzalcoatl. Far to the edge of the city, the roads were lined with people come from far away; merchants from the Maya to the south and zapotecans from the mighty city of Monte Alban in Oaxaca. They came to trade for the most valuable commodity in Meso-America, green obsidian, from which beautiful pieces of art were carved and where ceremonial daggers for bloodletting were made. In its day Teotihuacan, the great Toltec community whose name means, "The Place Where the Gods Gather, had been the mightiest city in the world." Below, on the Avenue of the Dead, he imagined priests emerging from their temples and beginning the ablutions and necessary rituals to maintain the favors which the gods bestowed on the city. He saw thousands of Toltec soldiers marching to war dressed in gay colors, festooned with flowers and adorned with quetzal feathers, nose plugs, and embroidered regalia. They carried shields of many colors, stone clubs, and swords edged with razor-sharp flakes of obsidian. The armies of Teotihuacan had controlled an empire ranging from the present-day southern United States on the northern periphery of Mexico, to what is now Guatemala in the south. Fifteen hundred years ago it had been the largest city on earth, commanding enormous tribute and endless captives to sacrifice to famished gods who controlled the celestial movements of the sun and moon.

The eastern horizon continued to brighten. Linda stirred, murmuring something barely audible, but Juan sat engrossed in the spectacle parading before his imagination. He had been here before; twice with Linda and four times with Marco. He preferred, though, to come unaccompanied and unencumbered by the presence of others. At those moments the history and mystery became so immediate and real that he lost himself in the fantasy.

Bright white needles exploded over the horizon, piercing the morning sky with their brightness. A blood-red orb began its ascent until it hung suspended above the eastern horizon. The Monkey god Ehecatl had blown the Sun god into the heavens again. The promise had been kept. The world would endure another day.

The sun burnished the ancient city in a golden light. An ethereal morning fog dissolved into clarity, revealing the environs of the abandoned city. Juan stood to enjoy the view. Taking Linda's hand, he began to gesture and talk, explaining what he knew of the Toltec mysteries. He prattled on about Mexico's celestial deities—the sun and the moon—and how human sacrifice had become necessary to ensure the movements of the sun, moon, tides, and animal migrations. He described how captives were sacrificed, the importance and influence of priests and the relationship between the Valley of Mexico and the rest of the country.

***

Linda sighed and shifted her weight, trying to appear interested. A smile tugged at the corner of her mouth. She'd heard it all before, but it felt good to see him excited about his work again. Nonetheless, she tuned him out rather than hear the lecture again. It was romantic to come at this hour when the ruins were empty, and so she had agreed to accompany him. But her thoughts turned inward and her mind strayed.

On their return to Mexico City as they topped the mountains surrounding the Valley of Mexico, a morbid fear had sent twinges of anxiety racing down her spine. This was the place she had been beaten and nearly killed. But the three of them—Juan, Marco, and herself had made light of it and adopted a boisterous bravado, a comradely, "we're all in this together" attitude.

123

Since returning to her parents, life wasn't too bad. They treated her like a prodigal daughter returned to the nest. Her father, Mario, had even behaved civil towards Juan. The boys had taken an apartment, and a week later David had called and scheduled a meeting at the university. They spent the entire day reacquainting themselves and reaffirming old ties. Marco, surprisingly, had begun work five days earlier. David was building a list of projects for Juan, and had encouraged them to go slow and become comfortable with the city again. "Have some fun," he said, "take a few days off."

Much to her amazement, the professor had offered her a job also, entrusting her with a special project. It entailed examining historic, but poorly made maps of Tenochtitlan and Lake Texcoco from the Conquest Era and comparing them to old Mexico City maps, drawn after the construction of the Cathedral in the zocalo of Mexico City.

The professor wanted to identify reference points and locate the old Aztec causeways. These roads, buried five-hundred years now, had connected the Aztec island city of Tenochtitlan with the mainland.

Dr. Wolf had already discovered similarities between an old route to Chapultepec on a map from the Conquest and another drawn by Juan Gomez de Transmonte in the sixteenth century. David would teach her the process of drawing maps to scale on transparencies and overlaying them on the old maps. He had alluded to the possibility of finding something more exciting than the causeways, but wouldn't be specific, even though he claimed to have two of the three reference points he sought.

Beside her Juan continued his boring lecture—now talking about the Temple of Quetzalcoatl. Linda locked her arms over her chest, cocked her head impatiently, and interrupted.

124

"Juan?"

"Huh?"

"Enough, querido! It's time for a kiss…can't you be romantic? Why are you always so serious?"

"Huh?"

"I don't care about cutting out hearts or building temples. Hold me and tell me you love me, goof. Talk to me. You didn't drag me out of bed and force me to climb the highest pyramid in Mexico without so much as a kiss, did you?"

Taking the obvious clue, he reached for her and placed an arm around her waist. His other hand stroked her long brown tresses. He seemed to hesitate, then pulled away. A look of distress crossed his face and he tried to speak, but stammered instead. As she watched his composure dissolve, he mumbled something about being "glad you came," and it being "really special," and, "I had intended to talk to you about something real important."

She'd never seen him like this and his awkwardness surprised her.

"…anyway, I guess what I'm trying to say…is that I love you…a lot. I can't imagine not being with you and…" he stopped, confused, seeing the bewildered expression on her face. He took a deep breath and said, "Just a minute," and thrust a hand into his pocket to extract a small, felt covered box.

Linda, barely breathing, stood mute with surprise, knowing it was finally happening. She could barely hear him now, only a loud ringing in her ears. Juan opened the lid and exposed a beautiful ring with a large diamond centered in a heart-shaped cluster of tiny red rubies. Gorgeous! She gazed wide-eyed, speechless.

"You know I love you. You mean more to me than…than…I mean

…you stayed with me through the worst time of my life. I can't imagine living my life without you. Will you marry me?"

She felt herself tremble all over. Part of her wanted to snatch the ring and scream with joy, but instead her eyes began to water. She had waited so long, and when she looked at Juan, she saw that he too felt vulnerable—afraid of being turned down.

She took the ring and looked into his eyes. They embraced at length then Juan began a long, passionate kiss that ended with his hands beginning to wander. Linda pulled away, saying, "Not here silly, the whole world can see us!"

"Come on, it's so early, no one's up this time of the day. It might be the first time anyone's done it up here."

"Not a chance, mister. Control your hormones. Be romantic and put this on my finger."

"Sure, how's this?" Confident now, he slid it on the third finger of her hand. With a flourish of humor, he said, "Linda, if you refuse to marry me I'll cut out my heart and roll myself down this pyramid!"

She laughed, delighted with the charade. "Hey…I don't want your blood on my hands, so I guess I'll have to say yes."

"Bravo! Bravo!" came a cry from below. They looked down.

"You're a romantic dog, Juan Degas!" called Marco, waving from below. He was climbing the pyramid with two bottles of champagne in one hand, and three long stemmed wine glasses in the other.

As he climbed, he panted, shouting, "You're a defiler of young maidens…a womanizer, and a rake!"

Linda clapped her hands and turned to Juan. "You planned this

…didn't you?"

"Well…I thought it would be a nice touch…you know…a marriage proposal, champagne with friends, a few toasts to our success…"

She gave him a quick peck on the cheek, then turned and called down to Marco. "Careful you don't fall."

"Ugh…I hate pyramids," he panted. I'll take a trench over mortared rock any day." Continuing to chatter, he made steady progress until he arrived gasping and begging Linda to give him mouth to mouth resuscitation.

"Not a chance…no telling where that mouth's been. But maybe Juan…."

"No way. I know where it's been."

"Laugh you two." Marco extended a glass to each. "If my lungs collapse, you'll die guilty!" he gasped. "I left a warm bed to hazard the worst traffic in the world, to bring joy and companionship to the most special people in Mexico, and to brighten their day with carbonated spirits." He held the champagne bottles aloft. "I came to pay my respects to Tonatiu, the Sun god…though I see I'm a little late." He used his other arm to shade the sun. "Most of all," he turned to Juan, "I came to bail your ass out in case you blew it and Linda shoved you over the edge. How'd he do, anyway? I didn't come too early did I?"

"Marco you're impossible! I'm glad there was a back-up plan…but…yeah…every thing's okay. He did great. What a man!" She hugged Juan again, and they embraced.

"Okay you two…break before you asphyxiate. How about some champagne?" Marco brandished the bottles, swore an oath to the ancient Toltec gods, then popped the corks with great fanfare and non-stop chatter.

***

127

An hour into the fiesta Marco reached for an empty bottle and declared, "Monday's the big day, amigo." He began to peel the label. "Found your new office yet?" he added with a sly smile.

"Hey...I was in that place a thousand times when Raúl and the professor were working out of it. I know my way around. The zocalo's not so bad. I still don't know how you ended up at the University and me downtown. Here...let me brush that brown stuff from your nose."

Marco ducked beneath the slow swipe of Juan's arm.

"I guess David's worried about keeping me out of trouble...wants me to keep a low profile." Juan shifted his weight to the other arm, then drank the remainder of his champagne. He wiped his mouth. "I'll fix it up like my old place at the museum, but first it needs cleaning. I'll return some things David left behind and maybe move some dust around until I decide what I need...you know? What's your plan for Monday?"

"I'm off to the museum to locate books. There's a good looking librarian who helps me navigate the dark corridors of the library. She can't keep her hands off me."

"She must need glasses," mocked Linda. Marco ignored her. "Well," she continued, putting her nose in the air, "I have my own office at the university...right down the hall from the professor," she giggled, tipsy from the champagne. "Actually...truth is...he stuck me in a lab on the fourth floor. It's full of old bones and broken pots...the place is a mess." Juan reached for her hand. Looking first at Linda then Marco, he said, "It's going to work this time. I'll avoid that bastard Raúl, even though I'd like to cut his cojones off. Marco, you do the same, okay?"

128

"You're preaching to the choir…take care of yourself. Let's stick to business, okay? No crusades." He held Juan's eye. "This time we follow the professor's instructions…agreed?"

"Agreed!" Juan extended his hand and they shook.

They sat atop the Temple of the Sun, in The City Where the Gods Gather, enjoying the last of the champagne. They feasted on the fruits of seeds planted and cultivated over many years of friendship. They drank to love and talked of old loyalties. Linda and Juan tipsy, love-struck, hung on each other.

Finally, the bottles empty and the morning sun grown strong on their backs, Marco declared, "Breakfast on me! There's an open-air restaurant down the road. How about some chorizo and coffee?"

"Sounds great. Linda?"

"Sure, why not…but…uh…I don't know if I can get down without falling," she giggled.

"Huh?"

"Too much champagne…here take my hand."

With Linda in the middle they descended the two-thousand-year-old pyramid. After gaining their breath, Juan and Linda walked hand in hand toward his Mustang, their backs to the abandoned city. The City Where the Gods Gather, Teotihuacan, had yet another story to tell. The town where countless people had lived, worked, prayed, and died stood eternal and unconcerned. It sat unmoving, essentially unchanged, a witness to man's aspirations, delusions, and failures.

Juan And Raúl Argue

Monday, June 23, 1984, 8:00 A.M. Tacuba Site, Mexico City

The wind gusted suddenly, capturing bits of paper, dust and grit, swirling them into a charging dust devil that raced along a gravel strewn, rutted road leading to the Tacuba excavation site. Two starlings screamed and battled over a broken tortilla thrown to the ground by two men cooking corn shells on a barrel lid set above an open fire. On Monday morning no one appeared in a hurry to begin work. Indeed, little was accomplished in the last two weeks. The workers stood around leaderless, aimlessly talking and waiting.

Juan sat heavily on a pile of rubble, then immediately stood to rub his eyes and spit out the grit and dust blown into his mouth by the dust devil. When he sat back down, a blinding mid-morning sun caused him to cringe. Raising his arm to block the light, he crawled to the shady side of the rock pile.

A pulsing headache commanded his attention and his mouth tasted like a den of jaguar shit. His hands trembled in an alcohol palsy. He hurt, and having to be at work early on a Monday morning only made matters worse.

Returning to Mexico City had so far been a success. His meeting with David had gone well, and Saturday Linda had said, "Yes!" to his proposal of marriage. Their rendezvous atop the Temple of the Sun on a Summer Solstice morning was romantic and joyous. The champagne and outdoor breakfast had piqued their celebratory impulses. Thus they spent the day and night commemorating the occasion with a salvo of champagne bottles in the Zona Rosa, followed by a night of dancing.

Linda, exhausted from the non-stop partying, went home in the early morning. Juan collapsed in sleep, satiated and debilitated, only to be awakened by Linda, asking that he attend mass at Our Lady of Guadeloupe. This memory elicited a groan and a shake of his head. Tired and sick with alcohol poisoning, bereft of his common sense, he agreed to go, proving to Linda, he hoped, how much he loved her.

After mass and a late breakfast, he urged her to return to the apartment for more lovemaking, but she demurred, convincing him to go to her parent's instead. Upon arrival the door flew open and a long line of relatives surrounded the Mustang, cheering and crying, "Felicidades!" congratulating them on their engagement. The festivities began anew. Brandy toasts were offered until lunch at 2:00 when a troop of purple-sequined mariachis, complete with wide-brimmed hats, arrived to serenade the blushing, tipsy, couple.

As evening approached, Linda retired for a two-hour nap. Juan, meanwhile, continued to drink and talk with her father, Mario, under a shady avocado tree next to a bubbling water fountain within a Spanish style, open-air patio. They raised toasts and talked of Linda until Mario became maudlin and his

131

eyes moist. Plucking a lime from a nearby tree and cutting it with his knife, he confessed his former dislike of Juan, then declared his new-found approval. Mario, drunk but filled with equanimity, stated that he was proud that Juan would be his son-in-law. They continued to drink, each toasting the other's family, raising cup after cup. They toasted Mexico's soccer team, their favorite cars, their favorite movie stars, Mario's German shepherd and more, until they sat drunk and near somnolent. Neither seemed willing or capable of leaving the patio table. Linda awoke from her nap and helped her mother break up the drunkest by shooing her father to bed and having a barely sober Marco drive Juan home.

Juan, concerned that he make a good impression, rose on time and visited his new office near the zocalo. It was a mess, and so he had half-heartedly moved a few things about and stirred the dust, then went to Tacuba upon seeing the professor's message to him on the chalk- board, '**GO TO TACUBA**.' The message struck him as a little peculiar, but he assumed David intended to meet him there.

Now he sat above a twenty-meter wide ditch on a pile of volcanic rock. The incongruity of so much stone in a former lake bed of silt and clay should have piqued his curiosity, as it might be part of an old road or structure built by the Aztecs. Today, however, archaeology must compete with his hangover for attention.

"Buenos dias, Señor Degas!" called a cheery voice from below.

Juan, raising his head, tried to emit a civil response despite a throbbing head and worsening mood. "Buenos dias Sebastiano," he replied to the stocky, round-faced former shovel man. "Long time no see...how's the new wife?"

132

"Fine…just fine," smiled Sebastiano. He looked away, momentarily embarrassed at the question.

Juan smiled benignly at the friendly construction worker, seeing it as a good omen to encounter someone he knew first thing on the job. Sebastiano remained a favorite from previous excavations and Juan recalled him as contented, very hard working, and like many of his brethren, surprisingly knowledgeable of Mexico's pre-history. Sebastiano had been a common laborer for the city utilities when his shovel inadvertently came into contact with a large circular stone carved in relief of the goddess Coyolxauque, sister to the war god Hummingbird-On-The-Left. His discovery ultimately led to the excavation of the great Aztec Temple and uncounted archaeological finds. Sebastiano's life improved measurably with his new found notoriety. After attending technical school, he secured employment as a heavy equipment operator and had recently married a willowy young girl from Sinaloa.

"So, what's the plan?" Juan inquired absently, looking down the long ditch toward Tacuba. "Is the surveying finished?"

"Si…si, they're finished," replied Sebastiano, "a long time ago. We're waiting for Sr. Cordoba to give approval to widen the tunnel."

"Cordoba!" exclaimed Juan. "He isn't here, is he?"

"Why…yes…he is, Sr. Degas," the workman hesitated, seeing the look of malice on Juan's face. "He's about fifty meters west, examining a wall of rock like this," he pointed toward Tacuba.

Juan's mood darkened immediately. Although inevitable, he had yet to encounter the museum director since returning, and the prospect of doing so this morning caused a quick, white anger to seize him.

133

"That bastard son of Malinche!" he jumped to his feet. "Always meddling…and he doesn't know shit about archaeology. Why's he holding up everything?"

Cowed by Juan's sudden anger, Sebastiano stepped backward. "Don't know," his round shoulders shrugged. "He found something a couple of weeks ago, a small statue I think. He closed down operations until he finishes his investigations."

"Investigations!" Juan snorted. "Cordoba isn't an investigator…he's a bureaucrat, and a piss-poor one at that! Where is the shit?"

"He, Sr. Degas, is right behind you, listening to your insults," said a voice oozing contempt. "I heard you were in town, but didn't believe it. You have no right to talk in such a manner in front of the workers!"

"Raúl!" Juan spun around, momentarily embarrassed, but his mood and his ire were not be denied. Though in an awkward situation, he knew he must say something. He began badly.

"So…what's in the bag? Something to sell to your buddies?"

"Careful, Degas!" hissed the museum director. "You never had any sense…always talking loudly and to the wrong people. Be careful you don't keep making the same mistakes!" Raúl's voice dripped innuendo.

Juan, understanding the implication, shook with long-suppressed rage. "Listen you bastard," he said in a hatred soaked voice. "If I ever hear you threatening me and Linda again, I'll kill you! Hear me, scum bag?" He stepped forward, his fists doubled, the menace in his voice unmistakable.

"Don't try to intimidate me, Degas!" Raúl stepped backward. "I don't know what you're talking about." He cast

134

about for help. "A dozen witnesses heard you threaten to kill me. What are you doing here, anyway? You have no right to be at this excavation. I'll be calling Professor Wolf to report this incident and insist on your removal!" The museum director slung the bag over his back, took another two steps back, eyed Juan warily, then turned to walk away, glancing over his shoulder to ensure that Juan didn't jump him.

The young archaeologist stood with fists clenched, abandoned to a helpless anger as he watched the diminishing back of Raúl Cordoba move east toward a distant line of cars. Stillness gripped the rubble-strewn construction site. Only the sound of the museum director's boots crunching the earth broke the fierce quiet as he retreated from unfinished business.

No one spoke. Several people had witnessed the exchange, but had no understanding of the situation. Why the argument? If the bulls were fighting over the cow, where was the cow? A few of the workers gave each other knowing looks, silently communicating something left unsaid. Sebastiano recovered first.

"Sr. Degas..." he waved his large arms from the trench, "...calm yourself...this is no place for a fight!" he pleaded. "Don't follow him...you don't want trouble, señor. Please, I have hot coffee and tortillas we can share until you feel better."

Juan's mind raced. What the hell had happened? How had the situation deteriorated so quickly? He had threatened to kill the museum director in front of twenty witnesses. Had he lost his mind? But the bastard had provoked him...talking about not making the same mistakes. That spineless son of Malinche!

The argument sealed his conviction: he felt certain that Raúl had ordered last year's attack in the Zona Rosa. The

135

unwelcome memory of the fight caused his stomach to clench and an involuntary spasm shook him. He felt like throwing up.

"Señor Degas…are you okay?" pressed the worried Sebastiano, now climbing from the trench. "My thermos is over here and I have an extra cup." He moved toward a nearby bulldozer, walking slightly stooped, as if his huge arms hung too heavy to carry.

Juan clenched and unclenched his hands. Though angry, his passion had receded to be replaced with a clumsy embarrassment. He hesitated, noticing the staring faces of the construction crew, shifted his weight from one leg to the other, then walked toward the bulldozer where Sebastiano stood unscrewing the lid to his thermos. He accepted a steaming cup of coffee.

Neither spoke for a moment, then Juan offered blandly, "I know you probably don't understand why that happened." He took another sip then added, "He paid some people to hurt my fiancee' and me about a year ago. I have unfinished business with Raúl Cordoba."

Thinking of his own pretty wife, Sebastiano's round face lit-up with understanding. "If that's true, he deserves to have his ass kicked. No one here likes him. You and the professor talk to us like men," Sebastiano's big fist thumped his chest for emphasis. "But Raúl acts like he doesn't have to shit; his nose is always in the air, and he's afraid to get his hands dirty." As an afterthought, Sebastiano added, "I wonder what he had in the sack?"

Juan stood quietly and sipped his coffee. All around, people returned to tasks they had begun before the argument. Juan's hangover clamored for attention and his stomach began to waffle. Maybe it would be better if he did throw up. When Sebastiano offered the thermos again, Juan waved him off.

He placed the cup on the bulldozer tractor-tread and said he had to make a phone call. He said thanks for the coffee, then traipsed in the same direction as Raúl, toward his car.

He drove toward the National University, thinking of what he would tell Professor Wolf. The traffic moved slowly, and thirty minutes had passed before he reached the entrance ramp to Insurgentes, then another thirty to drive to the university. He took his time. Urgency had fled like a field of startled crows, leaving him hesitant and feeling guilty. How had it happened? What would Raúl do now that he knew Juan had returned? He groaned and struck the dash with his fist.

After parking his Mustang in the Staff Parking Lot, he walked to the Department of Anthropology. He had promised David that this wouldn't happen, but it had—his first day on the job. After agonizing over what to say, he decided the truth was best—as usual. He had shot off his big mouth and nearly gotten into a fight. Now he must take his lumps like a good boy. He felt no remorse for what he'd said—he hated Cordoba, but he didn't want to cause David any problems.

Twenty minutes later he sat in the back row of a big lecture hall with two hundred students listening to the professor finish the morning's class. Dr. Wolf was lecturing on the prehistoric cultures of northern Mexico: the Mogollon, Hohokam, and Anasazi. Nearly out of time, he quickly reviewed the day's lesson by drawing parallels between the three. He cited ball courts, agriculture comprised of maize, beans, and squash, human sacrifice, and well-built stone architecture, especially among the Anasazi which had constructed very elaborate cliff dwellings.

Juan thought the argument for diffusion of ideas to the Anasazi to be weak. Mexican Archeologists routinely espoused the diffusion of ideas from Mexico as the source of nearly

137

everything. According to some, even the pre-historic effigy mound builders of the Mississippi and upper Ohio valley received their ideas from Mexico. Nonetheless it was true that no other New World civilization had come close to the social and material complexity of Middle America's, although the Inca in South America came close.

Juan slumped in his seat, enjoying the familiar environment of the classroom. He was tempted to close his eyes, but the lecture ended suddenly. Hundreds of students stuffed their books into bags and exited the room. He had caught David's eye when first entering the lecture hall, so he waited patiently while the professor visited with inquisitive students. Finally, he made a break and headed up the aisle toward Juan. Inexplicably, the biblical phrase, "The hour of judgment is at hand," jumped into his mind and took on a newer and clearer meaning. He took a deep breath and waited as his judge approached.

Professor Wolf Chastises Juan

Monday, June 23, 1984 10:30 A.M. Mexico City University

Restless, David pushed away from his desk and leaned back in his chair. He glanced at his wristwatch. A meeting was scheduled in thirty minutes and he didn't want to be late. Juan was talking, barely visible over the books, binders, and reports on the professor's desk. Stacks of papers, assorted books, and more lay randomly strewn throughout the room. The office appeared a mess and smelled musty. Aged, smoke-stained ceiling plaster hung broken and limp, defying gravity and threatening chaos to the clutter.

The plaster walls were cracked, but decorated with memorabilia. Photographs of David and Alicia in the Yucatan and Oaxaca decorated the rear wall. On his desk sat a picture of Guatemalan Voladores, the original bungee jumpers, hurtling downward from the tops of poles with only rope attached to their ankles at the Guatemalan Festival of St. Tomas in the town of Chichicastenango. Numerous artifacts were placed about the room.

The mess was so complete that he had given up trying to organize and routinely refused offers of help from graduate students who, in reality, only wanted to peruse the treasures of forgotten academic accrual. His students gleefully discussed excavating the office after he died. David had an unvoiced fear that he would be unable to find any- thing ever again if someone other than himself cleaned the room. A surprise would occasionally reveal itself from a neglected pile. Once he found a four-year-old Tupperware container with a mold-encrusted sandwich, and on another occasion, an un-mailed wedding anniversary card that had gotten him into trouble with Alicia.

He was half-listening to Juan's narrative, thinking instead of his upcoming field trip to Veracruz, when a key word startled him. He lurched violently and turned to face Juan.

"What? You went where?" Incredulity spread across the professor's face. "Say it again," he motioned with his hand.

"I went to Tacuba, and…"

"What the hell were you doing at Tacuba!" thundered the professor, striking his desk. "I sent you to the zocalo," he fixed Juan with a glare. "Look around, I said. See what you need, I said. Bring me some of my stuff, I said." He crossed his arms and stared angrily.

"David, I went to the…"

"You got any Murphys in your family, boy?" he interrupted, sarcastically. "What…Murpees? What are Murp…"

"Never mind…" The professor waved him off, disgusted. "A great Irish sage who gave us Murphy's Law."

"Which is…?" Juan sat stoically, crossing his arms, also.

"Anything that can go wrong, will go wrong. Get it?" David leaned back into his over-stuffed chair.

140

"Well," shrugged Juan, considering the question seriously, "maybe I do." He looked at his shoes.

"Just a minute." The professor stood and walked toward a window, perilously navigating between piles of reports. He looked through the pane, took a few calming breaths then began, "Okay…let's start over. What were you doing at Tacuba?"

"I tried to tell you…" Juan half-turned in his chair, looking for his boss, "I went to the zocalo like you said. I swept the floor and did some organizing, then I saw your message on the chalkboard."

"I didn't leave you a message," Dr. Wolf protested.

"Somebody wrote a message that said `**GO TO TACUBA**' in big letters. I thought you had written me a note."

"Aw…for Christ's sake." The professor shook his head in disgust, then returned to his desk. He took a deep breath and sighed. "Okay…tell me all about it."

Five minutes later, David held up his hands, palms outward to signal a stop to the narration. It was the same old problem. Juan's big mouth had gotten him in trouble again, but this time it might spill over onto the professor.

"So…you're telling me that you stepped on your dick again, right?"

Juan paused, "Well…yeah…but like I said, he provoked me. He told me not to keep making the same mistakes. His meaning was obvious."

"Are you?" asked David, quietly. "Am I what?"

"Are you making the same mistakes? Are you being indiscreet, talking in front of the wrong people, talking to the wrong people…you know?" "Well, I…" Juan stuttered, "I was talking to Sebastiano about Cordoba stopping construction at

Tacuba for an investigation. I said, what investigation? Cordoba isn't an investigator, he's a bureaucrat!"

"Then what?" coaxed David.

"Well...I can't really remember. He showed up carrying a canvas bag and...I mean...hell, I admit it, professor. I hate the man! You know he's the one who had Linda and me beaten because of the inventory project. Every time I think of him I want to smash his face."

"Juan! You're going to have to quit saying that. Listen boy...if Raúl Cordoba dies of an ingrown toenail and word gets out that you've threatened to kill him, you'll go to jail for a long time. Think!" he pointed emphatically at his head.

David continued. "I know this is an emotional issue for you. I understand...but if you don't act rational, it will hold you back professionally—might even get your ass in a sling." He leaned forward. "Make no mistake about it...Cordoba will get what's coming to him. You've heard the old saying, 'what goes around, comes around?' Raúl will get caught stealing or selling artifacts to his powerful friends, and he'll fall. His friends won't, but he will. They'll sacrifice him to save themselves. He's built a tangled web from which he won't be able to escape. Can't you see that?"

"It just doesn't seem fair that Raúl..."

"Fair!" the professor exploded, slamming his palms onto the desk. "Life isn't fair, boy! Was it fair that I lost Alicia the way I did...run off a cliff by bus? Listen!" The professor scooted his chair forward. "This is Mexico. Fifty million Indians were starved, beaten, killed, or died of disease during the Conquest. During The Revolution from Spain uncounted thousands died because of injustice and the need to rid ourselves of the Hacienda System and the colonial government of Europe. Then King Louis forced the monarchy

142

of Maximilian on us and thousands more died of gunshot, hanging, starvation, and cholera—all for fairness, mind you."

David shrugged, then spread his arms, palms upward. "What do we have today? The new rich of The Revolution own all the land, the government owns all the natural resources, and twenty-five percent of Mexico's Indians can't speak Spanish well enough to get a job in the city. We have the fastest growing, poorest population in North America." Professor Wolf paused for effect, then said "What's fair about that? Are you listening?"

"I know all of that David, but..."

"Hush and listen, boy!" the professor continued, angrily. "I'm going to tell you something. You were one of my best students and you have the potential to be one of the best field archaeologists in Mexico." The professor opened a drawer and removed a ruler, then watched in dismay as several reports slid to the floor. "The point is this," he shook the ruler at Juan, "it doesn't matter how smart or talented you are. The world's full of intelligent people who'll never realize their potential because they have an infantile concept of fairness. To be an adult is to realize that society has expectations and that it's your responsibility to measure up." The ruler repeatedly sliced the air for emphasis.

"The system in Mexico is less than perfect—most would say corrupt—but it's your responsibility to accommodate the system or you'll never work, never realize your potential. That's the only "fairness" that's relevant."

Juan bent to retrieve the reports and set them back on the desk.

David stood, pointed the ruler, and said, "You're smart, but you have repeatedly used poor judgment when dealing with authority figures. Grow up!" He plunked the ruler down and looked at his watch. "I've got a meeting. Think about what I've said. I'll take care of Raúl and you learn to keep your mouth shut and stay out of trouble, okay?"

David reached for his briefcase, glanced at his former student and said, "Go home...you look awful. Why don't you stop and see Linda, then check out early." He opened a drawer to extract a pencil and the paper stacks shifted again.

"By the way...I'm leaving for five days to check on some excavations in Tobasco and Veracruz. Plan on being here while I'm gone." He pointed the pencil at Juan. "I'll check on Raúl when I get back. In the meantime, Marco can do the rat killing and odd jobs until things calm down, okay?"

"Sure...anything you say, boss," replied Juan, miserably.

David snatched a legal pad from the academic refuse on his desk, and started for the door. He turned.

"Juan?"

"Yeah?"

"Stay as long as you like, but don't clean or straighten anything, okay?"

Juan's face cracked a smile. "Sure...wouldn't dream of touching anything in a Nobel candidate's office."

Outside in the hall, small parties of students gossiped of teenage frivolities. When the bell rang signaling the beginning of class, the groups reluctantly broke up. David acknowledged greetings with a nod of his head and an occasional "Hi!" He turned the corner, passing up the elevator for the stairs, and shuffled down four flights before arriving at a set of glass entry doors.

Marco had just entered. "Professor...I was just on the way to see you." He seemed agitated and filled with urgency.

"Marco, I'm in a hurry." David held up a hand to stave him off. "Don't mean to be rude, but I've no time for a conversation." He attempted to step around.

"This'll just take a quick yes or no," pressed Marco, maneuvering to stay in front of his target. "I know this sounds crazy, but I have this friend who just won a trip to the Rocky Mountains and I've been invited to come along—free!" A munificent smile exposed white teeth. "It's too good to turn down, but I need to take off a few days," he begged. "I'll work weekends, overtime, or until the end of time if you'll let me off!" he began to clown. "What do you say?"

"You just started this job! This couldn't come at a worse time." David glanced at his watch, impatient. "I just left your buddy in my office looking for the pieces of his ass I chewed off."

Marco, undaunted, pressed the attack. "Professor, I'll paint your house or clean your toilet. I'll empty your cat's litter box for a year. I'll do anything! What do you say?"

"Okay...okay," David cracked a smile. "When will you return?" "Next Wednesday if everything goes okay." Then Marco added, "The bad news is that I'm leaving the day after tomorrow."

"No...so soon?"

"I have no choice...really, sir."

The professor paused. "Okay...it's just as well. I won't be here anyway. Remember," he waggled a finger benignly, a smile tugging at the corners of his mouth, "you owe me another one, young man. One of these days I'm going to call in some debts!"

Marco went into his best groveling act, bowing repeatedly and reaching for the professor's free hand, his lips puckered to kiss a ring in parody of religious ritual.

145

"Knock it off." David retrieved his hand. "I'm in a hurry. Go see Juan. I'm sure he could use a friend." He stepped around and out the door into the milling crowd. As he walked it occurred to him that Marco never indicated whether his friend was a man or a woman. A free vacation to the Rocky Mountains? Sounded suspicious. What's that boy up to this time?

He glanced at his watch—five minutes late. No matter, he assured himself. No one was ever on time except for the Education Department and the Dean's staff. He navigated the shuffling crowd of thousands and headed for the splendidly mosaicked library. A dark gray cumulus mass had coalesced into a brooding, dark thunderhead and rolled over the western range of the highland valley. It began to sprinkle, threatening the long dry spell of three weeks and raising a chorus of approval. Everyone picked up the pace, hurrying to find shelter before the deluge.

"It's my fault," he mumbled, berating himself as he hurried toward the library. Poor planning and execution. Too damn many projects. He had dropped the ball on this one. David contemplated the Raúl/Juan problem at length, then decided it wouldn't be possible to go to Tacuba until after his field trip to Veracruz. He would visit with Raúl and offer him an olive branch at the same time. Matters couldn't stand as they were. The museum director behaved like a jerk, but the professor couldn't afford to ignore the altercation.

Satisfied, he put the issue aside and made a mental list of needs for his trip. Two of his graduate students were conducting excavations near the ancient Olmec site of La Venta in Veracruz. A familiar swell of excitement rose within as he contemplated the prospect of being in the field again. He entered the library and was headed for the elevator when he remembered Juan's statement. Did he say that Raúl had stopped excavating two weeks ago and that he had been carrying a heavy canvas bag? More suspicious behavior. Had the museum director found something? *Damn!* thought, David, knowing he should have gone to Tacuba earlier. He punched the elevator button too hard. Damn, damn, damn!

Filth Eater

The gods have no reason to exist but to provide order to the universe and make meaningful the lives of their adherents. Order out of chaos and meaning out of mindlessness—these are the keys to understanding the relationship with the gods. These are the fundamentals of existence and belief, the spiritual cause and effect of The One Universe.

The faithful of The One Universe accepted these premises and were gifted by the gods with a triumvirate to sustain them—maize, beans, and squash. What greater gift could we give while they inhabit their corporeal bodies? Food sustains the soul as well as the body. There is nothing better except perhaps attaining The Paradise of the Sun itself. The bleached race recognize the same premises of order and meaning, but have somehow perverted their understanding of the gifts. Believing that God's gifts were gold, subjects, and souls, they pursued them with a vengeance. The soldiers came for gold, but the real soldiers of the Conquest were the friars and priests. It is they who must bear the responsibility for having destroyed The One Universe. Now the poor swell the Valley of Mexico like hungry ants in a jar. The poor and dispossessed bloat The One Universe like worms gorging on the entrails of a dying kitten. Hunger brings them despair and their lives are void of meaning. The new Christian Filth Eater has not remedied this, nor has He seen fit to gift them with food, other than his "Bread of Life," which must seem very unsatisfying to a hungry stomach.

The people no longer bring gifts to the gods. The air sickens people and plants, causing them to die. Lake Texcoco is gone. The most beautiful place in the world has disappeared from the face of the earth to be replaced with a polluted imitation. Is this a gift? For whom? How does gold for the rich, souls for their God, and subjects for the powerful put food in the inhabitant's bellies and sustain them spiritually? This is filth beyond comprehension. Truly, such filth has never cursed the earth.

Cholo Goes To Confession

Tuesday, June 24, 1984 Mexico City, 3:00 P.M.

Cholo Rodriguez shuffled along Calle Morales, his head down and hands in his pockets, intent on staying on the shady side of the street. A large man with wide shoulders, he moved effortlessly in and around the sidewalk traffic. He ignored everyone, determined to remain unobtrusive—just one of twenty million in the city. He avoided the bright sunlight, as it hurt his eyes, and he paid no attention to sidewalk conversations, met no one's eyes, or stayed anywhere too long. He had chosen this circuitous, quiet route to the church in order to avoid as many people as possible, stopping only once to watch a pack of feral dogs fight over a filthy, disposable diaper. Becoming bored with the contest, he continued onward when his watch reminded him that the hour of his rendezvous drew nigh.

His gut hurt and his eyes ached from squinting through pop-bottle-bottom lenses—but that was normal. It certainly wouldn't keep him at home. The Bull's concubine had brought a note that said, "3:00 p.m., south confessional, come alone." Signed like the others, the typed name "Toro" appeared at the bottom. A silly-assed code name, he thought. Nevertheless, he had no intention of missing this important appointment. His livelihood depended on it.

The high cost of maintaining his small, but elegant six-room stucco with courtyard increased yearly. His woman of three years, Lupe, was a cheerful, childless divorcee who had left her drunken husband in a Nogales slum, where he belonged. Upon returning to Mexico City to visit an aunt, she had encountered the unusual Cholo in the Coyohuacan outdoor market, haggling over a pair of huaraches.

A strange sight to behold, he wore khaki pants, a white guayabera shirt and sported a pair of red Keds tennis shoes — one of them untied — and a Panama hat. He had a tendency to incline his head toward whomever spoke and he squinted at the world from behind a pair of thick, gold, wire-rimmed glasses. His Spanish was excellent, but his accent placed him out of country. Cholo made no friends, so one knew him or what he did for a living. He occasionally disappeared for weeks at a time and returned with no explanation other than he had been "learning his way around Mexico."

Lupe had felt an immediate attraction to the broad-shouldered barbarian, and rather than return to the slums of Nogales, had moved into his house on Calle Oso and set up housekeeping. They both knew she had never had it so good. He sometimes yelled or hit her, but this, of course, remained the prerogative of the Latin male. He smoked marijuana, and this bothered her, but not as much as her ex-husband's drinking, beatings, and bed-wetting — unquestionably the best trade she had ever made.

151

Because of his glaucoma Cholo had become nearsighted. He smoked pot three or four times a day, but he didn't drink anymore. His stomach resembled an ulcerated sieve, which required that he take prescription Tagamet tablets. His glaucoma was diagnosed as incurable and he had been warned that the condition could result in blindness. A former compadre in the Medellin Cocaine Cartel vacationing in Aspen had brought him a news article from the U.S.A. The story espoused the benefits of marijuana for glaucoma, so he had begun smoking the high-grade Colombian readily available in Medellin. Sure enough, his glaucoma went into remission, although it was nearly too late. The years of undiagnosed high blood pressure had taken its toll and destroyed much of his vision. But what he truly thought amazing was how much better his stomach felt after smoking marijuana. Thus he gained a dual benefit from each joint smoked which, he reasoned, was a good rationale to toke-up often.

Cholo had been an ambitious, bright boy of seventeen when he joined the Colombian Armed Forces. He came to the attention of his commanding officer when, as the leader of his platoon, he rescued two female Peace Corp workers from guerrillas in the Cucuta river valley. As a reward, he received Special Forces Training. He followed orders well and could be as brutal as the situation required when dealing with Colombia's numerous enemies: college students, dissidents, priests, and the highland coca-leaf growers.

After massacring twenty-five percent of a village sustained solely by growing coca, he drew the attention of the Medellin Cartel. Obviously, they could use a man of such talent and temperament. He became a first-round draft choice, and after going to work for the cartel, he earned more for one month's work than he would have in five years for the Colombian military.

Cholo grew to like the cartel and became an expert in terror, intimidation, and death. He learned the art of making powerful back yard bombs out of every conceivable material from petroleum jelly, fertilizer and gasoline, to soap. Occasionally he had to perform a beating upon a conscientious partisan, or, in a bad week, an assassination or two. Great pay, great benefits—women, drugs, and cars—but his stomach couldn't tolerate the stress. He went progressively from whiskey, to brandy, to wine, to beer, to Tagamet. Then the headaches began, and his already poor vision became occluded.

Because of the holes in his gut and his failing eyesight, he became a liability to his Bogota bosses. Employing a nervous, near-sighted terrorist was not an intelligent thing to do. After fifteen years of successful thuggery, Cholo was put out to pasture. Most of his buddies had been rewarded with a bullet in the head or a rope around the neck, but Cholo left peacefully, his life intact, and with a small gift of $200,000. His friends helped set up important connections for him in Mexico, and so he moved to Federal District in hopes of securing an occasional job that required his talents.

He quickly found work. 'El Toro,' the Bull, had placed him on retainer. Cholo had split a gut upon hearing his boss's pseudonym and had allowed himself countless hours of mirth with it since, even though they had never met. He had his suspicions as to who El Toro actually was, but declined to follow up on them, deciding the identity made little difference.

El Toro rarely contacted him, and when he did, he usually wanted to place an order to buy heroin. Never a large amount mind you, always a small packet. This remained a source of curiosity, but the Colombian had been in the business long enough to know the advantages of minding your own affairs when it came to the boss.

Since coming to Mexico, he had worked three times in four years; two bombings and the beating of a young couple in the Zona Rosa. Some jobs paid more than others, and he was hoping for a bomb or a bullet this time. Beatings didn't pay shit and too many people were involved. His health, poor and deteriorating, didn't allow him to do kidnappings, especially without the muscle of the cartel to protect him anymore. One had to be careful.

Today, he wore the clothes of a campesino; stained cotton pants, huraches, and serape. His face and hands had been rubbed in dirt and his hair was uncombed. He wore no jewelry. Long ago he had learned the value of anonymity, and during the course of his career he had acquired a trunk of used uniforms; clothes, hats, canes, gloves, and more, for his work. Filled with guile, he had learned to plan ahead and blend with the setting. More than one buddy had been caught because of carelessness, haste, and or no planning. Study and preparation equaled success. If you stood out in the crowd, someone noticed you. Some people made a living noticing the incongruent and the odd.

His head downcast, deep in thought, he approached his destination brooding of unresolved issues. Had he been alert and able to see better, he would have noticed the policía cruisers and the crowd in front of the church. Cholo found himself nearly in the middle of the fracas before realizing that something had gone awry. People milled about aimlessly, and the policía asking questions of the bystanders lent a confusing note to the scene. No one seemed to listen, except for a priest

154

who stood slightly bent, holding a white, blood-stained handkerchief to his head.

Cholo, cursing his stupidity, remained on a slow, steady, course while his mind worked double-time. What had happened? Did it have anything to do with him? Should he keep walking or enter the church and check out the possibilities of completing his task? Chingada! He wished the cabron would use the mail for these assignations, but the postal service remained too unreliable, even dangerous in Mexico.

Choosing to ignore the furor, he climbed the stairs of the two-hundred year old church as if he belonged there. Moving past ornate oak doors replete with carved saints, he stepped aside and out of sight of the crowd outside. A dark interior, lit only by rows of flickering votive candles near the altar, made it difficult to see. When his eyes adjusted, he squinted and surveyed the interior of the church. Then he checked his wrist watch: 3:12 P.M. glowed from its face. The voices outside had quieted somewhat, except for one, which was clearly heard above the others. It belonged to a cop, and he was asking questions of the padre while the other policía shooed the crowd away. Cholo decided to do it. Everyone was outside and this might be his only chance. He didn't want to blow this one. It might not be there anyway, but he had to know before leaving.

Quickly looking around, he walked to the end confessional, pulled the purple curtain aside and stepped in. The remarkable thing is that Cholo had entered the small quarter reserved for God's intermediary, not the side for the penitent. He sat and reached between his legs, stretching to the backside under of the seat. He found it! He jerked the taped envelope loose, put it in his pocket, and stepped from the confessional.

155

The voices had drawn near—they were walking up the stairs! What to do? If they searched him and found the letter, he was dog puke. Rapidly walking the aisle along the west wall, he swiveled his head to glance over a shoulder. They were entering the door! A pillar blocked his view of the entry, so he moved into a row of pews and knelt as if in prayer. Unaware that he was in the church, the priest and detective conversed about the incident.

***

"I was just walking around and straightening…preparing for evening services. I stacked the missals, then returned to the Sacristy to get Holy Water to replenish the reservoirs. It's important that God's children have an abundance of the blessed water available; the people insist, you know? Anyway…I thought I heard someone come in, so I went and looked, but I didn't see anyone. So I left the sacristy and went to refill the reservoirs."

The big detective asked, "Padre, did you make any noise when you did this? I mean…is there a possibility the attacker didn't hear you, or didn't know you were around?"

"Well…I guess…" agreed the priest, unsure of himself. "After forty years of parish work and celebrating the Sacraments every day, one learns to be contemplative in the presence of the Host."

"Of course…look…padre, when did you become suspicious? How did you come to notice that someone was in the confessional?"

"I saw his feet!" exclaimed the old priest, gesturing with one arm while holding the bloody rag to his head with the other. "I saw a pair of white shoes beneath the curtain.

"What did you do then, padre?" The suited detective scribbled furiously on his tablet.

The priest became animated and removed the handkerchief from his head and waved his arms for emphasis as he narrated the event— obviously the most exciting thing to occur in years.

"At first I was surprised. No one was scheduled to give confession, and priests don't wear white, shiny shoes with gold buckles. It isn't appropriate for men of God to wear fancy white shoes! I became angry that someone would profane the church with this sacrilege. I yanked the curtain back!" he gushed, his arm mimicking the pulling motion.

"Suddenly," he continued, "a big man with an ugly expression jumped up and ran out. I grabbed him, but he pulled me along! He kept trying to shield his face. He was very big and strong. I yelled for him to stop...and...and I hit him once, but then he turned around and picked me up! I nearly died, captain! I'm an old man. I begged him not to hurt me, but he threw me down the steps." The arms dropped and the priest's shoulders sagged. "That's all I remember until the policía came." He placed handkerchief on his wounded head.

"Padre...was anyone in the church, or standing outside who might have witnessed it?"

"I don't remember...lots of people were here after the policía came, but...I don't know."

"Let's go over your description again. Think hard; is there anything about him...anything he wore that seemed unusual?"

"No...I don't know," said the priest, looking at the handkerchief again. "Maybe...he seemed pretty well dressed. I think he had a bracelet."

"A bracelet, padre? Could you describe it?"

157

"Lets see…it was a big thing…you know…kind of wide," he said, "I think it might have been gold…and it had an old design on it."

"An old design? What do you mean?"

"Well…you know…like the pagan carvings and statues you see at the museum, something like an Indian would make."

"You didn't recognize the design?"

"Of course not. It didn't have our Blessed Mother, or the Lord Jesus on it!" he grumped. "I was scared to death and trying to keep from having a heart attack!

"I understand, padre," soothed the cop, "and that's very valuable information. Anything else?"

"He was hairy."

"What?" The detective's head shot up.

"He had a hairy chest. Not too many Mexicans have hair on their chests, you know."

"Really…how interesting." The detective wrote again, then asked

…"Anything more?"

The priest slumped visibly, looking faint. "Listen…captain, I feel like throwing up. Can we do this some other time?"

"Certainly, padre. Perhaps you'll remember more later. In just a moment we'll take you to a medico."

"Captain Alvarado?" interrupted a gray-suited policía.

"Si, Arguello, que paso?" The detective continued to write.

"Nada from that rabble. No one saw anything. Two old ladies found the padre bleeding on the ground…so they called the policía. How about the priest?" asked Arguello.

"No witnesses…doesn't remember much." "How about that guy?"

"Huh? What guy?"

"Over there, behind in a pew behind the pillar."

158

"Didn't see him." Luis stretched to look. "Go talk to him…get his story. I'll finish with the padre, then be over."

Arguello, walking slowly down the center aisle, called softly, "señor," but received no response. "Señor, please!" he said louder and more insistently.

***

Cholo's gut simmered with boiling acid. Someone was popping wheelies and spinning their tires in his stomach. His hands trembled and he felt on the verge of panic. He had overheard their conversation and knew he had blundered into a disaster.

El Toro or somebody had panicked when the priest surprised him. He had to think fast. The policía would come to interrogate him. He'd been in tight spots before, but never like this. He took a deep breath to compose himself, then acted. He quickly pulled the envelope from his pocket to see if the tape was still attached. He straightened the tape strips, then placed the envelope of money on the underside of the pew. He had just finished when he heard the gray uniformed cop approaching.

"Señor!"

Cholo pretended not to hear, staring vacantly toward a crucified Jesus.

"Señor…please!" repeated the voice.

He turned to the voice, squinted and said "Si?"

"Sorry to disturb your prayers. There's been an incident of violence committed against a priest. I need to ask you a few questions."

"I saw the crowd out front, but I don't know anything."

"Please…if you will…come with me," coaxed the policeman, motioning with his hand. "The captain will have questions for you."

***

Forty-five minutes later Cholo slowly threaded his way
through narrow streets, his stomach on fire, lurching towards
collapse, certain that he would die before reaching home. He
groaned, cursing himself for not bringing the Tagamet. His
legs trembled and his hands still shook from the interrogation.

That damn detective! Cholo knew he was suspicious. Jesus!
They'd even searched him! Thank God he wasn't holding. He
usually carried a joint for emergencies, but had decided not to
since it was important to remain lucid in business situations.

A calamity had occurred. He had lost the money envelope!
The policía had locked the church for a couple of hours so that
the padre could be taken to the medico. Now what? How
could he get inside to retrieve the envelope? Surely they
couldn't close a church for long? "Chingada!" he said to no one.

Who had beaten the priest and botched the pass? Toro?
Whoever it was deserved a good killing.

Now what? he wondered. No money, no job, and that smart
detective didn't believe his story. If they followed and saw
where he lived, he would face a firing squad for sure. Worse,
they might hang him.

Two blocks later he decided. He would go to evening mass
when the church re-opened and get the envelope. The tape
wouldn't hold for long, it had barely stuck to the well-oiled
pew. If it fell on the floor before he returned, someone would
be very rich. He picked up his pace in order to get home to
Lupe, his Tagamet, and a joint. He must retrieve that envelope!
It would be dangerous. Hanging out at the church would be a
dead giveaway. They would book him and run a check
through Interpol. Christ! He wasn't even a Mexican citizen. If
they discovered his real identity, he would be executed here,
or extradited to Colombia. Either way he was a dead man. His

160

stomach did two back flips, then the after-burner to a three-stage rocket lit up his gut. He slumped momentarily and groaned aloud, holding himself in pain. Two more blocks and he would be home. He willed himself to keep moving.

***

Blazing sunlight pierced the windshield and blinded Hector as he drove onto the Periferico Sur entry ramp. "Chingada!" he cursed, flipping the sun visor down, then squeezing the steering wheel in anger, imagining it to be the priest's neck. Adrenaline percolated in his bloodstream and his and his heart pounded painfully. The black robe had tried to be a hero. Cabron! What was the priest doing there so early? Confession began at five o'clock and mass at six. Didn't he know his own schedule?

Hector knew that chances were slim that they would associate him with the incident, but what of the money? The envelope would remain under the seat unless Cholo retrieved it, and what were the chances of that? The policía would arrive first and search the confessional. Ten thousand dollars pissed away! A hundred thousand pesos in unmarked, untraceable bills. He groaned and slapped the steering wheel. Chingada! It had always worked smoothly before. Priests were obsessive-compulsives with very strict routines to which they adhered. They were always on time. Chingada! Why today of all days?

Breathing deeply, his runaway heart gradually quieted and his fists unclenched. He slumped back into the seat, driving his silver Mercedes south on Anillo Periferico Expressway, his mind in turmoil. He must act now, and as he drove a plan took form as he drove toward the university. He would move fast. The money might be lost, but he had to know for sure.

Turning east onto Avenida San Jeronimo, he drove by the Olympic stadium. He needed to see Amparo before she left for Colorado tonight. After giving her a message to deliver to Cholo, he would drive the remaining few miles to his Coyohuacan suburb. If everything worked according to plan, Hector had a very important call to make and he must be in place early. The Raúl problem needed to be taken care of quickly, but first the money—he had to know about the money.

Filth Eater

Sacrilege beyond comprehension! Filth beyond credence! Hubris—the worst filth imaginable. Who but the descendants of the bleached faces would profane and commit such sacrilege against their Filth Eater by entering into a sacred enclosure designed for the purpose of absolution by their Filth Eater, then misuse it, as if absolution is not the greatest gift of the gods! What kind of person would casually desecrate a holy place and such a sacred rite?

This demonstrates a complete lack of morality and a total absence of piety. Indeed, the bleached souls sometimes demonstrate the worst filth imaginable—to have no faith or belief system at all. How does a pilot navigate without his sextant? Such hubris is filthy beyond description and an act totally alien to the old inhabitants of The One Universe. Forgiveness of one's filth is the cornerstone upon which the great pyramid was built. Absolution is the great equalizer. All who wish to penetrate the great void into The Paradise of the Sun know they cannot enter with their burden of filth intact.

Captain Alvarado Makes A Call

Tuesday, June 24, 1984, Mexico City

St. Francis Xavier Church, nearly three hundred years old, lay nestled within a middle-class barrio that had grown up on its periphery. Originally a pile of mud bricks in the Valley of Mexico, the church began as a small chapel within the confines of a larger mission built to proselytize the Indians. The mission no longer existed, but the church remained, and the Bishop of Mexico City had ordered a larger, permanent structure built to serve a burgeoning Indian community which hovered near to receive the spiritual favors, dispensations, and petty largesse of the church.

Today the church was bordered by wide, busy streets lined with broad-limbed, thick-trunked, one-hundred-year-old bald cypress, coconut palms, and shagbark hickory trees whose branches had lengthened to create dappled shade and protective canopies over the streets.

Captain Luis Alvarado exited the cavernous limestone church. He loosened his tie and rubbed his neck, slowly descending the worn, granite steps. It was 84 degrees. Hot for the highland valley, and a slight breeze molesting the leaves did little to dissipate the heat.

He walked to his car, took one last look around the neighborhood, then started his 1955 Mercury convertible and slowly maneuvered it onto Calle Medrano. A cursory glance in the mirrors showed the road free of traffic, so he relaxed and looked around the inside of his vintage automobile. The interior, a spectacular display of customized red and white leather, had rolled-and-tucked seats, floor boards that boasted a thick red carpet, and a new bonnet for its convertible top. Its chromed grille gleamed smooth and shiny and its wide, white-walled tires were free of blemish.

Luis drove with leisure, primarily because the car drew stares of envy, smiles, and an occasional thumbs up. He ran his hands over the seat and smiled. This was his car; Angela drove the old Chevy Impala. It, too had been restored, but an old Chevy didn't measure up to a `55 Merc, did it? A homicide detective with fifteen years' experience on the Mexico City Police Force, Luis had left his home one hour earlier to search for a wit- ness on another case when he stumbled onto this mess. Now he could get back on track, and he began searching a row of look-alike stuccoes that were all singularly different in a way that only a native could explain. Luis was trying to find a recalcitrant witness whom he believed had watched the murder of a prostitute in the Zona Rosa. He worked as hard on the murder of a puta as he did on any other case. They were all God's children. Besides, he hated murderers with a passion.

After ten years of tracking and apprehending scumbags, Luis believed he had seen it all—until the next one. Somehow each murder was a little different. He had acquired an extensive knowledge of human behavior working as a cop and he knew that large cities were a refuge for emotional cripples. You could find ways to hide in the big city that were simply not available to those living in small towns and communities where everyone knows your business. Sicko's seemed to gravitate to the city. During the course of his career he had met murderers whom he unknowingly would have allowed to baby-sit children and world class thieves with winning smiles to whom he would have lent his car. Someday he planned to write a book, estimating he had material for fifty volumes with an endless supply of character sketches.

He slowly cruised, continuing to look for the right house. The incident at the church was an aggravation – and a bit incongruent. He had wasted an hour on something that wasn't even his case. But it struck him as a peculiar, no question about it. He had left with an uneasy feeling. More had occurred than a simple assault. In retrospect, the whole episode seemed bizarre. He would write up a report and give it to Jose when he returned to the precinct house. Jose could do as he wished, but Luis hoped whomever got the case checked with him first. Something wasn't quite right about the dirty guy with the bad eyes. Luis had heard a lot of tales, but that guy's story smelled like donkey manure. Born in Puerto Rico, he said? Maybe, maybe not. One thing for sure—campesinos couldn't afford gold wire-rim glasses. Those things must have cost $200 Nah, he was dirty. Luis would write it up so that they would have to investigate the Puerto Rican—if that's what he was.

He checked his rearview mirror, then pulled into a "No Parking" zone alongside the park, turned off the key, and walked into the Farmacia Reyes to use the telephone. Luis had heard a story from a buddy who claimed that U.S. cities had telephones on every street corner, and that some people had

166

them in their cars. This sounded amazing, but the detective doubted it. He knew people would steal the phones if they were left outside.

He waited five minutes for his turn, then called the office. No messages. Well, maybe he write up a couple of reports, then talk to Jose about the dirty foreigner with the nice glasses. He should do it now before he forgot. The search for the missing witness could wait until tomorrow. He paid ten pesos to the girl at the counter, then climbed back into the Mercury and headed for the precinct house.

Cholo Recovers The Money

Tuesday Evening, June 24, 1984, Mexico City

Lengthening shadows stretched long and misshapen, casting stark angular shapes in the early evening light. Cholo moved like a wraith, concealed in the dark umbrage of baldcypress trees and walled, fortress-like stuccoes that insulated and protected the inhabitants from a fickled, restless government. A purple-flowered hedge of mescalbean raked his leg when he veered too close, so he jumped the bushes and crossed the street, walked one block, then turned north, treading the shady side of the street. He felt tired from walking the two-mile distance between his home and St. Francis Xavier, but relieved at the outcome.

He had dressed in his finest — white polyester slacks, a dark blue collarless shirt, and black loafers. A polyester jacket hung from his right arm, and he wore a fake Rolex and gold pinky ring. A camera hung from his neck. He looked just like any other tourist gawking at Mexico City's old churches.

Unable to contain himself, he grinned ear to ear. Hot damn! After fortifying himself with two joints and a Tagamet, he had returned to St. Francis for six o'clock mass and found the envelope dangling by one mangled strip of masking tape. *Maybe there is a God!* he crowed, silently. The envelope hung from his neck in the empty camera case, and he walked with purpose, anxious to get home and count the contents.

He felt certain that he would be hearing from "Toro" soon — maybe even today. Should he tell of the recovered money? Who would know if he had recovered it? He pondered this moral dilemma while following his circuitous route home. Honesty was not his strong point. On the other hand, if Toro suspected him of lying, Cholo would be out of work and possibly dead as a result of his greed. Best to play it safe, he decided. He hadn't lived this long by being stupid.

He continued to pace off the distance, ignoring waves of shimmering bougainvillea climbing white-walled houses, and disdaining to notice the yellow blossoms of blue paloverde shrubs lining the nearby park. Money. Money was on his mind. The envelope felt thick — a sure sign of a big job. Toro didn't pay in small bills. But what would he want for such a sum? The more the money, the more the risk as a general rule. It would be best to wait and see what the job required before making plans to spend the cash. One screw-up and he would be dead, or in Lecumberri, the National Penitentiary. An involuntary shiver shook him.

Mexican jails had a terrible reputation, and Lecumberri might be the worst prison on earth. A vision of the huge, brown monolithic walls crowned with barbed wire surrounding the legendary festering hell, floated in and out of his imagination. If you didn't expire of disease you would die a violent death. Worse, you would live, but become the thrall of a prison kingpin and be required to perform sexual favors until your rectum prolapsed from overuse. His flesh crawled and he shuddered again. Why was he thinking of this shit?

169

What was happening to him? He would have to cut down on the weed. Nowadays paranoia arrived suddenly and unexpectedly, gripping him like a boa squeezing a monkey, until he became incapacitated by fear. He groaned audibly. It had started again. Why couldn't he just turn it off? Chingada! His bile burned and his gorge rose as the smoldering coal in his stomach put to rest by the Tagamet and marijuana sent a wakeup call. "Cabron!" he moaned. Didn't it ever stop?

Aware that he was near home and Lupe, he slowed his gait to traverse the final two blocks. The camera case no longer hung from his neck. He had rolled the strap around his hand and hugged the case to his stomach cavity. Despite his mental and physical disarray, he regained his focus. As he turned the corner on his block it occurred to him that he would probably have to move soon. Too many things had gone wrong and he still didn't know what Toro expected of him.

Looking ahead, he saw someone, a woman, closing his wrought-iron gate—and it wasn't Lupe. He squinted, trying to identify the woman, giving her time to leave so that he wouldn't have to talk to her. She appeared young and attractive and Cholo didn't believe he had ever seen her before. Wait a minute, he thought. It's the Bull's concubine! He waved, certain that she had come looking for him. Toro had sent her— he knew it!

***

Amparo glanced down the sidewalk and spotted the Colombian as he turned the corner. A look of recognition spread across his face, but she headed quickly for her blue VW. She was going to Vail, Colorado and didn't have time for a conversation with Cholo. He could get the message from Lupe. As she drove away, she watched him in her rearview mirror. He

170

was clutching something to his stomach, and as he opened the front gate to his home, already calling for Lupe.

Captain Alvarado Makes A Report

Wednesday, June 25, 1984, Mexico City

Luis looked through the plate-glass window of his office into the central investigation area of the lower echelon detectives, and into Jose's room, a larger version of his own. The superintendent was talking on the tele phone and Luis watched, fascinated, as Jose's pencil thin handle-bar mustache bobbed and jerked.

The detective's eyes returned to the report one more time to ensure that it included everything; initial contact, narrative, witnesses, descriptions, etc. He took his work seriously and paid strict attention to detail. The streets were full of gray-suited, uniformed cops who still paid $15.00 a day to their bosses to have a job, their livelihood solely dependent on graft and corruption. He had worked hard to move up the ladder and knew he couldn't be a slouch now that he'd made Detective First Class and received a livable salary.

Two of the six desks in the central area stood empty. The other four were assigned to detectives according to department. Luis looked at the ragged collection of misfits being interrogated—two putas, a thief, and a junkie. The prostitutes sat with their mini-skirts hiked to crotch level, their faces caked with makeup, and dangling jewelry swinging as they gestured and argued vociferously, disgusted at being inconvenienced. The thief wouldn't talk. He had picked a spot on the wall to examine and waited patiently for a revelation. A long-sleeved junkie hugged a trash can between his legs while retching and gagging, punishing his empty stomach while his mother, a wrinkled ancient, patted him on the back, consoling him.

Eight offices like his own, all of them newly remodeled with plate-glass front walls, composed the perimeter of the central office area. Luis hated it. No privacy. You couldn't pick your nose without someone watching. He guessed the architect must have seen too many episodes of Kojak.

When the superintendent hung up, Luis grabbed the report and hustled to the other side, waving off Pricilla, Jose's flat-chested secretary. He knocked once and entered. Jose, a thin man with curly hair, didn't look up. He pointed his pen to a vacant chair and continued to write. Luis slipped his brown-suited, lanky frame into a chair, scratched his pock-marked chin, and waited patiently for acknowledgment.

Three walls of memorabilia—daguerreotypes from the revolution, pictures, trophies, and other mementos—testified to Jose's political credentials. One wall contained photographs of Jose shaking hands with various PRI functionaries and posing with semi-important, now-forgotten nobodies whose light had faded with the ascendance of newer, brighter stars. The superintendent had reached his present position during the Lopez Portillo Administration. But Jose, an ambitious, pretentious man, suffered from the sudden onset of brain flatulence, resulting in poor judgment and arrant, stupid decisions when handling a crisis. 'Brain farts' the detectives called it—the smell of which pervaded the air long after the events in question had unfolded. This, of course, was a terminal disease for careers, and Jose had labored long but unnoticed, his grandiose visions unrealized, languishing in the purgatory of middle-management.

His bathroom door stood ajar, revealing a full-length mirror and an expensive, pinstriped suit coat. An open can of pomade, a bottle of Grecian Formula, and a comb lay on the lavatory. Luis glanced at his boss—starched shirt, tailored suit, and immaculate hair—even his nails were manicured. Jose had a sartorial obsession.

"Luis," Jose leaned back into his chair with his fingers steeple, "tell me you're here for a warrant. If you don't come up with something soon, we'll both be directing traffic and booking putas."

"I got an assault for you." Luis handed him the report.

"Assault? What about the puta killing?"

"I normally would've filed this with Rodriguez in **Assault**, but I thought you should see it first in case it connects with something." Luis told the story, leaving out all but the essentials, talking at length about a big guy who tossed a priest down the stairs, the dirty foreigner with the nice glasses, and ended with, "I can't help but think there's more to this than meets the eye."

"Did you check the confessional?"

"It was clean."

"The foreigner?"

"He didn't have a thing on him, no I.D. or anything. His address is in the report, but it's probably bogus. I almost brought him in…but he hadn't done anything."

174

"Luis, I'm going to give this to Lobo Morales in Narcotics. We've got so many illegals in the country that we can't identify them all. Lobo can call Interpol and check with the Fed's."

"Good." Luis stood to leave. So far the air smelled fine.

"Luis…on second thought…"

Chingada! It was happening, the cloying odor of a bad decision, a 'brain fart.'

"…I want you to follow up on this yourself."

"Jose…I work in **Homicide**, remember?" He spread his hands in a pleading gesture. "Give it to Morales."

"No," Jose shook his head, "this isn't a regular assault. If the Bishop's office calls, someone who's worked the case should talk to them. Don't worry," he said airily, "just bury it in a few days if we don't hear from them." Jose bent over his tablet to write, dismissing Luis by ignoring him. The scent of a decision gone bad pervaded the room.

"Jose…"

"Beat it…no whining, okay?" He glanced quickly at the detective, then reached for a roll of Tums. "And Luis…?"

"Yeah?"

"If you don't turn up something on that puta by tomorrow, let's drop it…" he waved the murder away with his hand, "get busy on something important." He bent to his tablet again and slowly chewed the Tums.

Kiss my ass, thought Luis, wanting to grab the skinny little prick by his handle-bars. Instead he said, "If you say so, Jose." He turned to leave, then stopped. "Jose, it smells kind of funny in here. You ought to have it checked out sometime."

"You know," Jose's head shot up with a quizzical expression, "Rodriguez said the same thing yesterday, but I don't smell anything." He sniffed several times and looked perplexed. "What's it smell like?"

175

"Smells like something's dead. It smells like shit, Jose." Luis turned to go, leaving a confused Jose looking at the bottom of his shoes for the mysterious odor.

Luis exited the precinct house. The sun, dipping below the mountains, extended red-orange wings to protect the horizon, pulling the day west as it slipped slowly and unmolested into its nocturnal abode. Luis slapped at one of the two concrete lions guarding the entrance, then walked east toward his car with his long, weak shadow preceding him. Seething with frustration at Jose's callous disregard for the puta, Luis forgot and slammed the car door—an unconscionable sin with an old automobile. He regretted it immediately, wincing as the thud vibrated through Mercury.

"An assault case," he bitched, tooling the Mercury onto the asphalt, and a crazy one at that. A large, well-dressed man with a hairy chest and a gold bracelet sits waiting on the wrong side of a confessional, then beats up a priest when discovered. It didn't make sense. If it had been a honest mistake and the guy sat on the wrong side, why didn't he just say 'sorry' and move over? What the hell was he doing in a church confessional if he didn't want to go to reconciliation? If he had been waiting, who had he expected to meet? The dirty guy with the expensive glasses? The second coming of Christ? Luis slapped the steering wheel again, venting his anger.

Detective Alvarado couldn't wait to get home and tell Angela about his day. She thought most of his cases were boring, but this one would be a hit, he knew. Besides, if he played his cards right, maybe she would give him a rubdown. God knows he needed to relax. You couldn't take Jose too seriously or you would end up a pretentious, pomaded buffoon just like him.

176

Luis would go home and wash the Mercury. He had purchased a can of Carranza's Carnuba and he looked forward to trying it. He settled into the traffic, driving toward his quiet barrio, brimming with plans for the evening. The weirdoes at the church could wait until tomorrow.

Hector And Cholo Make A Deal

Thursday, June 26, 1984, Mexico City

Hector sat reading a newspaper in El Restaurante Espanola. Located on a corner across from the park, the absence of walls on two sides created a refreshing openness to two streets and allowed a mélange of odors to confuse the senses. The aroma of baked chicken, onions, and shrimp contested with the sweet, acrid odor of diesel exhaust and rotting curb-side refuse. Caladium, diffenbachia, and blue paloverde line the shady park across the street. Several small businesses ran in concert on the south side. Hector, having strategically placed himself, had a clear view of all pedestrians and cars that came into the area. A sign boasting a Public Telephone in the Farmacia Buena Salud was clearly visible from where he sat, sipping a Tecate and eating shrimp cocktail.

The restaurant clock said 7:30 p.m. Hector had arrived early to check out the area in advance and watch Cholo Rodriguez when he entered the farmacia to await Hector's call. They had never met in person and Hector intended that it remain that way.

He was tipping his third Tecate and second glass of shrimp cocktail, brooding on the chaotic events of the day. The food and beer did little to assuage his disquiet. The fiasco at the church and the lost money weighed heavily on his mind. It had always worked before, he repeated to himself bitterly.

Vicario received a thrill from using the confessional for an occasional assignation because he despised the church and the weakness it represented. The black-robed priests had controlled the politics and people of Mexico for five hundred years by withholding or dispensing their spiritual blessings. The church controlled nearly a million hectares of land and had created a government within a government, content to outlast each succeeding oligarchy. As a child he had watched with contempt as his parents eagerly immersed themselves in what he viewed as barely palpable nonsense.

The fact that he had nearly been caught in a heinous sacrilege and had seriously injured a priest bothered him not at all. That he had left ten thousand dollars in an envelope taped beneath a confessional seat without instructing Cholo what to do, drove him crazy. This made him even angrier at the church and its stupid priests!

If the Colombian arrived on time he might have witnessed the fracas that followed. If there were policía, or any kind of investigation, Cholo would know. Hector wonder if his man had went into the church and looked around.

At 7:40 Cholo stepped from of a taxi, paid the driver, then walked a few steps to sit on a vacant park bench. Hector, hiding behind his newspaper, watched as the Colombian surveyed the area with suspicion. After a pregnant moment, he stood and walked casually toward the farmacia. When he

179

entered, Hector lay down his paper and turned to the owner, Emilio, and asked to use the telephone.

"Of course, Sr. Vicario, but there is a ten peso charge for local calls." Thief! thought Hector.

Shutting the proprietor's office door behind him, Hector quickly dialed the six digit number to the farmacia. The phone rang twice, then someone answered, "Bueno?"

"Is Sancho Bolivar there?"

"Un momento. Is there a Sancho Bolivar…you señor? There is a ten peso charge for the call. Yes, thank you…five minutes, no more!"

"Bueno?"

"The bull is always right," said the Minister of the Interior.

"The bull is never wrong," replied the Colombian terrorist. "Tell me what you saw!" commanded 'Toro.'

Cholo talked quickly, ending the narrative with the girl in the blue VW leaving his house.

Hector's smile almost cracked his face. The resilient hit-man had secured the money. "You are very resourceful," praised Hector, "but you took a chance and were almost caught!" he admonished, unable to bring himself to be effusive.

"Yes…but I wasn't…and I saved the money. But I don't know if I want it. What do you want me to do?"

"How are you with bombs?"

"The best. You know that."

"Listen closely," began Hector, as he described his next victim and where he wanted him to die. Three minutes later he asked, "Can you do it?"

With no hesitation, Cholo replied. "Yes…security's terrible there.

When do you want it done?" "By next Monday…no later."

"Done!" said Cholo with finality, "Where can I reach you?"

180

"You can't. I'll contact you," came the reply, followed by a click and dull hum of the dial tone.

Hector passed the counter, signaling another Tecate on his way to the table. He shooed a black halo of flies from the glass of shrimp, hesitated, then turned. "Emilio, another glass of shrimp, and more limes!"

"Si, señor!" the owner hustled into the kitchen, wiping his hands on a barely white, largely stained apron.

Hector watched Cholo leave the farmacia and signal a cab. He could see the Colombian more closely now and noticed that he seemed to squint and lean forward, and his hand held his stomach. As the cab sped away blowing black smoke, its engine pinging from low octane gasoline, Hector wondered what had happened to his hit man. Was he sick?

Filth Eater

The old inhabitants knew the world existed in cycles of fifty-two years. For many millennia the fragile continuity of time was maintained by performing sacrifices and rituals. Now the bleached faces teach that time is eternal and that it moves indefinitely on a linear continuum until such time as their God arbitrarily declares and end. This is filthy and heresy. It's also nonsense. The world came to an end when people no longer offered the appropriate blood sacrifices or performed the correct rituals.

If the world has not ended, why is the Valley of Mexico the most polluted place on earth? If the gods continue to provide order and meaning to the lives of the faithful, why is Lake Texcoco gone and the valley choked with twenty million people? Why do half of them live in poverty? Why are fish missing from the lakes and the rivers soiled with chemicals? Why do plants and children and the elderly sicken and die from the air in the Valley of Mexico?

The gods of The One Universe have exited and now reside in The Paradise of the Sun. The life-force used to exist in the land as well as the people. Now the world is dead, but unaware of it as it hastens to its filthy, cataclysmic end as the

Bleached Faces hurry to use up every resource available and sell it to someone else. Sometimes the living would be better off dead. When I look at The One Universe and see the filthy conditions of the cities and the few remaining "Indians" living lives of soundless despair, I mourn. They exist as social pariahs in their own land. I know the world has ended for my people. Quetzalcoatl will not come. The Plumed Serpent has gone to The Paradise of the Sun. Why should a god care more than the believers? Perhaps I should depart also? Why should I offer my services to an unbelieving and ungrateful retinue of heretics and blasphemers? But, alas, I am reluctant to leave. I must remain patient. Since filth is the most prolific of all human products, I know that I am still needed to provide absolution to the detestable off-spring of the bleached ones. Until then, I will wait. My services will surely be needed again.

Hector Receives His Deadly Gift

Friday, June 27, 1984, Mexico City

Hector paced the room, matting the carpet on an already worn path to Amparo's bedroom. Expectation and suspense muted his awareness and stole his caution. His patience had paid off. That rabbit, Raúl, had finally called and promised to deliver the Tlazolteotl statue. Hector glanced at his watch. Time. The museum director should be here any moment. Hector felt ebullient! So far everything was going according to plan.

Amparo had left for Colorado and wouldn't return until Wednesday. Cholo had been retained and was working the contract. The fools were placed just as he wanted and they would all get what they deserved. The museum director producing the Filth Eater was icing on the cake. It would be a marvelous addition to Hector's collection and he felt beside himself with anticipation. He glanced at his watch again. Now the rabbit was late. Damn him, anyway. The minister plopped into a chair, irritated at the worm's tardiness. Hector had promised his daughter that he would be home in time to take her to dinner.

His fingers tapped a restless rhythm on the arm rest. Finally, an unremitting tension lifted him from the chair and he paced the room with a glass of brandy in hand. A thick gold bracelet had caused his arm to perspire, so he stopped to remove it, placing it on top of the table.

He felt confident that everything was arranged as it should be. Every once in a while, a man had to take care of outstanding business, he reasoned. If he didn't, his career would be over, and that scenario was not plausible for Hector. He had built his career on the bodies of lesser, more compromising men who lacked vision and the determination to win at all costs. Lopez Portillo had once introduced him at a cabinet meeting with the statement, "This man's smile is nice, but he has a vicious bite!" Unlike most, Hector's bite was reputedly much worse than his bark and many of his rivals had discovered this too late. Though certainly not pretty, his style of politics ensured that he always won. He would be around long after wimps like Raúl Cordoba, Juan Degas, and others became discards in the game of life.

The doorbell startled Hector. "Who is it?" he called out forcefully, daring it to be the wrong person.

"Delivery for Sr. Vicario!" returned a muffled voice.

Delivery? Surely Raúl hadn't sent the Tlazolteotl with a delivery boy? Hector hesitated, suspicious. When he opened the door, there stood a skinny boy in a khaki uniform, his face horribly blemished with acne. Hector frowned, repelled, but stood his ground. "Who's it from?"

"Don't know, señor. There's no return address. Are you Sr. Vicario?"

Hector hesitated. What the hell was going on here? Why would Raúl send the Filth Eater and not come himself? Momentarily at a loss, he paused to think things through, then realized the blotched face was looking at him expectantly. "Okay…bring it in…put it on the chair. Do I need to sign for it?"

"No, señor. The sender requested that there be no unessential paper work."

Good, thought Hector. At least Raúl didn't expect Hector to sign for property that Raúl, had stolen. The thought seemed ludicrous! "Here…beat it," he said to the delivery boy, handing him a ten pesos.

"Si, señor!" replied the grinning gargoyle, eyeing the ten peso note. "Any time, señor." He turned and walked smartly down the hall, turning the bill over and examining its authenticity. Hector shut and locked the door.

Brimming with excitement, he carried the small, paper-covered box to the table, but quickly became frustrated when he tried to open it. The box was laced with fibrous strapping tape and he didn't have a pocket knife. His large, puffy hands jerked and pulled in vain, until he gave up and huffed off into the kitchen to get a knife.

The package, about twenty centimeters square, weighed nearly three kilos. He recklessly cut the strapping tape and bent the flaps aside. Shredded packing paper lined the box and he anxiously grabbed two handfuls and threw them on the floor. A flash of green jade appeared, exciting him greatly, so he quickly tore out more. There! He could see it! Green, grotesque, and barely human in appearance, it seemed magnificent. Hector began to tingle, feeling euphoric and light-headed. His heart pounded and beads of sweat appeared on his face and hands. He loved it! It was more that he had hoped! He grasped it with two hands and kissed it gleefully like a small child. "Mine, all mine!" he said emphatically.

He switched on the dining room light and placed the Tlazolteotl on the table for better viewing. It felt sticky, and rough edges lined its back side. He rubbed his itching nose, sniffed, and stood back to appraise his new jewel.

The statue stood about twenty centimeters high and sat in a squatting position as if to give birth. Her female genitalia were exaggerated. The vulva and vaginal opening appeared preposterously oversized, leaving a visibly gaping hole between the legs. Her breasts hung large and flaccid. But the statue's oversized head and mouth were the most striking features. The face was grotesquely misshapen because of a huge open mouth replete with large, sharp teeth studded with red jewels. The mouth's opening gaped large enough to take his fist.

Hector, hands trembling, picked up the statue and kissed her with joy! Feeling giddy, he danced with the Filth Eater, twirling about and talking to her in a parody of conversation. He stopped to rub his nose again, gave her another quick smack of his lips, then placed her on the table to admire her. He reached for the sweating drink glass to toast the Tlazoltcotl. He tossed down the remainder of his brandy with a gulp, then grimaced. Condensation from the glass wetted his hands before he rubbed them over the Tlazolteotl's back and buttocks. His nose kept itching and so he rubbed it harder, then his eyes. He drew close to peer at the roughened edges on her back. How had those gotten there? They didn't fit with the overall look or feel of the statue. He ran his fingertips over the edges and felt loose pieces of grit. Grit? "Hell, this looks like it was just made recently!" exploded from his mouth.

Suddenly the room twisted and his vision filled with red tinted distortions. Surreal landscapes of undulant, shimmering colors came at him like the foaming tide, rolling over him, one psychedelic wave after another. He gagged and tried to remain standing. The Filth Eater loomed larger and menacing and a stab of panic sliced his viscera like a white hot laser! Fear gripped him like a vise and crushed all hope as he fell to the ground unbreathing. He jerked and writhed on the floor for fifteen seconds, eyes open, fully cognizant that he was a dead man. From where he lay, the Filth Eater seemed to grow, her mouth opening wider with an inhuman smile. She laughed at him. His heartbeat quickened and surged, gradually diminished, then stopped from a lack of air and a complete autonomic shut down. Green mucus oozed from his nose and his sphincter relaxed, flooding his boxer shorts with excrement. With only a few agonizing moments left, the realization seized him. The rabbit! Raúl!

The Tlazolteotl sat on the table unconcerned and uncaring. According to Aztec belief a person could confess their sins only once to the goddess Filth Eater, and Hector couldn't breathe to talk.

Cholo Builds A Bomb

Saturday, June 28, 1984, Mexico City

Cholo sat in repose, legs resting on a chair, his arms folded to his chest, looking out the window of his first floor motel room. It looked like every other motel room in which he had slept, and he hated it.

The rainy season had begun late, but a steadily downpour had scoured the city for two days, washing curb gutters clean of refuse and purging the air of car and factory spume. He stared unseeing, watching torrents of water splatter onto the asphalt parking lot, then eddy in wide, shallow streams into curbside rivers flowing down the street.

He thought of retiring, and sometimes wondered if he had worked too long already. So far this job had been one of the strangest and most unsettling in which he had ever been involved. This 'Toro' cat was obviously rich and powerful, but something bothered Cholo that he couldn't quite understand. The guy acted kinky and weird about things. The church for instance. What could possibly be wrong with meeting in a bar

189

or a car to do business? Everyone knew you met in a bar or a car, or even in the fucking street. But a church? All professions had accepted standards, and liaisons in churches to plan murder was not standard. Too bad Toro was his only patron. It would be nice to have options, to be able to turn a job down when it didn't feel right. But that wasn't the case. He needed the pesos—big time.

Cholo had rented a room at the Motel Camino Real to prepare the bomb. He never worked at home; that entailed excessive risk. The neighbors were totally unsuspecting and Lupe was barely smart enough not to pry. Although she sometimes had the audacity to complain about the marijuana, usually a "leave if you don't like it" statement clarified the situation sufficiently for her to bite her tongue. Occasionally she would turn into a silly bitch and talk nonsense about families and children, but a few slaps usually brought her back to reality. Now that he was getting older, he found that he liked her more and depended on her for help, especially with his health problems seeming to balloon each day. She was a willing mate in bed, a good cook and she treated him well. He had no reason to complain.

The Colombian opened his suitcase to begin preparations, then thought better of it. First things first. He quickly chewed four antacid tablets, then rolled himself a very thin joint and went into the bathroom to smoke after turning on the exhaust fan. As he took a toke and held his breath, the smoke roiled and adhered to the interior membrane of his lungs. The percolating blood would transport it to his brain, neurons, and synapses and provide the calmness he desired, preventing nausea from attacking him. Finished, he flushed the roach and left the exhaust fan running. He shut the door to trap any lingering odor and returned to the motel room table.

He peeked around the edge of garish orange curtains then closed them, satisfied that no one approached. He extracted the contents of his suitcase and placed the components in an orderly fashion on the bed. His specialized training in the Colombian Army, and later with the Medellin Cartel, had provided him with the knowledge to make very powerful bombs from the items found in almost anyone's house or garage; petroleum jelly, sugar, fertilizer, sulfuric acid, gasoline, or soap. In addition to the explosive components which would have to be mixed according to recipe, he laid out a stop watch with a plastic lens, a small clean metal screw, a battery, connecting wires with alligator clips, and a small nail.

First he prepared the volatile ingredients, spreading the petroleum jelly on waxed paper, then sprinkled and mixed the remainder to specifications. After placing a strategically located dot on the lens, he unscrewed the crystal from the stopwatch and scraped the paint from the edges of the second hand, exposing its metal edge. Next, he heated the small nail until it glowed red. Using a pair of needle nose pliers, he pushed the red-hot nail through the lens, leaving a perfectly round hole, just slightly smaller than the metal screw.

He re-screwed the plastic lens onto the stop watch and wound the screw into the small hole, threading it tightly, but stopping before it made contact with the metal face of the watch. He wound the time piece, attached wires with alligator clips to the metal body and screw, then taped the watch to a spring-loaded plunger assembly that would initiate the explosive when the car door slammed shut. He finished by taping the timer assembly to the explosives. The bomb completed, he needed only to place it strategically in the car and attach the alligator clips correctly to the car's fuse box.

He felt fatigued and his eyes were focusing poorly from the intense squinting required to prepare the bomb. As his glaucoma had worsened it had become more difficult to see. The antacids were wearing off, but he couldn't take a Tagamet for another hour. The pills were costly and he had adopted a strict rationing. His stomach began a hat dance, so he ate four more antacids, rolled another, thicker joint, and returned to the bathroom.

This was the easy part, he reflected, taking a toke and leaning back against the porcelain toilet tank. Planting the bomb was the tricky part, requiring luck and nerves of steel.

Two of his best friends had bought it planting bombs. A security officer had gunned one down and the other had blown himself up. Cholo's stomach began a slow, rising burn as he thought of them. "Jesus," he moaned, visualizing the acid pooling in his gut. He wished he could find a job that paid enough to get a stomach transplant and buy some new eyes. He looked at the joint, took another toke, and waited for its magic to begin. As he sat, he reviewed what he already knew; where the museum director parked his car, the best time of day to plant the bomb, the lax security, the escape route, and alternative scenarios for each contingency should some aspect of the plan change. He needed a good disguise, he realized, and remembered his trunk of old uniforms at home. But they all seemed unsatisfactory for different reasons. This was a big job, he needed something new. After pondering the right disguise at length, he exclaimed, "That'll do the trick!" He recalled a job Jaime Lopez had pulled off successfully in Medellin, and with a satisfied smile and another long pull at the joint, he nodded and agreed with himself, "Yes, that'll work nicely."

He finished the marijuana and returned to the bedroom where he repacked the remaining bomb supplies in a brown paper sack. He pulled the curtain aside and saw that the rain had reduced to a light drizzle, although the sky remained black and gray and promised more moisture. He would have to move fast or risk getting soaked. In order to procure a few items for tomorrow's job, he needed to find a used clothing store.

He locked the motel door behind him and walked to the dumpster to dispose of the paper sack. The contents were such that no one would suspect a thing if they found and opened it. Everything was going according to plan. He flagged a taxi near the motel office and gave instructions to be taken to The Friends' Store, a business run by Quakers which sold second-hand clothing from the U.S.A. He always enjoyed this part of the job.

Cholo Plants The Bomb

Monday, June 30, 1984, Mexico City, 7:00 A.M.

Cholo hadn't slept well. His stomach hurt and he felt tired.
Sleep was always difficult before a big job, and last night had
been no exception. Lupe had pried, whined, then bitched at
him to tell her what was going down. The argument had
finally ended with two solid slaps to her pretty face, causing it
to swell and reducing her to tears. By morning he had become
a morass of exposed nerves. Damn her, anyway! He should
have just stayed at the motel, but he knew it would be even
harder to sleep there. Years of staying in second-class
Colombian hotels, sometimes for weeks at a time, had ruined
him. He hated the damn things. The only thing worse was a
hospital bed.

His stomach growled and he wished he could still drink
coffee. "The list of things I can't eat and drink would fill an
encyclopedia," he groused to no one, then frowned in
aggravation. He had smoked a joint earlier in the morning and
ate a breakfast of melon, cheese, and tortilla, but his stomach

had turned sour and hunger pangs reminded him of his neglect. Two Tagamets had helped quiet the holes in his gut, and he always carried a roll of Rolaids for emergencies.

A continuing succession of mottled gray clouds, the turbid residue of a storm, swept in front of a bright yellow sun, temporarily blocking, then revealing its evanescent splendor. The humidity had risen and his newly purchased work clothes caused him to perspire.

He glanced at his watch. 7:00 a.m., time to get moving. He had rented the blue '72 Chevy pickup from Jose's Rent-A-Wreck. True to the company's name, they had provided him with a rusty, belching tin can with bald tires. The radio was an exercise in frustration, the brakes squealed, and the truck lurched and groaned in protest, lumbering through the rental lot. He had hoped for a better ride. The magnetic signs he'd attached to each door read "Jaime's Auto Repair," and a mechanic driving a piece of junk might draw too much attention.

Under the seat, he had placed a tool box with only a few tools in the top tray. Beneath the tray lay the bomb. He fidgeted nervously, then used the back of his hand to wipe sweat from his forehead. He sat momentarily, tapping his fingers restlessly on the seat, worrying, hesitant to begin the day's work. He wished for tomorrow already.

The Colombian wore a stained workman's uniform purchased from The Friends' Store. The shirt fit fine, but the elastic in the pants had stretched to the point of being no use. He had safety-pinned the pants to the shirt keep them from falling. A greasy L.A. Raiders cap with the bill turned backwards and a pair of scuffed black boots had finished out the disguise. He had hoped to do a little better in the clothing

195

department, but this would have to do. They would be thrown out in an hour anyway.

He drove away from Jose's Rent-A-Wreck, slowly shifting the gears and familiarizing himself with the truck's operation. He maneuvered through a palm-lined, barely shady barrio before pulling onto Avenida Constituyentes. He fought the rush hour traffic for thirty minutes, then exited onto Paseo De La Reforma and pulled into the Zoo parking lot in Chapultepec Park. He parked, partially hidden behind the trunk of an ancient tree, but facing the road so that he would see Raúl Cordoba's white Chrysler Le Baron when it entered the museum's parking lot.

He hated this part of the job, and his stomach sent constant reminders. A stab of pain jolted him when his gut awoke to protest the strenuous conditions under which it was required to operate, rewarding him with an infusion of hydrochloric acid. He slumped onto the steering wheel, feeling like he had been shot.

"Jesus! Not now," he whispered, then began the inevitable search for his Rolaids. He had just placed three in his mouth when the museum director's white Le Baron rounded the corner and pulled into the museum parking lot. Cholo's stomach lurched with recognition. He chewed the antacids, waited five minutes, then started the truck and slowly drove toward the museum parking lot.

He made one pass through the parking lot to ensure that no one loitered unnoticed. The entrance faced south with only one other exit to the north. It appeared clear, so he turned back into the park and passed through and out onto Reforma again, then into the museum parking lot. He parked two cars down from the Le Baron and reached for the tool box, all the while trying to ignore the dripping sieve of acid in his belly.

Trying to appear casual, he quickly observed the area, then walked to the Le Baron, holding on to his pants to keep them from falling. He opened his tool box and extracted a long, flat strip of metal with a hooks on each end. He slid it between the driver's side window and door frame, jiggled until it caught, then pulled upward to unlock the door. His stomach began to convulse and he thought he might throw up. He leaned against the Le Baron and breathed deeply to calm himself.

A quick look around assured him that no one approached, so he hitched his pants, opened the car door, and knelt by the tool box and door frame. His flashlight quickly located the fuse box. He extracted the bomb and masking tape. He taped the bomb to the underside of the dash, then set the plunger assembly to activate the stop watch when Raúl shut the door. He tried the door a couple of times to be sure it depressed the pin, then crawled inside the Le Baron, shutting and locking it from the inside. He connected the two alligator clips to the fuse box, then quickly reviewed the whole process to make sure he had set it correctly. He turned to exit through the passenger side door and looked right into the face of a smiling uniformed guard!

Stunned, he nearly panicked! But a second glance confirmed that the guard was indeed smiling and seemed to be waiting for him to exit the car. Was it possible the guard didn't know what Cholo done? Feeling foolish, he smiled in return, then felt for the four-shot Franci pistol strapped to his ankle. The guard wore a gun also, but showed no indication of pulling it. The Colombian's stomach began to buck like an angry bull, but he steeled himself and opened the door, saying, "Como esta usted?"

197

"Bien, bien" said the pot-bellied, mustachioed guard. "You're working on Sr. Cordoba's car...yes? What's wrong with it?"

Hitching up his pants, Cholo glibly lied about a short in the brake lights, stating that he needed to leave and get a part in order to repair it. "Listen," said the guard, "since you're a mechanic, would you listen to my car and see if you can tell me what's wrong with it."

"Sorry...señor. I'm in a hurry and must go for the part," lied Cholo.

"This will only take a second," the guard waved off his protests, "just listen and see what you think. I don't want you to work on it...just listen, okay?"

Cholo's stomach threatened to erupt molten lava, but he managed to stay on his feet and stand erect. He quickly discerned two options; he could shoot the guard, or spend a few seconds listening to the simple bastard's car, then feed him a line of crap and leave. The first would be the quickest, but undoubtedly the messiest; and the guard had a gun also. His taste for gun battles had receded many years ago. The second option would waste critical seconds, but would probably result in his leaving alive and without anyone the wiser.

"Okay, but only for a quick listen." He grabbed his slumping pants and retrieved his tool box. In order to show his determination not to work on the guard's car, he placed the box in the pickup bed, then followed him across the parking lot, listening as the guard gestured and explained the history of his car's problems.

Time was of the essence. Cholo's back was to the museum and he couldn't see who came or went. Nervous, he glanced over his shoulder, then said, "Start it...I'm in a hurry."

"Un momento, señor," the guard fumbled for the keys, "sometimes it doesn't start so good."

The engine began to grind and turn over, but didn't start. "Jesus Christ!" Cholo complained, holding up his slipping pants. "Look...I've got to go...my boss..."

The car fired, choked and farted repeatedly, then began to knock loudly. "Rusty piece of junk," bitched Cholo. He waved the guard to turn it off. But the guard replied by goosing the engine and revving it to a roar so that Cholo could better hear the engine.

Behind him, a car door slammed and Cholo's heart skipped a beat! His head jerked around for a quick look. No! Raúl! Without hesitating, Cholo turned to run. The safety pin holding his pants popped from the sudden strain. Halfway through his first step they slid from his hips. Within a second they were at his knees. He reached to prevent them from falling further, but tripped and stumbled forward. He had arrived directly behind his truck and appeared to be suspended in midair when Cordoba's car blew.

The large picture windows of the museum flexed inward momentarily, then recoiled outward in a fury, shattering into millions of iridescent shards. The ensuing fireball incinerated Cholo immediately, blowing him toward the opposite side of the parking lot. The small pistol strapped to his leg broke loose and slid on the concrete thirty meters away where it lodged against the back tire of a parked car. Raúl Cordoba, of course, died immediately. The guard, roasted but alive, lived for another two minutes, then mercifully died, his body charred and flesh melted from the waist up.

Black clouds from the raging fire billowed into the skies over Chapultepec Park. Five or six cars burned at once, setting off a chain reaction. Every few minutes another gas tank exploded, starting yet another inferno, igniting the car next to it. All told, twelve cars were destroyed and eight more damaged in the bombing. Cholo's stomach didn't bother him anymore, and Lupe would probably be returning to Nogales sooner than she wished.

Filth Eater

The bleached faces tout their Filth Eater as having impeccable credentials since he is the product of a virgin birth. In their ignorance and credulity they fail to see the obvious— anyone of any importance was born of a virgin. Such myths and legends are rife throughout the world. A miracle is merely an unnatural event that occurs naturally. A virgin birth is simply a spiritual awakening and quickening. The vessel of delivery is unimportant, although some virgin births are more important than others. Perhaps this was the case with the Christian Filth Eater.

Death and birth are part of the same cycle. Without birth there can be no death. They are the temporal and spiritual realizations of existence—here and in The Paradise of the Sun. I myself gave birth to Centeotl, the god of Maize. It was a gift from me to the pious of The One Universe. I assure you it occurred without the aid of anyone, or any entity. The power of creation and invention resides in the very fabric of a god's being.

A virgin birth is a meaningless gift unless it benefits people by sustaining their existence. Any other purpose is a filthy presumption and a misguided attempt to promote purpose over benefit. If a god wishes to gift mortals, this questions must be answered: What is the purpose of the creation, and what does the gift achieve? The Christian Filth Eater was a gift to save the world from itself. A bizarre concept at best. Centeotl was a gift to nourish and sustain the inhabitants of The One Universe. You be the judge. Which gift has a purpose easier to discern? Which has produced something of measurable value? To this day the inhabitants of The One Universe consume maize on a daily basis. It nourishes them physically, but food also has spiritual properties. If mortals are not sustained physically, how can they live to embrace the supernatural?

The Christian Filth Eater's credentials are nothing out of the ordinary and his purpose is highly suspect. This is a filthy breach of covenant between mortal and immortal. Who but me could eat such filth?

Captain Alvarado Begins His Investigation

Monday, June 30, 1984, Mexico City

Captain Alvarado yawned with fatigue and sleep deprivation, tired from being up all night. He knew that he wouldn't be home for quite some time. "The cat has shit in the cake!" he bitched to no one, slowly cruising toward Coyohuacan and the Sanchez-Vicario mansion. Nothing made sense anymore, yet today was shaping up to be the most important in his life. This case could make his career, or send him back to the streets if he mishandled it.

Jose had given him one week to find a bad guy or the fed's took over. The murder of Hector Vicario was not a routine homicide; it was interpreted as an act of war in this socialist country. El Presidente had screamed at Jose and Jose had screamed at Luis. *Why me?* he thought. If giving him the case was a left-handed compliment, he didn't need it. Jose had made it clear; get results or you're finished as a detective on

203

this police force. Did Luis understand? Who could mistake his voice tone or the connotation of his words?

The matter had begun as a routine investigation. The Interior Minister's daughter called Sunday, alarmed at her father not returning home for two days. Coincidentally, someone reported a horrible smell and large black flies swarming outside an apartment door. Appearances are deceiving, and at first glance it appeared to be a case of an old man dying of a heart attack. Then two uniforms, gagging and choking, died a horrible death in the same room as the Minister while the landlord, his wife, and several apartment residents witnessed their deaths. This quickly dispelled the heart attack theory. Now three murders were committed. But who did it? Why? How? These were the sacred trinity of homicide.

That freaky-looking statue was probably how. The uniforms had died after handling it, and Luis could think of no other possibility at the moment. The sculpture had been sent to the morgue along with the bodies to undergo tests and Luis hoped to have the results this afternoon. He had left a crew of three detectives to search the apartment and the interior minister's car. Meanwhile he was ready to interview his first witness and he was driving to the Sanchez-Vicario home to talk to the daughter.

He casually navigated the Coyohuacan suburb, slowing to a crawl in order to admire the gleaming, white-stuccoes behind ornate iron fences and thick, brick walls that declared the homes off-limits. Carpets of bougainvillea with purple flowers rippling in the breeze flowed from rooftops and over the walls, providing a natural decoration and beautifying the expensive homes. He turned onto Nezahuapili Drive, so named after the Aztec philosopher-king of Texcoco, and pulled into the driveway of the palatial Vicario-Sanchez mansion. When he honked his horn, a servant appeared at the gate and attempted to shoo him away before seeing his badge and I.D. The servant frowned at Luis's identification, sniffed with disapproval, then instructed him to wait, and so Luis took a moment to look around the neighborhood.

He tried to remain expressionless, but his eyes grew wide with wonder. Impressive. Everything arranged perfectly. Rows of multi-colored croton guarded two rows of diffenbachia, and the south wall lay hidden beneath a mat of red blooming bougainvillea. Flowers erupted from the flat roof and cascaded down the wall. Vicario's colonial-style house, as big as a hacienda ranch home, was easily twice as large as any other residence on the street.

Money and power, Luis assured himself, had somehow led to Hector Vicario's death. In a country like Mexico, how many enemies would Hector Vicario have? Twenty? Fifty? Hundreds? Luis would bet a year's pay that somewhere people were raising toasts to the Interior minister's death, and one of them might be a murderer.

The maid returned and ushered Luis through several rooms and out into a Spanish-style courtyard where a plump, homely, well-dressed lady in her early thirties greeted him. She stood in the shade of two tamarindo trees and a percolating fountain in the center of the white, terrazzo-decked courtyard.

"Señorita Vicario?" Luis extended a hand.

"Yes...and you are?" She held a handkerchief to her eyes with one hand and her other clasped a woven straw fan. She ignored his hand.

"Captain Luis Alvarado, Detective First-Class." He dropped the proffered hand.

"Yes…I've been expecting you. Please sit." She pointed to a white wrought-iron table and chairs. "Thank you for phoning ahead. This is a terrible time for me and the newspapers won't quit calling. All they care about is their precious story. I'm changing the phones."

"There's more than one telephone in the house?"

"There are several, captain. My father was a very important man. He used different phones for different purposes."

Luis made a mental note to get a log on all the phones. Meanwhile his eyes surveyed the immaculately clean, opulent courtyard, all the while thinking of his own mean quarters on Calle Medrano. He turned to the puffy-faced patrician. "Señorita…I know this is tough for you, but it's important you provide us with any information you can in order to find your father's killer, okay?" He took out his writing pad and pencil.

She nodded, then stared down at the white terrazzo, resigning herself to this unwanted intrusion.

Luis continued, "Did the Superintendent tell you about the deaths of the two policemen who found your father?"

"Yes…it's too ghastly to think about!" she began to weep. "What kind of person would do such a thing?" she held the handkerchief to her mouth while tears leaked from her eyes.

"Señorita, do you know the woman who lives in the apartment where your father was found?"

She frowned, dabbed her eyes, then said, "I think it's Amparo's place."

"Amparo?"

A look of extreme distaste fixed her face. "An old acquaintance." Her handkerchief waved the idea away. "I introduced her to my father about a year ago and…well…I think the bitch was having an affair with my father."

"Was, señorita?"

"Was…is…what difference does it make!" she exclaimed angrily, freezing him with a hostile stare. "She's a slut and no better than a street puta! I hate her! She's the cause of this!" she accused, venom dripping from her tongue. "She's a nobody. Her father was a nobody. I hope she rots in jail over this."

Luis paused to let her recover, then quietly asked, "Did your father see her often?"

"How would I know, I'm his daughter! He didn't tell me about his love life!" she glared, then fanned herself, incensed at the indignity of having to answer such intrusive questions.

Ouch! thought Luis, deciding on another line of questioning. "Señorita, while walking through the house I noticed many objects of art. Some of it looks to be very valuable. Was your father a collector?"

"Of course…it's obvious," she swept her arm around the courtyard, indicating the numerous pedestals with statues and stelae. "Everyone knows my father amassed old pieces of art. The house is cluttered with his trash. There's way too much, if you ask me." She fanned herself. "Sometimes, I think he spent more time collecting archaeological junk than managing the country's natural resources. He was always after some piece, or someone to acquire something for him. Especially that nice little man at the museum, Raúl Cordoba."

Luis, scribbling on his pad, asked, "Did your father have any particularly valuable pieces?"

"Surely you jest, captain!" The fan started again. "Father probably has the most extensive private collection of pre-Colombian art in Mexico…maybe the world," she added.

"Where?" asked Luis.

"Most of the truly valuable pieces are in his private museum. Actually…it's more like a large vault." The fan stopped. "I've only been inside a few times. Very few people know of it or what it contains. He was very secretive about it."

"It's here, in the house?"

"There, through that door," the fan pointed to an unremarkable white door.

"I would like to see, if I may?"

"That isn't possible. There's a steel key in his bedroom wall safe and I don't know the combination. Tomorrow I meet with my father's attorney to straighten out his affairs. I doubt that we'll allow anyone to snoop through his personal belongings for at least a month or more…or at least until we have assessed the situation ourselves." The fan started again. "My father's investments and properties were extensive and a mystery to me. It will take a while to know where I stand," she said firmly.

Luis groaned inwardly, but kept a placid face. He needed in the vault now and this rich bitch was stonewalling. When her father was alive, he had lived as one of the untouchable elite and could have forestalled any investigation. But now he was at the bottom of the food chain, rotting in the morgue, and some of the señorita's privileges were about to be revoked. Though apparently unaware of it, her life would undoubtedly change drastically with her father's death.

Luis would have his boss fix the problem. Intuition told him that a connection between the art-collecting hobby and Hector Vicario's death was a foregone conclusion. Good Lord! The man had been killed by a piece of art. And this Raúl Cordoba at the National Museum of Anthropology—he was involved somehow. Much would be learned by examining the relationship between Hector Vicario and the museum.

"Señorita…did your father have any enemies?"

208

The girl burst out laughing amid tears, dabbing the handkerchief to her eyes, then waved her fan once at Luis. "You're a comedian, captain. My father was a very powerful person. You look like an educated man — you know the history of our country. Of course he had enemies!" she stated emphatically. "Who were they? Who knows? Not sure it matters." She spread her arms. "I heard him argue with many people over the years." She coughed nervously into the handkerchief.

"Mary save us," she continued, crossing herself. "I remember he had a terrible argument with El Presidente on the telephone. He argued with the museum director about art. Once, a horrible man who used to work for Sr. Cordoba...Juan Degas...caused them trouble." She sighed and dropped both hands into her lap. "Father argued with my mother every day until she died." The señorita Vicario shrugged her shoulders. "He was not an easy man to get along with, captain. He was demanding and used to getting his way...what can I tell you?" She blew her nose, "He was a difficult man to understand."

Luis finished his notes and put the pad away. Much remained to be investigated, but the señorita Vicario was reluctant to continue. She had a distant look and began to sigh, then ignored him altogether. The interrogation would deteriorate quickly now. She had absorbed enough pain for the day. He'd need to request the phone logs on the apartment and this house and Jose would have to get him into that vault as soon as possible.

"Captain Alvarado?" interrupted a servant. "Yes?"

"Telephone...in here, please."

"Perdon, señorita," smiled Luis. He followed the servant into a sitting room. The walls were decorated with hand-woven wool blankets of several styles; Zapotecan, Tarascan, Maya, and Aztec. Luis would bet a month's pay that they were priceless. He picked up the phone.

"Bueno?"

"Luis? Jose...where are you going after the Vicario home?"

"I'm nearly finished. I'll stop by the museum to talk to the director, then meet with the team later."

"That's why I called...get to the museum quick." Luis frowned, confused. "Yeah...why's that?"

"The museum was bombed. Half the precinct and all the fire trucks in Coyohuacan are there. Didn't you hear the sirens?"

"Bombed? Who..." Somehow, before the words had left his mouth, his intuition had already answered—Raúl Cordoba.

"The director and his car were blown to pieces. Get your ass over there!" Jose ordered, then added sourly, "Luis...come up with something quick, or we'll all be cleaning latrines at Lecumberri."

A bad joke, but Luis took the statement seriously. Consequences were a distinct possibility if they messed this one up.

"On my way," he hung up the phone. What next? Had the whole city gone mad? First Vicario, and now Cordoba?

Luis excused himself to señorita, promising to call again. His mind reeling with questions, he left Coyohuacan and drove rapidly toward the museum. Here, eight miles away, angry black clouds billowed above the skyline. The long night had left him fatigued, but now his adrenaline was pumping. Who was the crazy son-of-a-bitch killing everyone in his precinct? He angrily stomped and floored the accelerator, then backed off as a line of traffic approached.

The traffic crept along slowly, as most of the drivers had detoured for Chapultepec also, and Luis began a slow burn, frustrated at the perversion of men who always gravitated to tragedies. Finding it impossible to get closer, he parked six blocks from the museum. Cars and trucks were strung haphazardly, blocking roads as people from everywhere flocked to the carnage in Chapultepec. Flashing his badge repeatedly, he worked his way through throngs of voyeurs and curiosity seekers until he arrived at the scene. The museum had been evacuated and yellow ribbon cordoned off the area. Fire trucks lined the roads like huge blocks, sentinels intent on protecting the ancient heritage of Mexico.

The fire had diminished greatly, except for a burning VW and a car too charred to discern its make. Black, stinking smoke from smoldering tires stained the sky, sending a distress signal. He spotted Paulo and waved. The detective trudged near, notebook in hand, looking as if he'd been up a week without sleep. His suit was wrinkled and his round face sported a two-day growth of beard.

"Hey, stud," said Paulo, running his fingers through his hair. "Got a mad bomber—could be gasoline or dynamite. Incinerated guy in the car was Raúl Cordoba, the museum director. It'll be hard to tell, because there isn't anything left of him." Paulo pointed. "That guy over there, or what's left of him, is an unknown. He may have been a mechanic working on the guard's car. There's an old truck over there that says Jaime's Garage on the side that no one can account for, and the hood was blown off an old Chevy that belonged to the museum guard. He was torched inside it."

Paulo sighed, running a hand through his rumpled hair again, "The bomb was very professional. Looks like the mechanic may have been working on the guard's car when the explosion cooked them. The bomb boys arrived ten minutes ago. That's all they have so far."

What a mess, thought Luis, surveying the area. The debris of shattered glass, twisted metal, and broken concrete lay like the refuse of a battle field, the twisted Plain of Meggido, Raúl Cordoba's Armageddon.

"Paulo, close this place until further notice. Have some of the uniforms help question the staff. Get a roster of the administrators. Be sure and talk to the secretaries before sending them home; if anyone knows anything, they will."

Luis looked around for a bumper to rest a leg, then continued, "I want all of the museum director's files seized and brought to the precinct house. When you're done here, I'll have Pedro help you go through them. Two names—Hector Vicario and Juan Degas—see if you can turn up something, okay?" Luis hesitated, seeing the look of distress on Paulo's face.

"I know I'm asking a lot. This is the biggest case you and I will ever work. Bust your ass and I'll do everything I can to get you kicked upstairs. That's a promise…and you can tell Pedro, too. Don't plan on going home until late, okay?"

"Yeah…okay. Just harder to think when you're tired. I'm glad you're in charge, or I'd probably quit." He gave a weak smile, pocketed the note pad, and then turned to go to work, looking for witnesses and searching for Pedro.

Luis turned to go. The rancid, gritty smell of burning tires made him nauseous. He really wasn't needed here, so he threaded his way through the crowd and headed back to his car, breathing deeply of the clean park air.

Organization was the key, he reminded himself. He turned the key in the ignition and put the car in gear. He'd never get anything accomplished if he didn't stay on task.

***

212

Ten minutes later he pulled into El Texcoco Azul apartment complex and climbed the stairs to the third floor apartment. Tony, his occasional partner, stood near the kitchen table tagging evidence when Luis entered. "How's it coming Clousseau?" asked Luis with a feeble attempt at humor.

"Luis?" The large, square faced detective turned to see who entered. "Not bad. Been waiting for you. May have a couple of things."

"Yeah?" said Luis, pleased. "Like what?"

"Just intercepted a call from Vicario's concubine. She called to talk to him. He has a key and spends weekends here. He told her to check in, but never answered the phone, so she kept calling. Get this…she's in Vail, Colorado with a male "escort".

"She's in the U.S.A.? With another man?" Luis repeated, trying to discern the importance of the information. "How long did you talk to her?"

"About fifteen minutes…she's all shook up. Says she'll be on an early flight tonight if she can. Sounded surprised and scared. I told her someone would meet her at the airport and," he looked pointedly at Luis, "I don't plan on being up at that hour".

"Luis ignored the inference. "What else you got?"

"We got Vicario's car keys and went through the Mercedes. Found this under the seat." He handed Luis a sheaf of papers. "It makes for very interesting reading."

"What is it?"

"Oh…the regular stuff," panned Tony, "blackmail, threats, some rough stuff, and a lot of stealing have been going on at the National Museum. Looks as if our dead Minister of the Interior was a thief and extortionist. But then again, he was a politician, wasn't he?"

Luis felt a stirring of excitement. He walked to the balcony, looking first at the towering buildings of the National University, then at the street and parking lot. Maybe this thing was coming together. Soon they would know how; maybe this was why. Glancing at the report, he wondered if it might even tell them who.

He returned from the balcony and sat down to read. The title and author's name leapt from the page and onto his lips—Juan Degas. That name again. He read quickly while Tony worked. No doubt about it — this Juan Degas had a strong motive. An archaeologist with a grudge, he knew the dead men and had reason to hate both. Degas was beat up, lost his job, then wrote this report to keep Cordoba and Vicario away from him and his girlfriend.

"Tony...we need to find this guy as soon as possible!" Luis whacked the report against his leg. "The señorita Vicario says her father used to argue with the Raúl Cordoba about Juan Degas. We have our first suspect. Any idea where we can find him?"

Tony grinned. "Wondered when you'd ask. I mentioned his name to the girl and she volunteered that he works at the university for a professor David Wolf in the Anthropology Department."

Luis jumped from the chair. "You're a sleuth, Antonio! If we don't end up in **Traffic** writing parking tickets and stealing tourists license plates, I'll treat you to a night in the Zona Rosa." Luis turned, as if to leave.

"Luis?" "Yeah...what is it?"

"Did you know any of the uniforms killed here last night?"

Luis's shoulders sagged. "No...but Pedro told me they have wives and kids. One guy's wife was seven months pregnant."

214

"When we catch the son-of-a-bitch that did this, I want five minutes alone to interrogate him. Think that can be arranged?"

Captain Alvarado didn't answer. He normally despised the rough stuff. It gave the police a bad reputation and was strictly against the law, but it happened all the time. Old habits die hard in Mexico. If someone wanted a confession, the boys in the White Room were practiced at getting it—regardless of what it took.

"Yeah," he said, "I don't see why not. But you'll have to get your own witnesses for the questioning. I don't want anything to do with it. When you're done, I'll cuff him to a chair and let the widows interrogate him." Luis perused the room one more time. "How long before you're done?"

"Another hour...two at the most, why?"

"I know you've been up all night, but I need you at the station to help out. Paulo and Pedro are bringing in Cordoba's file cabinets and desk stuff. It's going to take hours to go through everything."

"Who's Raúl Cordoba? Oh! You mean the guy in the report?"

Luis turned, surprised. "Tony...I guess you haven't heard. Raúl Cordoba bought a harp and moved upstairs. He was murdered two hours ago by a bomb at the Museum of Anthropology."

Their eyes locked knowingly, then Tony said, "I'll wrap it up and be down. Luis?"

"Yeah."

"You can count on me. I'm in for the whole thing...whatever it takes."

"Thanks, amigo. If we win, I'll see that you get something out of this," promised Luis.

"I just want the bastard's cojones…here in my hands," continued Tony, extending a large clenched fist. "Don't forget about my five minutes," he repeated to Luis's retreating figure.

Fatigued and sleepy, Luis was fading. He needed a cup of coffee and a sweet roll, but knew he didn't have time. It was a long drive downtown to the morgue. Hopefully the white coats would have completed Vicario's autopsy and analyzed the sticky shit on the statue.

The sun grew stronger in the hazy sky, and he began to perspire. He loosened his tie and slumped into the driver's seat, fastened his seat belt, then thought about closing his eyes for just a moment. Instead he exhaled, fired the car, and drove slowly toward the zocalo. He thought about Juan Degas and Vicario's girlfriend. Why had she split to the United States with another man when her sugar daddy and his friend were getting themselves killed? Things promised to be interesting tomorrow. He hoped to be awake when it all went down.

Luis Makes A Serious Mistake

Monday, June 30, 1984, Mexico City, 11:00 A.M.

Luis's suit coat and necktie lay wrinkled on the car seat. His body odor reeked sourly and his nostrils flared. A two-day growth of beard grew unevenly on his face and his step had lost its spring. Tired. He was plodding along, trying to stay focused. The zocalo traffic seemed horrendous, as usual, and Luis was stuck following an old Chevy Biscayne with a ceramic Chihuahua dog near the back windshield. Its head bobbed continually and big red eyes lit up each time the driver applied the brakes, which happened frequently. The detective tried to stay calm, moving in and out of the traffic, carefully guiding his customized Mercury through the worst traffic in the world. Finally he arrived, parking in an underground garage, then walked the remaining distance to the world's largest morgue. Statistically, in a city of twenty million, someone would die every fifteen minutes.

He walked south along Independencia, breathing caustic car exhaust, trying to tune out the clamor of car horns and shrilling policía whistles. Numerous street vendors accosted him, hawking everything from paper air-filtration masks to children's toys. Unemployed laborers lined the street, patiently sitting on the curb. They held cardboard signs advertising their specialties: Plumbero, Electricista, and Carpintero. An occasional a car would exit the traffic, negotiate a price, and the worker would grab his tool bag and jump in the car.

Luis paused to work up his courage, took a deep breath, and entered the glass double-doors. He followed the signs to the Coroner's office, where he picked up the autopsy report, then went to view Hector Vicario's body. The morgue, a huge, semi-sterile refrigerator, had numerous bins of decaying flesh whose odor clung to the inner membrane of the nose long after leaving. Luis hated coming here. After fifteen years it never got any better.

He held a handkerchief to his nose as he stood over Vicario's body. *Stinks like hell*, he observed, looking at the dissected remains of the once powerful Minister—and so did the autopsy report, he decided. Disheartening and unrevealing, it listed the cause of death as poison—a neuro-toxin mixed in pine gum which entered through the mucous membranes of the three murder victims, Hector Vicario and the two policemen. It further described the poison as a derivative of curare, one of the world's deadliest known poisons, found in the skin of amphibians. It attacked the autonomic nervous system, suffocating the victim while causing hallucinations at the same time. Animal tissue membrane, urine, and lye soap were also identified. Probable use of these ingredients: leaching agents to remove the poison from its source.

"Good Lord," muttered Luis to no one, reflecting on this particular mode of dying. He had witnessed his share of death, but never anything quite like this. This was...was...almost exotic, he decided.

The report didn't identify the source of the poison. A rare substance, curare was used by South American Indians to make poison arrows. He tried to recall something he had read, couldn't, then suddenly remembered—Poison Arrow Frogs—that was it. Tiny, brilliant-colored rain forest frogs. But where would the murderer find a curare type poison or a poison frog? The National University? Brazil?

Luis found nothing amusing in this strange twist to an already complicated plot. The case had turned bizarre by any definition and he didn't need weird, esoteric poisons listed on a pathology report to bring to Jose as a cause of death. That would invoke the famous 'look,' accompanied with scathing criticism, sarcasm, and threats against your job. Probably best to wait a day or two before giving him the report.

He yawned uncontrollably, then stretched. The long, sleepless night and the activity of the morning had made him grumpy. He was tempted to call Jose and tell him to go ahead and call the fed's, but Luis knew it would result in latrine duty at the federal penitentiary. His career would never recover. Nothing to do but keep on working and hope for a break.

"Perdon."

Startled, he glanced over his shoulder, then stepped aside as a stainless steel gurney rattled by, its cargo covered with a blood-stained sheet and smelling of feces and rot. *Yech.*

His Timex informed him that his scheduled meeting at the precinct house began in an hour and his throat told him he might gag any moment if he didn't leave this stinking hell of white jackets and decomposing bodies. Tucking the report inside his jacket, he headed for the door. It would take the rest of the day to get the cloying odor out of death out of his nose. How did the doctors and technicians stand the smell?

He exited the glass doors of the morgue and walked toward Independencia. As far as the eye could see cars lined up in every direction. As he approached the intersection, a squeal of rubber and the resounding crash of crunching metal drew his attention.

Two drivers jumped from their cars with arms waving, each accusing the other and arguing vociferously. Suddenly one of the drivers kicked the other's fender. Enraged, the twice-injured party responded by grabbing a tire-iron and striking the aggressor's car. Seconds later, both drivers were circling the enemy's vehicle, repeatedly hitting and denting the offending automobile in a frenzy of revenge as they took turns demolishing the other's car. Hundreds of car horns honked and everyone shouted encouragement, inciting them to greater mayhem.

Good God! thought Luis, stopping to watch the circus. He started to intervene, then reminded himself of his last adventure with the priest and the assault case. He turned a blind eye and walked toward his car and four unsolved murder cases. Stay focused, he reminded himself, striding away. A tire-iron to the head would greatly impede his effectiveness.

***

Two hours later, Luis' team of detectives were deeply engrossed in the murders. Tony had commandeered a dusty, nearly empty storage room while Luis surveyed the evidence gathered from the bombing. Little clothing remained from the charred mechanic except a pair of gold wire-rimmed glasses and an old boot. The remains of his body were taken to the morgue for autopsy. The other detectives were systematically sorting documents, comparing witnesses' testimony and anecdotes, and trying to construct a chronology of events. Big gaps remained, but the killings were falling into individual frameworks.

Were they connected? Poison and a bomb were how, but a motive was missing, which, of course, precluded knowing who, especially if there was more than one perpetrator. This might take the intervention of the Blessed Virgin, mused Luis.

He decided to take the methodical approach and make a slate for each murder. This took only thirty minutes, but after completing and comparing them, it struck him as singular that both lists required that he question Juan Degas and his girlfriend. Degas's report could be interpreted as strong motivation for both murders. Vicario and Cordoba were both connected to him by the report. But why would he use such different methods to murder? This gave him pause to speculate, and he resolved to ask the other detectives what they thought.

***

Two hours later they broke for lunch. Luis had sent out for chicken tacos and colas, and all began to voice their opinions, wolf down food, and chase it with tepid soda pop.

Tony began with, "Cordoba's killer is a man." "How so?" asked Luis, chomping on a taco.

"It's a violent crime, women don't make bombs," replied Tony.

Luis didn't share his opinion. "How about the poison? You've seen the autopsy report. Poison is something a woman would use."

"Maybe the murders are related," offered Paulo.

This is what Luis wanted to hear. "Are they? What's your gut say, Pedro?" he asked the quiet, bookish detective.

221

After a slight hesitation Pedro answered. "Yeah...they're related."

Everyone stopped eating and waited expectantly for him to justify his answer, but he stared instead at the contents of Raúl Cordoba's office spread out on the table.

"Why?" Luis coaxed, unable to wait any longer.

"This looks like a blackmail and revenge case," Pedro took a swig of his soda, "and there's one thing that ties it all together—this anthropology and antiquities thing."

"How?" asked Luis.

Pedro held up a finger. "Number one...all the suspects and victims are involved with archaeology or the museum; Two...Juan Degas is an archaeologist and used to work at the museum; three...Hector Vicario was a big collector, and Cordoba the museum director; four...the thing that ties it all together is the report Degas wrote. It fingers both Cordoba and the minister as thieves. If half of what Degas says is true, then we have a major theft ring and a conspiracy by high government officials to cover up their crimes. Besides...look at the deaths. A poison statue and a bomb at the museum. Different methods I grant you, but linked by an archaeology theme."

"I agree," said Paulo, biting off the end of a jalapeno. He motioned with the chili stub. "Four different museum employees listed Degas as someone with a grudge against Raúl Cordoba. None of them loved the museum director, but they liked Degas even less. He's got a motive...plain and simple. Someone needs to get over to the university and bring him in for questioning." He took a swig of his pop. "I'd be surprised if he's still there."

"What about the blackmail part?" asked Luis. "The revenge motive is easy to see because of the report. Who's black mailing who? If Degas was blackmailing Cordoba and Vicario, why would he kill them?"

"It's still a good place to start," insisted Pedro. "We ain't got anyone else as a suspect, do we?"

Everyone agreed that Degas was the best place to start, so Luis gave in. "Tony and I will head for the university. Pedro, drive over to that excavation thing at Tacuba and find out what's going on. That's where Cordoba has been spending his time. Talk to as many people as you can. Paulo...I know this sounds crummy, but I want you to work on the phone logs. Take them home if you want, but I want addresses and names on as many as you can identify. Try to find a pattern or a call that shouldn't be there—anything out of the ordinary. See if you can make any sense of it. We'll meet here tomorrow morning at eight sharp. Don't be late. I've got a meeting with Jose at ten-thirty and I want to compare notes before I see him, okay? Any questions?"

***

Thirty minutes later, Luis and Tony descended the stone steps at the precinct house and headed for Luis' Mercury. Dark thunderheads rolled in from the northeast and wind gusted strongly, blowing dust and grit into their eyes.

"Come on...let me drive," Tony badgered.

"I've seen you drive. You'd have to put up collateral first...your wife or something in case you wrecked my car."

"I'll do it! Or...we can take it out in trade or something." He nudged Luis with his elbow.

"I'm going to tell her that you almost swapped her for a 1955 Mercury and see what she says, Tony."

"Don't do me no favors." Tony fastened his seat belt. "Listen...it's getting late. Let's just arrest Degas until someone

223

better comes along. It's obvious he's involved. None of these guys are wearing white hats."

"You know better than that. We'll listen to his story…maybe he'll have an alibi." Luis turned the key and the Mercury fired. He smiled with satisfaction.

Tony broke wind, then rolled down the window.

"Fucking donkey, why didn't you do that outside?" Luis hit the fan switch and rolled down his window.

"You know something that bothers me about Degas being the murderer?" he said. "He's smart…guy's got a Ph.D.…but he's left a trail that leads straight to his house. That doesn't make sense. If the contents of that report are leaked it could embarrass everyone connected to PRI, even El Presidente. On the other hand…I guess…if he's a hothead bent on revenge…maybe it doesn't matter to him. Hotheads don't think well.

"These academic types have their heads in the clouds, Luis. Most of them don't put on the same colored socks in the morning. He may be smart, but you've got to have the mind of a criminal to pull off something like this. How many Ph.D.'s are street-smart like criminals? These guys would commit a crime and not expect to get caught just because people wouldn't think they'd do anything like that. They're human, Luis, just like the other murderers and thugs. They love, hate, covet, and suffer from greed just like everyone else."

True, thought, Luis. He pulled onto Insurgentes and swung into the traffic. Intelligence and learning didn't insulate you from base emotions. Thinking you were smarter than everyone else might even delude you to thinking you could get away with something. Anything's possible, he reminded himself, and Luis began to remember other cases he had worked that involved surprise perpetrators.

224

Twenty minutes later they stood behind the mosaicked library and studied a map of the National University. The campus, a behemoth that sprawled endlessly in every direction, had tall buildings that impeded their sight, preventing them from identifying landmarks. While Luis looked at the map, Tony checked out the girls.

"Would you look at that…great legs!" crowed Tony…"and that tall one by the steps…look at that rear-end motion! Remind you of anything, Luis?" Tony made crude in-and-out gestures with his fingers.

"Tony…we're here to question a suspect, not feed unsuspecting maidens to your libido. Get your mind off your crotch and help me out here!" replied Luis, sternly.

"Sure…sure," agreed Tony, continuing to track the girls.

"It's on the other side of this building." Luis folded the map. "Come on, before you start drawing attention to yourself."

Luis Arrests Juan

Monday, Late Afternoon, June 30, 1984, Mexico City

The chipped oak floor was stained from numerous liquid spills and creaked loosely from fatigue and pulled nails as Juan shifted his weight to the other leg. Two of the five lamps suspended from the university's laboratory ceiling hung useless, emitting no light. The walls, formerly white, were distempered, stained, and putty-colored with age.

If there was such a thing as a living nightmare, Juan suspected this was it. He stared through the window, tracking a line of dark thunderheads that mirrored his mood, intent on his personal dilemma. The sword of Damocles hung above his head ready to fall at any moment. Gripped with a sense of impending doom, he considered running. The city had thousands of hiding places, but he knew that running wasn't a serious option. It would imply guilt and he didn't want to lead the policía to any erroneous conclusions. Best to wait, he decide. They would arrive soon and he must be ready.

Juan and Linda had driven to the museum as soon as news of the bombing hit the radio. A newscast had mistakenly reported that the museum had been blown up. But this was wrong, he realized upon arriving. Raúl Cordoba was blown up. The museum had only lost a little glass.

He stood wondering how long before the policía came. Restless, he shifted his weight to the other leg. Who would want Raúl dead? Why?

Had he double-cross someone? Juan hated his guts. But murder? He turned to his fiancee.

"When's David due back?"

"The professor said he would return tonight or tomorrow, depending on whether he stopped at La Venta," she repeated for the third time. "Quit worrying, Querido! You haven't done anything wrong."

"No…the policía will come," he said, resigned to an uncertain fate.

"Why? You keep saying that." She folded her arms in irritation. "Because Raúl was an important person of sorts, and they'll be pushed to find who did it."

"But you're innocent!" she cried. "You haven't done anything!" She glared at him, then softened her look. "What will you do if they do come?"

"I don't know, I can't run or they'll think I did it. If I'm not here to be questioned they'll assume I'm guilty and issue a warrant to pick me up."

I don't want to go back to jail again—that was horrible."

Linda, surprised, whispered, "You were in jail? I didn't know that. I thought you had told me everything?"

"Thought you knew," he shrugged. "Three days in 1968. Marco was with me. You were still in high school and probably don't remember the problems at the university. We were

227

protesting government policies…and they had troops stationed on campus. Everyone went on strike. El Presidente sent in more troops and three students were killed in the riot. Marco and I were rounded up with hundreds of others and put in jail. El Presidente closed the National University for six months as a warning. It worked for me," he added, facing the window again. "I don't ever want to go back. Mexican jails are shitholes."

"Well…you're not going to jail, what would they use for evidence? You haven't done anything," she repeated again, mostly to assure herself.

"I've talked to the wrong people. I've threatened Raúl several times.

They may have found the report by now." His fists clenched. "They'll be here…if not today, tomorrow. God, I wish David were here." He leaned against the wall.

"I told you not to write that stupid report! We should've just left it alone and got on with our lives. David told you it was a bad idea, too," she accused.

"He told me that after I'd already written and delivered it." "Well…you should've checked first. It was a dumb thing to do!" Her face had turned a mottled pink.

"Is it always going to be like this?" She glowered, hands on her hips. "Your big mouth getting us in trouble cause you've always got to be right?" her frustration erupted.

"They're here," he said, ignoring her tirade. "What?"

"They're here…look," he pointed, "two guys in suits with a map. It's them. I know a cop when I see one," he said with certainty.

They peered down into the courtyard and saw two men holding a map. The cops looked upward, then one of them pointed at their building, his finger directed at the upper floors.

Linda bit her fist and stifled a cry. Juan, choked with fear, stood paralyzed, his eyes transfixed on the pointing finger.

***

Luis stood in front of a scarred, pre-revolution oak desk with pad and pencil in hand. He watched Juan Degas intently to study his reaction to questions. The archaeologist had seated himself on the other side of the desk, his hands hidden from view, but wise to the fact that he was a suspect. Luis would bet a month's pay that the hands were shaking and that the boy's sphincter was clenching like a fist. Degas's armpits were soaked with nervous perspiration.

"You haven't been to work for three days? Why not?" asked Luis, incredulous that the young archaeologist didn't have an alibi.

"Professor Wolf, my boss, went south to check on the progress of some excavations. He told me to take some time off since he needed to be here to supervise my work," lied Juan, avoiding Luis's eyes.

Luis considered his answer, then asked, "Sr. Degas, you hold a Doctorate from the university. Why does your work require the supervision of another Ph.D? Surely you're a qualified to work independently?"

"Yes and no. Raúl Cordoba halted construction on a section of the metro line near Tacuba, and David wanted to check on it himself. He told me to do very little until he returned."

"And you don't remember where you've been, or with whom? Surely you understand how that creates suspicion?"

"I was home by myself last night." Juan reached a trembling hand for a pen on the desktop. "The night before, my fiancee and I had dinner and watched TV at my apartment."

"What about this weekend?"

229

"I went to the zoo Friday morning. Linda came over later and we went to El Mercado de Coyohuacan. Saturday, we drove to Puebla to visit archaeological sites and hike the foothills of the volcano Popocatepetl. Sunday, we went to Mass...and that's it." He shrugged.

"Where were you Saturday and Sunday nights? Can anyone vouch for your whereabouts?"

"Home all night!" Juan slammed the pen to the desktop. "Look...I'm a busy man. I have a lot of projects...and...and...I'm currently drafting a paper," he lied again, growing agitated. "I hope you're not implying that I had anything to do with Raúl Cordoba's death. Everyone knows I didn't like him. That's old news, but neither did a many others. He conspired to have my fiancee and me beaten-up. If you've read that report you already know that."

"Yes," agreed Luis, scribbling on his pad, his mind posing the next question. "You live alone?"

"No...I have a roommate...Marco Gonzalez, he's an employee of the university, also."

"And where can he be found?" Luis held his pencil poised to write. "He's in the United States with a friend. He's due back tomorrow or the next day. He's vacationing with a friend by the name of Amparo Ocampo."

The pencil stopped. "Amparo Ocampo, señor?" Luis's head shot up. "The secretary at the museum?" A look of amazement spread across his face.

"Si...si," agreed Juan, his face skewed with disdain. "She's Raúl's secretary...I personally can't stand the woman. She..."

"Let me get this straight," interrupted Luis, slowly choosing his words. "Your roommate is in the United States with Raúl Cordoba's secretary, who is also Hector Vicario's mistress?"

230

Luis watched Degas jerked visibly at the joining of both names in one sentence. The menacing connotation stood alone—a starkly simple meaning in a nebula of innuendo.

"Didn't know she was Vicario's mistress," the young archaeologist replied, lamely. "I knew her from when I worked at the museum."

"She isn't his mistress anymore, señor. Vicario's dead. He was murdered Friday night in Amparo's apartment while she and your roommate were in the United States."

As Luis watched, Degas' skin became electric with tension and goose pimples rose on his arms. Degas had killed them. Luis knew it. The archaeologist sat unmoving, struck mute at the implication.

"How did he die?" choked the Juan.

Luis fixed him with a stare. "Poisoned, señor, by a statue tainted with curare poison. You know…the kind of things an archaeologist might have access to?"

Degas shivered. The accusation was clear this time. He jumped from his chair and leaned toward Luis, his hands planted on the desk - top. "You're implying I had something to do with Hector Vicario's death? That's so ridiculous I won't even justify it with an answer!" he fumed.

Luis stood his ground, his eyes boring into those of his suspect, searching for an expression of honesty. He looked at his note pad to review the conversation, then made a decision. "Is there a telephone around?" He tucked the pad in his suit jacket. "Department Office, down the hall," replied Degas. He sat heavily, falling backward into his chair, as if exhausted.

"Don't go anywhere. I have to call someone, but we must talk again." Luis exited the laboratory and poked his head into the room next door.

"Got a minute?" he interrupted.

231

"Uh…sure…we were just about finished. The señorita has been most cooperative," said Tony, his eyes raking Linda's body.

In the hall, Luis said, "What do you have?"

"Not much…a good looking girl in love with a frog prince. Says she spent all day Saturday and Sunday with him. He's a wonderful guy, so on and so forth."

"Get this…Degas' roommate is in Colorado with Amparo Ocampo," said Luis, waiting for Tony's reaction.

"The museum secretary?"

"I'm calling Jose to see what he wants me to do. I can't figure this guy. If he's innocent, he won't be able to prove it. They must give college degrees to anyone these days. Come on." Luis led the way to the department office and flashed a badge to the secretary. She issued an accommodating smile and ushered them into a private room with   a telephone.

Luis dialed Jose's number, and Pricilla answered. "Bueno?"

"Pricilla…Luis. Is Jose there?"

"On another line…want to hold?"

He thought a moment. "Have Pedro or Paulo returned yet?"

"Both. Pedro just walked by…hold on."

Luis's fingers drummed the desktop. He didn't know the whole scenario, but after twelve hours of questioning, he felt sure that Juan Degas would write out a confession and sign it, probably sooner when Bolo and the boys were done with him.

"Bueno?"

"Pedro…Luis…what did you find at Tacuba?"

"More dirt on Degas. Nobody likes Cordoba, but Degas threatened to kill him last Monday in front of ten witnesses. Serious argument…lots of bad blood between them," he added.

232

"Anything else?"

"Nah, just a big ditch. Everyone's sittin' around. Whole area is taped off waiting for Raúl Cordoba to finish some kind of investigation. Must be ten or twelve guys laying around doing nothing."

"Stay on it. Paulo there?"

"Yeah...here scratching his crotch. I'm outta here. Call if you need anything, okay?"

Luis putt he telephone to his ear and said, "Paulo, the phone logs arrive?"

"Naw...I gave the eggheads a wakeup call and got a bunch of double-talk about computers. I asked Jose to rattle their cage. Luis...still sorting this stuff from the museum. Jesus! Did you have to bring the whole fucking place? It's going to..."

"Is Jose off the phone?" Luis interrupted, anxious to talk to his boss.

"Let's see...yeah...looks like it. I'll give you back to Pricilla." Two clicks later he heard....

"Luis? Where are you? Been on the phone all day with the fed's and they want the case now...claim it's their jurisdiction. I'm going to give it to them. Told them to come in and pick it up day after tomorrow. That'll give you time to tie up loose ends and write a report."

"Jose...listen!" Luis could smell the odor of Jose's office over the telephone. "Just listen...I may have our man." He methodically related the case step by step, detailing the results of the interviews, physical evidence, interrogation of Juan Degas, the report, everything he had.

"What do you think, Luis?" asked Jose, fishing for a decision.

"He's up to his neck in shit, Jose. Looks like he and his roommate spirited Vicario's concubine out of town, then killed

233

Vicario at the apartment and Raúl at the Museum. He can't account for his time Friday, Saturday, or Sunday nights, and he's been heard to threaten Raúl Cordoba several times.

"I don't know, Luis…" Jose hesitated.

"Then you should read the report Degas wrote. It's a "Who's Who" list of political crooks, and names both Vicario and Cordoba. If the names in the report are leaked to the public, we'll both be taking it in the ass on a Cuban freighter bound for Angola."

"Arrest him," said Jose, positive this time.

"You're sure?"

"Arrest him. When is Gonzalez and Vicario's wench due back?" "Eight o'clock tonight."

"Arrest him, also."

"You sure? We don't have any evidence…"

"Don't be so naive," Jose interjected, "they're roommates for Christ's sake. Been pals for years. How could he not be involved? He just ran off with the Minister's girlfriend. Arrest him. I want them both booked and interrogated until we have a confession."

"Jose, these guys are educated, white-collar types—good citizen material. I don't know if the rough stuff's a good idea this time."

"Quit your crying. I've got six dead people to account for. Raúl Cordoba may have been a PRI flunky, but Hector Vicario was Mexico's Minister of the Interior and a top advisor to El Presidente. I could arrest the fucking Pope if I wanted to."

"What about the girl?"

"Who?" asked Jose.

"Amparo Ocampo, Vicario's mistress."

"Why? Do you think she's involved?"

"Not yet…but who knows?"

234

"Question her, but no rough stuff. Use your own judgment…and Luis…nothing to the newspapers, you hear? Nothing. I've never been to Angola, but I'm sure I won't like it. Arrest Degas and bring him in. I'll tell the boys to expect you…Luis?"

"Yeah?"

"Good job. I'll see you get something out of this."

"Sure…thanks, Jose" sighed Luis, his shoulders slumping. "Had a lot of help."

"Get your butt moving so you'll get some sack time."

Luis cradled the phone, then turned to Tony. "Jose says to book him for murder. He's going to give him to the guys in the White Room until we get a confession."

"Let's do it," Tony turned to lead the way, "we don't want Degas to be late for his crucifixion."

Filth Eater

The bleached ones are a lower form of life—hypocritical and ignorant. Their religion presupposes correctness, righteousness, and redemption. They are a blight on The One Universe. The white faces are secure in their ignorance. It is their strength. Belief. The Conquistadors believed that their Filth Eater, their "Redeemer," died for their filth. This is a terrible thing, a god dying because of mortal filth, yet after witnessing their behavior in The One Universe, I see it must be true.

The bleached skins conquered The One Universe by exercising their audacity and greed. Do the wise shit in their own nest? Do the Pious foul their own habitat? Do the virtuous rape, enslave, and defile? I think not. Only those deluded by belief.

Prior to the mixing of the cultures I know that the inhabitants of The One Universe were born unpolluted and untainted. Unblemished, like the rare quetzal feather, they did not assume the filth of those who came before them as the bleached faces insist. Filth was the result of impious choices and acts of the will—not heredity. If the bleached ones are born tainted with the filth of their ancestors, then they are doomed to destroy, exterminate, and subvert. They were born cursed. They will consume the people of this planet because the pious are unsophisticated and unalloyed. They are without guile. They are cannon fodder for the bleached skins whose "beliefs" allow them to engage in pollution on behalf of their Filth Eater, their "Holy Redeemer." Whose plan is this? Who could take credit for such an idea or be allied to such beliefs? Is all truly lost? How can such filth exist uneaten?

Marco Loses His Woman

Monday Evening, June 30, 1984 8:00 P.M. Mexico City

The roar of jet engines preparing to land pulled Marco's eyes from Amparo's stoic face. Sitting in the aisle seat to her right, he looked beyond her, through the small oval window as the plane tilted and began to circle the metropolitan behemoth below.

Women! he thought with disgust. Who could understand the female gender? Happy one moment, sad the next. One minute voluble and flirting, the next laconic and indifferent. After boarding the plane, she had barely acknowledged his presence, answering with short, clipped responses; "yes…no…I don't know," or saying nothing at all. Initially angry, he had finally resigned himself to her mood. It would change again soon, he knew.

The trip to Vail could only be described as an abject failure, although the first two days were great. They hiked, drank wine, and made love non-stop. Then Amparo had become ill, shivering and vomiting, behaving annoyed and angry. Then

238

her illness had ceased as suddenly and mysteriously as it began. Yesterday she had called home, but had not spoken to him except to issue orders or bite off his head. Now she had become the ice woman; distant and unapproachable, diffident and terse, almost secretive in her behavior. What had happened, he wondered? Death in the family? Had she lost her job? Twice she had cried, then screamed uncontrollably when he attempted to comfort her. This relationship was doomed to failure. Something strange and hidden hovered around Amparo. She appeared overwrought and near an emotional breakdown, oscillating between tears and anger. For reasons unknown, she now showed no interest and no affection, no inclination to continue their relationship. But that was just fine, he reflected. She could be a fickle bitch if she wished. There were lots of fish in the sea. That had been his philosophy since his cousin Joaquin had first informed him at age 10 what was up the young girls skirts.

Continuing to stare past her, he watched the hydraulic pistons on the plane's wing adjust the flaps as the plane circled Mexico City, then drop precipitously into the smog-entrenched valley. The pilot's voice issued a request for all to stay seated upon landing until special passengers were escorted from the plane.

Marco looked around, curious as to who this might be. Hadn't noticed anyone special on the flight. Perhaps someone in first class? He glanced at Amparo, hoping for a sign, but she stared resolutely out the window, a black-haired expressionless statue, unapproachable and forbidding. The seat belt light flashed and the stewardesses flitted up and down the aisle collecting drink cups and napkins and checking seat belts. Five minutes later they rolled off the tarmac and taxied to the terminal to disembark. The same announcement as earlier reminded everyone to stay seated, and this elicited groans and complaints. Marco leaned back into his seat and waited patiently, curious as to when Amparo would acknowledge his presence and wondering if goodbyes would be said.

***

The plane stopped and everyone looked about expectantly. Amparo, still unapproachable, continued to look out the window toward the air- port terminal, purposely ignoring Marco. The heroin withdrawal in Vail had nearly sent her over the edge and home crying to Hector, but now he was dead. She was determined to enjoy this small respite with Marco and get away from Hector and Raúl, but now she was close to losing it again. She knew the signs, and felt intimately familiar with how she behaved prior to one of her schizophrenic bouts. Her sanity hung in the balance, connected only by a few tendrils of reason. She would have to be strong. She would have to pretend a while longer.

Two men in suits followed by four uniformed policía, slowly threaded the aisle, their eyes reading seat numbers. When Amparo jerked and stiffened, Marco turned to assure her that everything would be okay.

"Amparo Ocampo?" said a voice from the aisle.

"Huh?" Marco turned to the line of men, surprise on his face.

"Yes," Amparo answered, turning to face the policía. She smiled a welcome. "Thank God you came! I was hoping you would meet the plane."

"What?" Marco's turned to Amparo. "You were expecting the policía? What's going on here?" He stared wide-eyed, suddenly afraid.

"You Marco Gonzalez?" asked the other suit. "Yeah…why? Who wants to know?"

240

One of the suits said "You're under arrest," and nodded to the uniforms, who yanked him roughly from his seat and cuffed him while he protested. "Take him downtown with the other one."

Amparo sat rigid, staring stupidly at Marco's retreating back. Events in her apartment had rendered her taciturn and unable to share her fears with Marco. How could she have explained it? But why were they arresting him? My God, was he a criminal? She smiled weakly at the detectives, not quite knowing how to respond.

"Señora...you must come also."

"But...I haven't done anything! Where are you taking me?" she asked in a tremulous voice. Up and down the aisle, passengers craned their necks to watch the drama unfold.

"We need to ask you some questions, señora. Please hurry so that we don't inconvenience the other passengers."

Inconvenience the other passengers! Who gave a shit about them? She grabbed her purse, bent to avoid the storage bays, and stepped into the aisle. "My baggage..." she began, clutching her purse to her chest in a helpless gesture.

"Your baggage will wait, señora. Please..." The detective motioned, standing to the side, extending his arm toward the front of the plane.

Smiling to hide her fear, she walked past rows of seated voyeurs, intent on remaining composed. Her mind reeled with uncertainties, fearful that she would be arrested also and put in jail. That damn Hector—getting himself killed in her apartment. As they walked the concourse, a detective on each side, she felt tempted to scream and run. But she maintained her cool and allowed them to usher her into a room. She offered a tentative smile, then with a small voice, she said,

241

"Has something bad happened to Marco? He's not a criminal or anything, is he?"

***

One hour later, in a small office next to customs, Luis grew tired of asking questions. He shook his head in bewilderment. He couldn't get a handle on this one. The woman alternately beguiled with laughter, then cried and wept real tears each time he mentioned Hector Vicario's name. He felt limp with fatigue and wanted to go home to Angela. How many days had he been up now? Two? Three? Although her story lacked something, she came off as sincere and open to questioning. He must decide what to do and get it over with.

"Un momento, señora." Luis motioned for Tony to follow him outside. "What do you think?"

"Good looking piece, if you ask me, Luis. Let's take her downtown and do her in your office," he joked.

"Tony…" Luis's lips spread into a thin line and he cocked his head in irritation, "knock it off. I'm tired and want to go home."

"I don't know Luis." Tony extended his arms, palms up and shrugged. "Look…the bitch has the morals of a puta. She's been married and divorced…admits to being "very special friends" with Vicario, and she's been romping in bed with Degas's roommate for a week."

Luis dropped change into a coffee vending machine and punched a button. "Her morals don't concern me." He turned to Tony and poked a finger at his chest. "What I want to know is this—is she part of a conspiracy? What does she gain by Vicario's or Cordoba's death? It just doesn't make sense. Degas already has a girlfriend, and neither he nor Gonzalez have any money that we know of. There's no motive."

He took a sip of the coffee and grimaced. "Vicario was her sugar daddy...now she's out in the cold, and her secretarial job at the museum won't pay the rent on that coyohuacan apartment."

"What do you want from me, Luis? I agree. Look...we'll know more tomorrow after they're done with Degas and Gonzalez. Let's find out where she'll be and tell her not to leave or we'll issue a warrant."

Luis sipped his coffee, thought a moment, then capitulated. "Okay, let's do it."

They returned to the room. Amparo, sitting primly in an expensive suit, crossed and uncrossed her legs for their benefit, languorously moving her shapely limbs in an attention-getting maneuver.

"Señora," began Luis, trying unsuccessfully not to follow her leg movement, "we haven't determined the extent of your involvement in this matter, but I don't think it's appropriate that we detain you more at this time. If I decide to release you until we need to question you again, where will you be staying? Your former apartment is locked and unavailable to you."

Excited at the prospect of leaving, she stood and pulled at her dress, running her hands over her hips and stomach to check for wrinkles. She grinned at Luis. "I can stay at the Apollo...and I'll be happy to answer any questions you have, captain! I want to help you find the horrible person who did these things."

"Until I tell you otherwise, señora, call this number and check in at 9:00 a.m. and 3:00 p.m. everyday. We need to talk again tomorrow. Don't plan to go anywhere." He turned and pointed. "These two will drive you to the Apollo. Here's my card. If you remember anything more...call me...immediately. Nothing is unimportant, understand?"

Amparo, filled with relief, unexpectedly threw her arms around Captain Alvarado and gave him a quick hug. "Thank you captain," she said with a brilliant smile, "you're such a gentleman."

Luis, removing his hands from her waist, looked at the floor, flustered, his face beginning to color. Tony smirked and rolled his eyes.

"Señora, please!" protested Luis, his composure lost, opting to study the scuffs on his shoes. "Yes…well…as I was saying," he shot a murderous look at Tony, "you'll probably hear from us tomorrow…so don't make any plans without checking, okay?" Turning to the uniformed policemen he said, "Escort the lady and her baggage to the Apollo. Be sure to get her room and telephone numbers."

***

Amparo shook hands all around, her winning smile exposing perfect white teeth. Everything had gone perfectly. If only she could hang on a little longer. She grabbed her purse, and headed down the concourse for **Baggage Claim**. She walked with a sense of purpose and authority while the two uniformed cops followed, shuffling along like baggage handlers.

What now, she wondered? Hector and Raúl were dead. Marco was in jail…for what? Did she still have a job? Where would she live? A torrent of questions overwhelmed her as a flush of emotion, relief from the anxiety of the last two days, coursed through her like a drug.

What she needed, she realized, tears beginning to pool in her eyes, was a friend. Sadness overwhelmed her and she began to cry. She stopped and searched her purse for a handkerchief, then continued on, the two embarrassed Policía following. She stopped again and blew her nose, trying to

244

compose herself. She tucked the hanky into her purse, and reconsidered. No, she didn't need a friend. What she wanted was a good toot. She visualized the brown lines of powder on a mirror and shuddered with pleasure, wondering if that creep Cholo was home.

Her baggage in tow, and feeling relieved at being released, she walked towards the appointed police car, oblivious to the stares of the curious. Thank God, she repeated to herself, beginning to think she might have the luck of the bitch Malinche.

Bolo Learns Something

Tuesday, July 1, 1984, Mexico City

Juan's head exploded in pain when the liquid gushed up into his nose. It was a small thing to the interrogators in the White Room, but they found it diverting and never tired of the amusement it provided. Juan, naked with his hands tied behind him, slumped in a hardwood chair that stood firmly fastened to the floor. He gasped for breath and sputtered. The big one, Bolo, grabbed Juan's hair and pulled his head back while Ernesto shook the bottle and fired yet another stream of Coca Cola into the victim's sinuses, sending him into convulsions, interspersed with coughing and screams of outrage.

"You bastards!" he spat, his teeth clenched and brown mucous oozing from his nose. "I'll kill you when I get out of here!" he slobbered.

"That's why you're here, Sr. Degas," said the pock-faced, beady-eyed Ernesto. "You're a killer. But that's over now. Tonight you'll write us a scholarly dissertation on how and why you did it, then you'll sign it and plead for mercy." He grabbed Juan's head by the hair and lowered himself to within inches, his sour breath wrinkling Juan's face into a grimace. "Make no mistake asshole. There's no one to save you now."

"I demand to see a lawyer! I know my rights!" Juan sputtered.

"Rights?" Ernesto, smiled perversely. "You're an enemy of the state and Mexico has special solutions to deal with assassins and saboteurs."

He stood back to assess his naked prey. Pausing for effect, he continued, "I can see it's too early to ask for a confession…have to soften you up a little first. Bolo, get me the bag of grapefruits."

Bolo, a block of neckless granite, dutifully brought the bag of grapefruits, then yanked Juan's head back and waited. Ernesto hefted the bag to test its weight, then with a big wind up, slammed it into Juan's solar plexus and chest. Twice more he repeated the routine until Juan slumped in the chair, groaning and insensible.

"Hang him up and I'll give him a few in the kidneys, then we'll see if he's ready to talk."

"There's faster ways…" began Bolo.

"Not yet," hissed Ernesto, irritated. "I don't want to leave any marks. If he makes it through tonight, we'll try some of the other tomorrow. This is an art, you big lunk! Pay attention and you'll learn something."

Bolo strung Juan to a pulley and hung him by his arms, pulling the rope until his toes dangled six inches above the floor. Trembling, naked and humiliated, Juan twisted and jackknifeed his muscular body against the taut rope as anger and fear drove him to escape.

"What do you think?" grinned Ernesto.

"Nice tight ass." Bolo slapped Juan's buttocks. "The maras (gangs) at Lecumberri will like this one," then he moved his hips in a gross imitation of anal intercourse.

They laughed at the pantomime, then Ernesto added, "Yeah, maybe we should go ahead and pull his teeth now. Save them the trouble of knocking them out." They roared with laughter again, then returned to the business at hand.

Exhausted and gasping, Juan's frenzy ceased, leaving only the pain of breathing. He thought that his sternum must be cracked and his stomach clenched as rivers of pain flowed from his center. If he confessed he was a dead man. If he didn't, he might die from the torture. He knew what he had to do, and he began to concentrate, to pull his consciousness inward and move to the beta plane as an old Lacandon shaman in Chiapis had taught him many years ago.

He began to recite all 206 bones of the body in order to focus his mind and redirect it from the chaos and fear that clamored for attention. He started with the bones of the head, and had recited the parietals, occipital, and sphenoid when the bag hit his kidneys. It occurred to him that he might have every bone in his body broken by morning. With wry humor he told himself that he would have no trouble telling them where it hurts. A paralyzing fear seized him, and tears burst from his eyes. He soiled himself—much to the disgust of his two torturers—then began the recitation again.

Dr. Wolf Returns To Mexico City

Wednesday, July 2, 1984, La Venta, Veracruz

Professor Wolf was loathe to exchange the tropical splendor of Tobasco and Veracruz for the highlands and Mexico City. The heat and humidity were enervating and the endless rows of green mountains were flush with banana, papaya, and mango. The road, winding like a cat's cradle through the verdant countryside, curved tortuously up, down, and around the mountains. He always enjoyed this part of the trip; gazing at ripe orchards and fat cattle, all interspersed between small towns of a few thousand people neatly tucked away into a lowland niche.

Today he wrought no joy from the torpid pastoral scenes or colorful garb of the town's women. He slumped in his seat, tired. He knew eight o'clock approached because the sun would soon set. He would enter the highlands of Puebla in two hours, and the air would begin to cool, but for now the heat remained intractable. Shimmering curtains rose from the asphalt, distorting the road, causing his eyes to fatigue. His cotton shirt hung damp with sweat and glued to his skin. The air smelled heavy with moisture and the odor of decaying vegetation. Soon it would exchange itself for the dry coolness of the higher elevations.

The news had jolted him and sent his mind reeling back to Mexico City and its twenty million people. He didn't know the whole story yet. The radio reported the bombing at the National Museum on the five o'clock news, but had given no details. The university offices were by the time he reached a telephone. Two calls to friends produced nothing. Unable to get it off his mind, he decided to return a day early and see what happened for himself. He hurriedly met with his graduate students, then departed La Venta around noon. He hoped the bombing had nothing to do with him or his staff, but didn't really believe it. David leaned forward and squinted into the sun. Deeply etched crows-feet around his eyes twitched with fatigue. He drove determinedly toward the distant snow-capped volcanoes, Popocatepetl and Iztacciutlatl. Then the jabber of the radio again caught his attention: "Mexico's long-time Minister of the Interior, Hector Vicario, is dead of unknown causes. He was found in the apartment of a friend and had been missing and apparently dead for several days. The circumstances of his death are suspicious and it's believed that several policemen died at the same location…also of unknown causes."

The news report continued. "Little is known at this time, but the matter is being investigated as homicide, possibly the work of someone with a grudge against the powerful minister, although terrorism has not been ruled out according to Superintendent Jose' Ledeno of the Mexico City Police. When asked if the murder was related to the bombing death of Raúl Cordoba, the long-time director of the National Museum of Anthropology, Ledeno said it was not known at this time."

250

"From the Yucatan come reports of an explosion at the Pemex Refinery…"

Stunned! The professor sat riveted to his seat, barely conscious that he was driving. Raúl Cordoba dead in the bombing? Hector Vicario murdered? My God! A twinge of fear twisted his gut and his skin tingled, hair rose on his neck. Were the two related? Does a jaguar shit in the jungle? Of course they were related! With a rush of premonition, he knew his students were in danger. Swinging the green Plymouth Volare into the curves, he drove automatically, trying to recall the contents of Juan's report. Then he remembered; the names of people, the stolen artifacts, and more. Urgency gripped him as he looked at the speedometer, then pressed the pedal downward. Though surrounded by tropical mountains, he was in the lowlands. Another twenty kilometers per hour wouldn't hurt anything on this stretch of the road.

The sun, a yellow-white inferno, slid behind the mountains to his left, casting dark ominous shadows across the road. Dense jungle foliage bordering the road appeared impenetrable and forbidding, encroaching and strangling the asphalt snake on which he drove. At that moment a machete-wielding boy with feral eyes darted from the jungle and crossed the road!

He slammed his brake pedal and swerved. "Chingada!" he yelled, slowing to stop. He glanced at his rear-view mirror, but the child had fled into the jungle, a phantom like the mirages on the road.

"Nearly hit the little bastard," he growled. He punched the accelerator in a fit of anger, held it to the floor a moment, then backed off.

"Chingada," he muttered again. Tonight would be a long haul.

Professor Wolf Calls In A Favor

Thursday Morning, July 3, 1984, Mexico City

A magenta haze pulsed in the east as the earth slowly turned on its axis, revealing its face to the Sun god, bringing life to the darkness and hope to those who despair. David yawned uncontrollably and stretched, loosening the binding tendrils of fatigue that pulled him toward lethargy and sleep. He had driven all night and his face was creased with squint-lines. Two dark, half-moon bags puffed noticeably below each eye. Upon arriving and locating the right precinct house, he learned that the policía were not releasing information, no visitors were allowed, and that Marco was arrested also. Had the world gone mad? A cabinet minister poisoned and Raúl Cordoba blown up? Juan and Marco accused? Unbelievable! he shook his head, bemused. Was he in an alternate universe?

He stretched again, then shook his head to clear the fatigue of driving hundreds of miles with no sleep. It was 7:30 a.m. and the city was resurrecting. Electric trolley cars rattled the rails two blocks away and car horns blared aggressively as impatient drivers finessed for position. He stood on his balcony, hands grasping the protective rail, letting the energy of the city replenish his faltering reserves. Lightening, back-lit in a line of thunderstorms, flashed to the south, threatening the morning serenity. The cloying perfume of nearby rose gardens mixed with the odor of cooking breakfasts and rode the warm morning breeze to his balcony. He breathed deeply to invigorate himself, hesitated, then returned to his apartment living room.

He called Linda's house earlier, rousing the whole household and reawakening last night's unresolved hostilities. Anxious to escape her father's wrath, she eagerly agreed to join David at his house. She sat brooding and preoccupied on the couch, her hands in her lap, staring listlessly at the floor. Occasionally, she raised a hand to cradle her belly. He knew that her worst fears had become reality.

Her appearance worried him. She seemed drawn and pale, and dark pouches hung below red-rimmed eyes. She gripped a rosary in her hand, and he surmised that she had cried or prayed herself to sleep last night. David knew her father well and felt sure that Mario had gone into one of his familiar "I told you so", rages. Mario was rarely wrong, just ask him.

"Linda..." David began, then stopped and watched her touch her lower abdomen again, a gesture peculiar to females. This morning it struck him as curious and he wondered where he had seen it before. Aw well...he began again.

"Linda...we won't get anywhere by demanding our rights and calling lawyers. This case is too big and important. It involves people at the highest level of government...and I think that's where we'll have to go to get answers."

"But where, David? Who?" She held up her palms in a helpless gesture. "I don't know anybody in politics, do you?"

"Well…I used to know a couple of people," he offered, running his hands through his hair. "Haven't talked to them in years. Don't know if they'll help or not."

"Call them…please!" She buried her head in her hands. "You know what they're doing to Juan and Marco don't you?" She touched her belly again.

This time he remembered, and blurted out without thinking. "Linda…are you pregnant?"

Stunned, her mouth gaped wide and her eyes grew large. The unspoken was finally voiced.

"How…" then her faced colored and she burst out crying, engulfed in a flood of unresolved conflict.

"Linda…I'm sorry…I…" he stuttered, feeling like an ass. Nice going, he told himself, walking to comfort her. You're a real sensitive guy, David.

Strings of bulbous tears issued from her green eyes. He sat next to her, unsure what to say.

"Haven't you told anyone?" He placed an arm over her shoulder.

"No."

"Not even Juan?" He reached for her hand.

"No."

"You must be scared to death."

"Yes." She reached for him, seeking comfort like a child in the grip of night terrors.

Two minutes later she sat back, wiped her eyes and moved long strands of hair from her face. "I must look awful." She sniffed loudly, then appealed to him.

"David…please?" She looked hopeful. "Can't you call? If we don't get something done today, they might never get out of jail. It's been two days. Every minute counts," she pleaded, her fingers tightly interlaced and her arms extended between jeaned legs.

"I'll try." He looked doubtful. "I'm not even sure I can get through to them. They may refuse talk to me if I do. It's been fifteen years."

He rose to go, then turned. "Why don't you make a pot of tea? I need to be private when I call." He stretched again, then stood and headed for his office. Linda scurried into the kitchen with her head bent in worry.

His office was in the same state as he'd left it—a mess, and ten minutes later he was still digging through piles of papers strewn about the room. Nearly ready to give up the search, he spotted it—an old invitation to Miguel's 40th birthday. Stain rings from tea cups marred the expensive white invitation which had yellowed with age. He opened the card to the phone number, then sat down at his desk to dial. He began with a number at the National Palace, knowing that it would be almost impossible to get through.

"Bueno, please hold," followed another click, then, "...Palacio Nacional, may I help you?"

The professor, trying to be persuasive, explained to whom he must talk. This, of course, elicited a giggle of amusement from the palace operator.

"Surely you're not serious, señor! Even if I tried to give him a message, no one would let someone like me close to him."

"Señorita, tell him that Professor David Wolf wants to talk to him. I'm sure he'll take my call."

This evoked additional mirth, and the operator said, "Maybe I should say that I'm Queen Isabella...maybe he'll see you!" She laughed at her own wit, clearly enjoying the exchange with this fool. "Perhaps you should call his home and discuss old times," she suggested sarcastically, then

"Sorry, I can't help you. You can write a letter to the following address if you wish...."

Annoyed, David cradled the phone. No surprise there. He hadn't expected to get through. Picking up the invitation, he located the other number, then dialed with trepidation. If this didn't work, he didn't know what to do.

"Bueno?"

"Is the señora in please?" "Who's calling?"

"Professor David Wolf, from the National University." He leaned forward to rest an elbow on his desk. God help us! he pleaded silently.

The soft tap of high heels on terrazzo floor grew louder, followed by muffled conversation.

"David...is it really you...after so long? Is everything okay?"

"Concepcion, thank God you're there!" He exhaled with relief. "Sorry I haven't written or called. I don't...really have a good excuse...I guess we just have different circles of friends now. I'm not a political person, just an old professor with nothing to offer people like you and Miguel." He could feel the beginning of a lump in his throat.

"Nonsense!" she snapped. "That's hardly what I expect to hear from an old family friend. We are eternally indebted to you. I should be angry that you never contacted us. We were worried sick about you when Alicia died."

An uncomfortable pause followed, then he said, "How's Isabella?"

"Isabella? Isabella is wonderful, thanks to you and Alicia. She's married, has four beautiful children, and her husband is a successful business man. If it wasn't for you and Alicia, God knows where she would be. We were ready to have her committed." She paused, and he knew that the events of twenty years ago had been recalled.

"The sixties were a terrible time for children to grow up," she continued. "When I remember the drugs, sex, the screaming fits…then look at her today, I can't believe she's the same person. Her six months with you two in Guatemala changed her whole life. Miguel and I know we are in your debt."

That's what he wanted to hear, and now he set the hook. "Concepcion, someone who means a lot to me is in very serious trouble. I need to talk to Miguel as soon as possible. I tried to call the palacio, but they won't let me leave a message."

"That's all? You want to talk to Miguel? That's easily arranged, but I won't do it unless you promise to come for dinner. It's been too long, David. You've treated your friends poorly," she chastised.

"I promise," he said. "When can you get through to Miguel?"

"When? Now! He may run the country, but he still answers to me.

Give me your number and I'll have him call."

Thirty minutes later, their tea cups empty, the phone rang and David shooed Linda from the study.

"Bueno?"

"David?"

"Miguel? Thanks for calling I…"

"David, what the hell's going on! I meet in five minutes with the Ambassador from Venezuela," he fumed.

Bad start. He'd have to set the hook quick. "How's Isabella?"

"David…you don't want to talk about Isabella. I'm sure you and Concepcion talked about her. I'm in a hurry…maybe you should come for dinner if…"

"Miguel, I need a favor," interjected the professor. "This is the only time I'll ever ask...I promise. But I've got to have it," he pleaded.

"A favor? That depends David," El Presidente began back-pedaling. "I don't have the power people assume I have. I probably can't help you. Maybe you should write a letter?"

David sensed that he was losing him, so he repeated, "How's Isabella?"

A long silence ensued, and the professor held his breath, afraid his old friend would ignore an unpaid debt and hang up.

"What do you want, David?"

"The policía arrested two students of mine for the murder of Hector Vicario and Raúl Cordoba yesterday. They're innocent. You've got to help me get them released. You know as well as I do what's happening to them right now as we speak. They may already be dead!"

"David...you're not asking for a favor, you're asking for the moon! You're asking for the return of Moctezuma's gold!" he yelled. "Ask for something I can give. Just because I'm the president doesn't mean I don't answer to anybody. Do you have any idea how important Hector Vicario was? Half the ministers on my cabinet are in place because of him. How long do you think I would be president if I let his murderers go free?"

Thinking quickly, David replied, "Then do this, Miguel. Keep them in custody, but put them together in a cell by themselves? Make sure they're treated well? No torture..."

"We do not torture people in Mexico!"

"Oh...horse shit. Miguel...listen! If they need medical attention...see that they get it." David paused, then added,

"Give me access to all evidence and one week to prove their innocence."

Silence. Trepidation. Finally, El Presidente replied, "You should see my grandchildren, David," he began wistfully, "they're beautiful and so full of life. It's one of the few pleasures left to a man like me. I'm not free anymore. I belong to everyone, and everyone wants something."

"Miguel...these boys are innocent...they're like my sons. Alicia and I never had children, and she's dead. They're the only family I'll ever have and the policía snatched them just to claim they've solved a crime. If you don't help, my children are dead men and you know it." David gripped the phone tightly in a hand wet with perspiration.

"Okay...I'll give you what you ask...but no more." Miguel faltered, then said, "Next time you call don't ask for anything. I'm going to take a lot of heat for this. My debt to you is paid."

"Miguel I..."

"Forget it. I've endured worse. Come to dinner, David. We want to see you again, and Isabella would love to show off her babies. Stay in touch this time, Okay?"

"Thanks...I won't forget...well...I'll be calling. When can I go to the police station?"

"Within the hour. I'll take care of it immediately. Good luck with your children, David." Mexico's president hung up.

David's hands trembled with emotion and memory as he sat at his desk and let the years whirl through his mind. Recollections of his first years in Mexico, the National University, and his new friends flooded his awareness. Concepcion, rich and smart, sashaying across campus; Miguel, full of fire and promise, wanting to change his country for the better; and Alicia—beautiful Alicia. He retrieved her photograph from the corner of his desk. Tears distorted his vision as he studied her smiling face. He brooded over the picture and recalled the smallest, most intimate details of their life together.

"She was beautiful."

"Eh? Linda…didn't hear you come in." He wiped his eyes.

"You must miss her very much."

"Yes…she was my best friend. I miss her terribly." His voice cracked, raw with emotion.

Linda put her hands on his shoulders, "Did you find out anything, David?"

"Yes…we need to get going. Get your stuff and I'll fill you in on the way. We have a brief reprieve for the boys, but we must start immediately."

Professor Wolf Tries Detective Work

Thursday Afternoon, July 3, 1984, Mexico City

"Okay...see you at one o'clock." Jose smiled with satisfaction and hung up the telephone. He leaned back into his chair and stroked the handlebars of his mustache. Certain that a promotion would result from Luis and the boys solving the Vicario-Cordoba murders, he had just made an appointment to be fitted for a new suit. True, they didn't have a confession yet, but the boys in the White Room never failed. A man needed clothes to be taken seriously, and Jose had his eye on one of the double-breasted outfits at Julio's. They should all celebrate, he told himself, continuing to smooth a pomade-slicked handlebar between his fingers. A case like this didn't happen very often, and this one had ended happily, so he had given in to his compulsion and called for an appointment. He thought to call the White Room and check on their progress, then hesitated.

Maybe he should invite Luis along to Julio's? God knows he could use a new suit. The captain's suit jackets were old and rumpled looking. Although Jose planned to take most of the credit, Luis might receive a promotion if Jose saw fit to throw him a bone. Looking through his plate glass window, he glimpsed Luis shuffling reports on his desk. Jose reached for the phone to ring him with the invitation when a well-dressed stranger approached Pricilla. Tall, fit, and gray-haired, he oozed authority, and his suit fit very well. When he flashed his badge, Jose became annoyed. Chingada! What were the federales doing here so early? They weren't due until tomorrow at the earliest.

With a plaintive expression, Pricilla swiveled in her chair and looked into his office. Annoyed, he waved for her to send him back. Jose would give him a piece of his mind. A deal was a deal, and the fed's had reneged again. The tall federale smiled, complimented a blushing Pricilla, then walked to Jose's office door. Knocking once, he opened and entered. Without hesitating, he walked straight to Jose's desk and proffered a hand.

"Please excuse this unannounced visit. I'm Manuel Antonio de Marchena, the Director Superior of the Federal Policía for Mexico City. Sorry I'm early. I know we had an agreement, but something unexpected has come up."

Jose blinked, then a look of amazement spread across his face. The second most powerful man in the city, maybe the country, stood in his office apologizing for doing his job. Why had he come himself? He must have hundreds of agents at his disposal to complete a routine prisoner transfer. Jose quickly forgot the ass chewing and assumed a diffident, fawning attitude toward the powerful man.

Mexico's top secret service agent continued by saying, "I'm afraid the situation has changed dramatically. El Presidente has requested that we intervene and supervise the new conditions of the investigation for the Vicario-Cordoba murders. I assured him that we could count on your help." He smiled knowingly at Jose.

New conditions? Hadn't he come to snatch the prisoners and take them to the zocalo?

"I'm not sure I understand…er…Director Marchena. What did you or…uh…I mean…El Presidente have in mind?" stuttered Jose, obsequiously.

Five minutes later he said, "I see…er…un momento," and he made two calls.

"Bueno?"

"Are Degas and Gonzalez in the White Room?"

"Just finished with one…we're ready for the other. We'll do them every other hour until they break."

"The interrogation is to cease immediately and both men put in central lockup. Get a doctor to check them out. Feed them. Get them a bath and some clothes," he ordered.

"You're kidding!" came the response.

"Get your ass moving before I come down there myself!"

"Si, señor!"

Jose dialed Luis. "Captain Alvarado, can you come to my office?"

***

Thirty minutes later, the Director Superior nodded his head in agreement, "I agree…it looks like a conspiracy. I think you have the right men, however, El Presidente has agreed to honor a….how can I say this? A commitment…yes…a pledge to a very concerned person; out of fairness to him and in the best interest of justice."

This, Jose knew, was bullshit. El Presidente appeared to have granted a favor to an old friend, and Jose would likely take it in the shorts as a result. He knew from experience not to use the words `fairness' and 'justice' in the same sentence when politics were involved. He frowned. Maybe he should call Julio and cancel the suit.

To the Director Superior he said, "You have my assurances that you'll have our complete cooperation. I'm leaving our best detective, Captain Alvarado, on the case," Jose gestured toward Luis and smiled.

The phone rang and Jose grabbed it, annoyed. "No calls, Pricilla, I'm busy! Huh? You're kidding, this isn't a good time for one of your jokes, Pricilla. Really? Sure, put him through. Yes it is! This is such a great honor, your Excellency! Of course we understand...but of course your Excellency. You can count on it, sir! Really? Why... thank you! Yes sir, we'll do everything we can to assist. This is a great honor, sir. Yes...good-bye...good luck to you also, Sr. Presidente."

Flushed with excitement, Jose cradled the phone and turned to a disbelieving Luis and the smiling Director Superior who said, "Persuasive, isn't he?"

"Was that El Presidente?" asked Luis, his mouth gaping.

"Yes...of course," Jose dissembled, straightening his tie and looking at his fingernails. "Ahem," he cleared his throat, "I was just assuring El Presidente that we'll do everything in our power to assist this gringo...uh, David Wolf, in his investigation." Momentarily ignoring the two, Jose eased back into his chair and reflected on the vicissitudes of change. His luck was holding. Maybe he should go ahead and meet Julio for that appointment? He thought the gray tweed would look best. The hounds tooth was too flashy, not appropriate for business.

***

Two hours later, David and Linda Maria sat and listened to a disgruntled Captain Alvarado narrate the events of the investigation from the night of the dead minister's discovery to the arrest of Marco.

Strong circumstantial case, thought David. The boys had really screwed up. The professor swore that if he got them out of this jam, he stake them to a trench in Quintana Roo excavating fish bones and wheel-barrowing dirt.

"Captain…I agree the boys appear guilty at first glance. However, I'm certain that we can uncover the truth in the matter." He tapped the desktop with his finger for emphasis. "I've known these boys ten years and worked with them in unusual circumstances for long periods of time. Neither is capable of planning and executing a murder. I would stake my career and reputation on it."

***

Luis, ambivalent and disgusted at the turn of events, bit his tongue and gave the professor a sour expression. He didn't know whether to scream in outrage or laugh at the parody being played out. This was the brain fart from hell. Jose's office had the worst odor he could ever recall. Today's decision would be the beginning of tomorrow's recriminations. *Why me*, he groused silently?

The case was nearly complete: evidence, arrests, everything but the confessions—but these were inevitable. Now this: a middle-aged, overly sincere gringo with an accent and Degas' girlfriend, both with expectant looks, wanting to be taken seriously. Jose would owe Luis one for this mess. He looked askance at his boss, then turned to face his antagonist.

"Professor…"

"Call me David, please."

"David?" the captain paused, trying it out to see if bitterness remained on his tongue. "Okay…David it is. Anyway…I hope you're right. I've never worked with an

266

archaeologist before, but you're a detective in your own way, correct? I guess I'm at your service," he glanced quickly at Jose, "but I'm not happy about it. If not for your political friends, I wouldn't give an amateur like you the time of day. What do you know about murder?" Luis crossed his arms on his chest and stared at the professor, disgusted with the prospect of kowtowing to an egg-head civilian.

The professor, however, met Luis's stare straight-on. "I'm not an expert on murder, but I know something of human behavior, and I know that these boys are innocent."

They glared, each at the other, until the detective blinked, looking at Jose for support. But the superintendent merely watched, content to watch the duel play itself out. An experienced politician, he had placed himself in the role of an observer now, deflecting the pressure to Luis. His passive look revealed everything. Luis would have to handle it now. Shit rolls downhill.

They returned to Luis' office, circumnavigating the chaos of the central waiting area and its multitude of misfits. Luis called Tony to assist, then reluctantly turned to face his new partners. Knowing he had to make the best of a bad situation, he took a deep breath and put forth his best professional demeanor.

"There are some leads that haven't been investigated and a few people who haven't been questioned. I'd like to suggest some places to begin, but first I think it's time for Degas and Gonzalez to have completed their cleanup. I'll call and…"

"Did you use any special techniques while interrogating them? The professor interrupted.

"Such as?" replied Luis, picking up a model car from his desk, then looking through the plate-glass to Jose's office where he still talked with the tall federale.

"Such as torture and coercion," said the professor. "Let's not cat- about and mince words if we are going to be working together."

Luis winced, thought a moment, then said, "I think it's safe to say that both men have been coerced, and how can I say...strongly encouraged by force to confess. This is not a routine criminal case. Both are charged with the assassination of a high public official and murdering the museum director. It's a political matter as well as a reprehensible crime," explained Luis. "They will have special treatment during the next seven days. They don't merit it, but they'll have it. Jose says you can talk to them any time, and they'll be treated fairly. However, if you haven't produced evidence to the contrary within a week, the charges stand and they'll be transferred to the federales." He set the model down with a plunk.

***

Fifteen minutes later, feeling out of place, Luis left the room, unable to witness the emotional reunion of friends and lovers. Juan limped and his face bulged with purple golf balls.

"You've really done it this time, boy," chastised the professor in a quiet voice.

"Yef fir, do you haf a gun to pleeve shoot me?" mumbled Juan, barely able to enunciate.

"If I had a gun...I'd shoot you" said Marco. "I'm pissing blood, and my ribs are cracked." Linda, crying softly, had taken Juan's hand and led him to a couch in the corner. It was a pitiful sight. While Juan lay unmoving, Marco sat on the floor with his back to the wall, a couch pillow supporting his head.

"I didn't do it, Dafid," Juan whispered.

"What didn't you do, Juan?" interjected Marco. "Why am I here? Did you have an affair with El Presidente's wife or something?"

268

"You immature dope-head!" growled the professor. "If it wasn't for El Presidente, you'd both be rotting in a cell and preparing for a firing squad."

"Excuse me if I seem ungrateful," replied Marco. "I know I should be appreciating this much more than I am." He turned away from the professor's glare.

Frowning, David turned to Juan. "I need your help. We've got one week; then you belong to the federales. I pulled some strings to do this, but if you don't put your thinking caps on, you'll be back where you were. Ready to get on with it?"

"Fire auay," said Juan, his tongue swollen.

***

Two hours later little had been accomplished. Luis sent Pedro and Tony to question the Señorita Vicario and search for the missing vault key. Paulo still pursued the elusive phone logs. Marco, up and moving around, had joined them as they alternated between the evidence room and Luis's office. Juan slept fitfully on the couch, contributing an occasional moan. He had been beaten badly, and they sent for a doctor when he began coughing up blood.

"This isn't working. We're going about it all wrong," said the professor. "How so?" replied Luis, irritated. He tossed his pen on the desktop and sat heavily on the desk's edge. "We're proceeding in a logical manner. In order to test a hypothesis you gauge the validity of your premises. If our premises are accurate, the conclusion will reveal itself." He leaned forward aggressively, his neck slightly extended. "It's always worked for me."

"That system doesn't always work well," argued David. "It's possible to start with a good premise and draw the wrong conclusion. It happens all the time in anthropological studies when trying to determine cause-and-effect relationships."

269

"I'm not following, David," said Luis, waving him off. He stood up. "I'm just a cop, not a philosopher."

"Look…this is what I mean." David began to count, holding up a finger for each statement. "We're assuming that Juan's hatred for Raúl Cordoba, the report he wrote about the stealing at the museum, his desire for revenge, his threats to kill Raúl, and his lack of an alibi are all related, correct? These are the premises that lead us to conclude that he murdered Vicario and Cordoba." The professor planted his arms on the desk and leaned toward Luis. "If I presented a paper with such faulty reasoning I'd be laughed out of my profession."

"I'm still not following," said the miffed Luis, pacing the room. "I've successfully investigated hundreds of murders using deductive reasoning." He stopped and turned to address the professor. "We're not talking about pottery and bones, we're examining human emotion and behavior, and I have more experience than anyone here in that area."

"Under normal circumstances that line of reasoning would be adequate, but…" the professor paused, searching for the right analogy…"Okay, look at it this way. Do you think this is a routine hate-revenge murder?"

Luis frowned, his brow lining with furrows as he considered the question. "No, absolutely not."

"Why?"

"Because of the manner in which the victims died. Vicario was poisoned with an ugly statue and Cordoba died in a bombing."

"Doesn't it strike you that these two methods of killing are singularly different? Almost as if they're not related. Maybe even committed by separate people for different reasons?"

"I've considered that, David" said Luis, nearly losing his patience. "Unfortunately, there's no evidence for that scenario."

"That's my point, Captain!" said the professor, slamming a flat hand on the desktop. "We're looking at the wrong kind of premises to support our conclusion. In Anthropology, there's a paradigm called 'Galt's Problem.' It's essentially a cause-and-effect challenge. For example, in this room, three of four men wear the Mexican mustache and wear glasses. Do glasses cause mustaches, or do mustaches cause glasses? Are the two even related?

"Eh...you're talking in circles, gringo." Luis, shook his head in bewilderment. "What's the point?"

"The point is...we should consider other possibilities from different perspectives. We already know what Juan Degas has or hasn't done. Let's investigate Raúl Cordoba's and Hector Vicario's relationship. Maybe they were involved with something totally unrelated to a scenario in which Juan caused their deaths."

Luis began pacing again. "I've thought of that, David, but there's little to go on." He stopped and looked at the professor. "We know they were friends. We know Raúl procured art for Hector, and that there's a common archaeology theme in the case," he glanced at the sleeping Juan. Confused, he threw up his hands. "I'm open for suggestion...let me know when you figure it out."

"Maybe we need to get into Vicario's vault?" offered Marco. "No telling what's in there."

"That'll be difficult, at least for a couple of days," said Luis. "Maybe the federales can help us out on that one."

***

One hour later the doctor had come and gone. Luis and the professor were looking at the evidence table and checking the tags on each item recovered from the bombing and from Amparo's apartment. David went immediately to retrieve the gaping-mouthed statue of Tlazolteotl. It had been scoured clean at the morgue and brought to the precinct house.

"What is it?" asked Luis. "It's a Filth Eater."

"What?"

"A Filth Eater, the Aztec goddess Tlazolteotl. She gives absolution from filth. She eats your sins so that you can enter the Paradise of the Sun."

Bizarre, thought Luis. But it was something he hadn't known before.

Maybe the gringo would be good for something after all.

***

They talked at length and the afternoon sped by swiftly, but they reached no agreement on how to proceed. David considered his options, then decided.

"I'm off to Tacuba to see what Raúl was working on before I left.

What time is it?"

"Four-thirty," said Luis, glancing at his watch, "almost time to go home. Time to lock up your boys for the night."

Marco groaned and his chin hit his chest.

Professor Wolf walked to the couch. "Juan...wake up!"

Juan shuddered, then rolled to face the professor, his pain evident. "Leaf me alone. Ith Linda still here?"

"Juan...listen...are you listening?"

"Yef."

"Who would know what's been going on at Tacuba?" A long pause. "Thebathiano."

"Who?"

272

"Sebastiano," said Marco. "You know, the guy who accidentally dug up the Coyolxhauqui stone."

"Linda...call Dina at the Anthro office and get his address. I'm heading to Tacuba. Would you find Sebastiano's house and talk to him?"

"Anything you want, David," she agreed, looking at Juan and touching her belly."

"Captain, even though we accomplished very little, I appreciate your help. We'll start again tomorrow. Can I count on you to see that the boys are properly cared for?"

"Of course. We're not a bunch of incompetents!" Luis huffed, offended. "Tony...you know the new rules? Put them away for the night.

***

Thirty minutes later Linda departed for Sebastiano's and the professor was en route to the Tacuba excavation. Luis busily cleaned his desk top and prepared to go home when Lobo Morales called.

"Luis...just called to thank you for the lead on that assault case you worked last week. I think we've got a positive I.D. from Interpol on that foreigner with the gold wire-rims. He's a Colombian national and a former hit-man for the Medellin Cartel. Colombia will extradite him if we can find him. We've issued a warrant. Thanks for the lead."

"Yeah...well...glad it turned in to something."

As he descended the stone steps of the two-hundred-year-old precinct house, Luis had the distinct feeling that he knew something but had somehow lost it. He'd be glad when things returned to normal. He'd been riding a roller coaster of emotions. Things were looking great until this professor character had showed up. It was tough being civil to the gringo. An academic had no business interfering with professionals. The case had been a wrap up until the fucking politicians intervened. Still, Luis thought grudgingly, the professor seemed a likable sort of guy—and that Galt's Problem thing of his merited some thought. Who knows? Maybe his ideas would turn into something. And too, maybe Luis didn't have anything to lose? If David failed, Captain Alvarado won. If the David's idea proved to be right, Luis still won, because he had helped. This reassured him and placed the day's events in a better perspective. He would leave it alone for now. Time to go home and hug Angela and change the oil in the Mercury. They both required a lot of attention.

Sebastiano

Thursday Evening, July 3, 1984, Mexico City

The cavernous concrete bowels of the subway system thundered with the sound of trains lurching and squealing, transporting millions to and from work through its intricate web off arteries. Sebastiano stepped off the metro at 6:15 p.m. Tired and dirty and preoccupied with thoughts of his new wife, he climbed from the cavern floor, passing the small, recently excavated Aztec temple to Ehecatl, the Monkey god, which excavators discovered during the building of the subway. He surfaced alongside thousands of his brethren, all walking familiar paths and performing similar rituals of work and play.

A pungent mixture of food from the street vendors, exhaust spume, and body odor accosted him. The sky was painted an insipid gray from noxious, airborne poisons ejected into the atmosphere by hundreds of factories and thousands of automobiles. Massive dark thunderheads in the nebulous countenance of Tlaloc stalled on the southern range of the highlands. Poised for assault and gaining strength, they slowly slid into the valley, threatening to purify the stagnant air.

A smog alert was issued. Street salesmen wove in-and-out of bumper-to-bumper traffic, competing to sell filtered breathing masks, braving the traffic like fearless bullfighters. Palm trees stood motionless and dejected, their leaves withering and the palm fronds a brownish yellow from the smog. Some were dead — the rest dying.

The policía, waving martinets in blue-gray, shrilled their whistles and gestured emphatically, directing multitudes of automobiles. Paseo De La Reforma, the grand boulevard, was lined with thousands of automobiles. The drivers ignored the policía and changed lanes at every opportunity, maneuvering between cars, threatening pedestrians and creating chaos as a matter of course.

Moving his heavy arms in rhythm, Sebastiano began the thirteen-block walk to his one-bedroom apartment. Towering stone and concrete buildings walled him in on each side. Aged, grandiose, and staid, they suffered the same benign neglect as the roads and highways of the entire metropolitan area.

He moved with the shifting masses, oblivious to a distracting, cacophony. He had worked the metro excavation for four years and thought himself fortunate. He had a job. After graduating from a nine-month technical program in heavy equipment operation, his brother-in-law had helped him find a job on the excavation crew. Sebastiano's notoriety as the shovel man who inadvertently discovered the Coyolxhauqui Stone six years earlier had opened a few doors to him. With a salary of one-hundred dollars a week, he considered himself part of the growing Mexican middle class. He had saved a little over three hundred dollars which he

276

planned to put toward the purchase of an old GMC pickup truck.

Continuing his trek into the barrio, he resolutely paced off the steps and daydreamed of Maria, his wife of one year. He stared into the distance, he imagined her smiling face, long hair, and the lithe ripples of her body beneath colorful floral print dresses. His abstraction moved to the bedroom and crystallized on images of yesterday's lovemaking. A sense of urgency held him tightly. Part fantasy, part memory, his reverie was broken by a shove from behind and an elbow on his left as the crowd jostled him.

He picked up his pace, moving with the flow, and concentrated on the errands he must complete. Entering the corner farmacia, he purchased items from the señora at the counter while three shoeless children in dirty torn clothes sipped warm cokes and observed curiously. Bag in hand, he exited and walked two blocks to the zapateria to pick up his repaired boots. Three blocks later he entered an abaceria, a small grocery store, and bought corn tortillas, sweet bread, and toilet paper.

With Reforma to his back, he ambled north into the littered, dirty streets of the barrio, the noise from El Centro dissipating as he walked. The familiar odor of cooking food, curbside refuse, and dog mess welcomed him home. Ahead, a group of six youths noisily worried a soccer ball up and down the asphalt pavement, pausing only when the ball lodged beneath a car. The ball recovered, the game continued, shifting from one curb to the other as Sebastiano passed. Laundry hung above from makeshift clotheslines and balcony railings. Drying mops and buckets sat next to potted croton and diffenbachia. A gesturing matron from the balcony above directed a vitriolic voice at an adolescent girl. He quickened his pace, thinking only of his wife and home.

Turning right onto Calle Madero, he walked thirty meters and entered a stairwell; He lumbered to the third floor, turned and walked to his apartment. Pausing to retrieve a key, he unlocked the door. He crossed the threshold and placed his goods on the table, then returned to reset the latch on the door. Doors were never left unlocked in Mexico.

"Maria, I'm home!" He placed the sacks on the table, then, sensing her presence, turned to a slim, smiling girl and accepted her embrace and welcoming kiss. His shoulders tensed and he began to touch her expectantly, his desire growing, but she giggled and stepped away. "Sebastiano, we have a guest. Linda Maria, Sr. Degas's fiancée, wants to talk with you. She's in the back room looking at our wedding pictures. I'll go get her."

Seeing his crestfallen expression, she smiled and teased, "Don't worry, silly, there's time for that later." She sniffed and made a face. "You need a bath, anyway."

The Professor Finds A Grave

Thursday Evening, July 3, 1984, Tacuba Site, Mexico City

A ceiling of clouds hung dark and brooding, promising more rain for the already soaked earth. Lightning had not yet shown itself, but rumbles of discontent echoed from the south. The air felt heavy and thick. It would be pouring soon. David parked his car nearly a hundred meters from the site. He hesitated, considering whether or not to change into boots, then succumbed to his impatience and followed a wide muddy trench, examining it as he walked for stratigraphic irregularities or other evidence of man's handiwork. Virtually all the excavated dirt had been trucked away.

With the exception of an occasional pile of rubble, a clay composite layered much of the Mexico City floor. Formerly a prehistoric lake bed, it occasionally presented a surprise. At the time of the Conquest, Lake Texcoco, though quite large, was all that remained of the ancient body of water. The Aztecs had transported rock from the surrounding mountains to build causeways to connect their island city of Tenochtitlan with the mainland and to construct their temples and pyramids. Because of the valley's clay base, anything of any weight usually sunk to the lake bottom, never to be found again. Indeed, one of the major frustrations of building in Mexico City was the ever-settling lake bed. It was difficult to find an old structure that hadn't settled or tilted, and in some areas the problem had resulted in churches and buildings becoming uninhabitable.

As David walked, he noticed scattered rock lying about. This, he thought curious. The stone appeared to be volcanic; basalt, granite, and larger pieces of very light volcanic rock called tzontle, formed by violent gasses. The Aztecs used tzontle, a very light, porous rock, for buttressing the interior of their pyramids and roads in order to inhibit sinking and settling.

Here, one hundred meters away, he saw the outline of heavy equipment and what seemed to be a large pile of rocks. This excited him greatly, and he picked up his pace, hurrying west alongside the trench. He forgot about Juan and Marco, his mind shifting immediately to the implications of so much rock in the middle of the lake bed. He was thinking of his old maps and the project he had assigned to Linda, when someone hailed him.

"Hola, Professor Wolf," called a security guard. "Haven't seen you for a long time. You're late. Everyone's gone home."

David approached the waiting guard and shook hands, saying, "Best time to look around…when no one's here to bother me."

"Nothing but mud and rock." The guard lifted a mud-caked boot. "The policía came twice asking questions about your man Juan and Raúl Cordoba. I read about Sr. Cordoba in the paper. Bad way to die, but a man like him must have lots of enemies."

"Eh…why do you say that?" asked David.

The guard shrugged. "No one liked him. He talks down to everyone and is rude to the workers. No tears were shed around here when we heard he died."

The professor considered the guard's words. He heard the same thing everywhere he went. The museum director was universally scorned and vilified.

"What's happening here? Juan tells me that Raúl halted construction two weeks ago. Why'd he do that?"

The guard shifted his weight to the other leg. "He told everyone that he found a pile of bones, then cordoned off the area. No one's allowed in that area except for Raúl. That rope," the guard pointed, "is as far as anyone goes without getting their ass chewed."

"That's ridiculous!" snapped David. "This is highly irregular and unprofessional. Why wasn't this reported?"

"I'm only a night watchman, professor." The guard shook his head. "Even when Raúl worked at night he wouldn't allow me to cross the rope. Didn't trust anyone. A couple of times he brought a woman with him in the museum pickup. They would load it with something, then cover the truck bed with a tarp."

Alarms went off in David's head and his excitement grew. The whole scenario had the appearance of Raúl robbing a grave or stealing something. He looked directly into the guard's eye and said, "You don't expect me to believe that you haven't been on the other side of that rope, do you?"

The guard coughed and extracted a pack of cigarettes from his pocket. He offered David a smoke, then said, "No…Raúl didn't believe it either. He accused me of taking something once, but I didn't. Yeah…I've been over there a couple of times." He tapped the end of an unfiltered cigarette on his

281

thumbnail. "There's no one here at night except for Sr. Cordoba, and I was curious. He used to come and work every night, but he's dead now and no one goes over there but me."

"Would you like to give me a tour?"

"Be my guest...it's just a bunch of old bones and trash." The guard led the way through the muck. They hadn't walked thirty meters before standing next to an imposing pile of rock, much of it the light, porous tzontle.

The professor's heart quickened as he surveyed the pile, then he walked to the edge of the trench. There! The causeway! A blind man could see it...about ten meters wide and fifteen meters deep— the old Aztec causeway from the island city of Tenochtitlan leading to Tacuba!

Raúl had discovered it and not told anyone. Why the secrecy? He would have received credit for the discovery, but instead had shut down construction, leaving the excavation crews idle. The answer appeared like revelation! He had discovered something important and didn't want anyone to know. He'd been stealing!

"Is there a ladder around here?" David looked around helplessly.

"You can't be serious," grumbled the guard, looking askance. He peered up at the dark sky and roiling thunderheads, then, seeing the professor's look of resolve, he added, "Awful muddy down there, professor. You'll to ruin your shoes." The guard went to retrieve a ladder while David gazed into the trough.

The trench, cutting through the causeway just northwest of the old road, ran roughly parallel before heading in a straight line for Tacuba. The archaeologist stood on the north side looking south into a newly created, heavily eroded cul-de-sac. A wall of moisture-sodden clay had collapsed, causing a small

282

avalanche of mud to balloon, then cascade into the trench. Large pools of muddy water lay everywhere, and plastic tarps were spread to cover the areas in which Raúl had worked. The site hadn't been measured and staked. There were no visible lines of string to demarcate distance, no controls or boundaries for scientific reference. Raúl had definitely been in a hurry and up to no good.

Gripped with impatience, David nearly jumped into the trench before the security guard produced an aluminum extension ladder, allowing the professor to scurry downward before sinking into muck above his ankles. He carefully placed one foot in front of the other, trying not to slip on the treacherous, wet clay. Sucking, squishing sounds accompanied each step as he slogged his way toward the tarps. Lifting an edge, he rolled a tarp back, draining the water from its top as he moved it aside. Underneath lay a large skeleton.

Visibility was poor in the trench because the overcast sky, and dark shadows hindered visibility. He called out, "Throw me your flashlight." Catching it in mid-air, he switched it on and swept the beam through the area, revealing the bones of a large animal—probably a horse.

Rusted pieces of iron, heavily corroded and not immediately identifiable, lay adjacent to the bones, and the ribs looked as if they had been pulled apart and moved. The excavation area was a mess. This was not the work of an archaeologist. A grave robber had worked here.

He moved around the skeleton and rolled aside another tarp, exposing skulls and long bones, some cast aside in a haphazard fashion. Something caught his eye, causing him to turn and walk toward a large hole in the middle of the trench. His foot tripped on a heavy object. Shining the light beam on the oval, he reached to pick it up—when a thunderbolt of recognition shook him! The skull of a nameless Conquistador, permanently entombed in its helmet, stared vacantly at the professor. It was impossible to mistake the helmet's style.

His breath came in shallow gasps and a surge of adrenaline-induced euphoria cloaked him, allowing his mind to focus on the discovery. This was it! This is what he had dreamed of discovering as a small child sitting under his uncle's shady avocado trees in Veracruz, reading books on the Conquest.

He placed the helmeted skull on the ground and swept the beam over the eroded south wall. Rains had caused large sections to collapse, exposing a jumble of artifacts. Human bones were clearly visible. He sloshed forward, nearly falling as he waded through the mire. Carefully moving the light over the mud pile, a glint of metallic caught his eye. He knelt onto the pile to stretch upward and extract the shiny piece. It was heavy and had lodged in the wet earth, requiring several hard yanks to extract. With shaking hands, he scraped the mud from the piece and placed it atop his knee. His fingers revealed a raised design, so he focused the flashlight on it. It appeared to be a ceremonial shield with a motif. He cleared more mud, then, suddenly, he recognized the image of the War god Huitzilopochtli embossed on the front! He scraped the mud from an edge with his fingernail to verify the find.

Just as he suspected; Raúl Cordoba had stumbled onto the largest graveyard of Conquistadors in the new world and had discovered the lost gold from Moctezuma's temple! David shivered, filled with awe at the discovery. "My God!" he whispered. "I've dreamed of finding this my whole life!"

The flashlight beam swept the area again and stopped on the skull-encased helmet of the Conquistador. According to historical records this area would contain hundreds of bodies;

dead horses, cannon, and the gold of Moctezuma's treasury. It had been thrown into the watery grave of Lake Texcoco by the Conquistadors fleeing the angry Aztecs. The gold was never been recovered, and its value would be impossible to calculate —easily worth millions. In the form of art objects, sculpture, etc., it was priceless.

Light rain fell and beaded on the muddy shield, issuing armies of concentric circles across the flooded trench. He looked around, shining the light everywhere, his excitement reaching a crescendo when, unexpectedly, thunder cracked like a rifle shot, startling him. Lightning traced an incandescent web across the heavens, illuminating the area and creating an eerie, surreal reality.

"Professor...you all right? Did you find something?" called the concerned guard. "Professor, you're getting filthy in the mud. Come back tomorrow when conditions are better. It's raining! Professor...are you okay?"

Mute with wonder, David knelt, unmoving, loathe to do anything other than bask in the euphoria of discovery. Squatting in the mud alongside the collapsed wall, he lovingly ran his hand over the gold shield. The rain quickened and fresh gusts of air swept the trench in curtains, causing him to wonder if the rain god Tlaloc was angry. He would remember this night forever, he thought with joy.

But he was strangely alone in his discovery. A moment of regret tugged at his mind as his thoughts moved fleetingly to Alicia. Too bad that she hadn't lived to share in the discovery. That would have made everything perfect.

"Coming...coming," he called to the worried guard. "You've done a marvelous job of guarding this place. Starting tomorrow this site will be filled with guards, policía, and people from the university. I'll put in a good word for you," he

285

promised, slipping on the ladder. "Here take this," he ordered, struggling to keep his balance, handing the heavy gold shield to the guard before breasting the top rung. Covered with grime, panting and slumped in exhaustion, the joy of discovery coursed through his veins, giving him the strength of a younger man.

"What is it, professor?" asked the bewildered guard, turning the heavy shield over and over in his hands.

"It's Hummingbird-on-The-Left," replied the professor. "He's been buried along with his victims for five hundred years."

Professor Wolf Phones Inspector Alvarado

Thursday Night, July 3, 1984, Mexico City

The storm's fury had abated to the pattering of rain drops against the glass balcony doors of David's apartment. Jagged veins of lightning flickered and illuminated fluorescent nebulas in the swirling thunderheads. The air was fresh and moist and reeked of ozone.

Linda and David, flush with the excitement of their discoveries, sat drinking hot tea and sharing stories. The professor had showered and donned a robe. Unable to contain his excitement, he would rise from the couch and talk about his discovery at Tacuba, recalling different written accounts and comparing them to legend.

Linda listened politely, but was unable to share in his excitement. "David...what about Juan and Marco? How does it all fit together? Sebastiano told me that Raúl found a gold statue with a really big mouth. He staked off the area so that no one else could go in and bother it."

The professor, deep in thought, paced the room. He stopped, his face went blank, then a smile lit his face as insight congealed into understanding.

"Got it!" He held up a finger. "Raúl has been robbing the excavation site and selling the pieces to Hector Vicario. They got into an argument and somehow both ended up dead: a falling out among thieves. That's it! It's simple." He spread his arms. "That's the motive—gold and greed!

I'm going to call that cop at home." David went into his study and dialed the number on Luis' business card.

"Bueno?"

"Captain Alvarado?"

"Yes…is that you, David?"

"Got it…listen close!" He detailed the findings at Tacuba and Linda's visit with Sebastiano and his new wife.

Twenty minutes later the captain grudgingly said, "I'm happy for you, gringo. It sounds like an incredible discovery. It seems that Cordoba was…how is it you said…robbing graves? However, unless I'm missing something, there still isn't any evidence to blame Hector's or Raúl's deaths on anyone except Degas. We already know from the report that they stole from the museum. Maybe Degas discovered that Raúl Cordoba had discovered the Aztec causeway and they argued. Maybe he killed both men because of it. That fits with the scenario and provides an additional motive for the murder. I've need evidence that implicates Vicario or Cordoba in the death of the other."

"What about the statue? Sebastiano saw it!"

"That was a gold statue. You saw the one that killed the minister in my office. It's made of cheap green onyx."

"Then he switched them! Don't you see?"

"Then where's the original, David? Find that one and we'll have a place to start looking. I need evidence to prove a link between the two men."

The phone to his ear, David slumped into a chair, deflated and tired. He ran his thick fingers through his hair and frowned, unable to rebut the detective's scenario. Neither spoke, each assimilating the new information. Then the professor said, "Tell me this…don't you think my discovery at Tacuba, Raúl's grave robbing, the gold statue, and the murders are all related?"

Luis considered the question, then replied, "I've been thinking about your statement that we are approaching this investigation from the wrong direction, focusing on the wrong sets of relationships, and confusing cause and effect. Yes…there's a possibility they're related. But again, we must link the murders to someone other than Juan and Marco. I'll give it some thought and you do the same. We'll put our heads together tomorrow, okay?"

"Yeah…sure…sorry I bothered you," mumbled David, vexed at his failure. He hung up and turned to Linda.

"Tomorrow we quit looking for reasons why Juan and Marco are innocent. We're going to look for evidence that Vicario and Cordoba are guilty."

Captain Alvarado Wakes Up

Friday, July 4, 1984, 3:00 A.M. Mexico City

His legs twitched and jerked, then Luis bolted upright in bed. Soaked with sweat, his pulse raced and he gasped for air; the nightmare remained vivid and recent. What was it? Who in his dream had caused him to waken? The glasses, those gold wire-rim glasses sitting on the evidence table. They belonged to Lobo's Colombian terrorist! Luis had seen them on the dirty guy with the foreign accent, and they had screamed for attention. The charred, dead guy at the museum hadn't been a mechanic, he was Lobo's Colombian hit-man! He must have planted the bomb that murdered the museum director and inadvertently killed himself doing so.

The clock said 3:00 a.m. and Luis sat wide-eyed on the edge of his bed. Unresolved issues frequently turned him into an insomniac. He threw the covers aside and padded into the bathroom to wash his face in cold water. He peered into the mirror. Who would know a Colombian terrorist or avail themselves of his services? Not Juan Degas, that's for sure. Only a wealthy, politically powerful man could afford or risk it.

Hector Vicario. The name came to mind immediately. Vicario had hired the murder of Cordoba. Why? Double cross? Blackmail? Did Cordoba poison Vicario? If so, why? What was the motive? Who did what to whom? Questions— never resolution.

The thug at the church who dumped the priest down the stairs—Luis remembered the description; big man, hairy chest, gold bracelet, white patent-leather shoes with gold buckles. He tried to recall the clothes Vicario wore the night of his death. A gold bracelet lay on the table, and Luis would bet a year's pay that the minister had worn white patent-leather shoes the night of his death. Why had he gone to the wrong side of the church confessional? Waiting for the Colombian? Bizarre, thought Luis, absolutely bizarre.

He continued to stare into the mirror, weighing the evidence within the new framework. Maybe Degas and Gonzalez were innocent? Suddenly he remembered, "Aww shit!" and hurriedly left the bathroom to call the morgue, even though he believed it to be too late. If not claimed within three days bodies were routinely cremated and Luis felt certain that no crying, distraught family member had come to claim the Colombian's body.

Five minutes later a morgue attendant confirmed his fear. The body had been cremated the previous evening. Luis requested the autopsy report and photographs, then thanked the attendant. He cradled the phone. It wouldn't be enough, he realized with gloom. He had to have a body to do a positive I.D., and a John Doe autopsy and pictures wouldn't suffice. He would show it to Lobo tomorrow and see what he thought.

291

At 3:30 Luis returned to bedroom, thinking that perhaps the professor had been right. Degas and Gonzalez were innocent and the gringo's fantastic discovery at Tacuba would be powerful motivation to murder. If so, the policía had made a move of incalculable stupidity by arresting Degas and Gonzalez. It shocked him to think that he had encouraged Jose to arrest them, then passively acquiesced when his boss had decided to torture them. The policía had proceeded in haste, nearly convicting and executing the wrong men. He considered the gringo with new respect. He truly believed that his boys were innocent and he might be right. Luis berated himself. He had just been taught a valuable lesson by an amateur. Tomorrow the Mexico City Police Department would bust ass to find the real murderer. He would put everything he had into the investigation. Nothing mattered but the truth.

Captain Alvarado lay next to his sleeping wife, deep in thought, his mind still sorting and sifting. It occurred to him that he still couldn't release Gonzalez and Degas, but things were looking better for them. He didn't know the link between Cordoba and Vicario, but now they had some idea where to look. The professor would be delighted at the new development. He closed his eyes and exhaled. His breathing became shallow and two minutes later he lay sound asleep.

Filth Eater

The Conquistadors did not understand that the Flowery Wars were pre-arranged engagements with selected opponents for the purpose of securing captives. If you took a captive you won great honor. If you became a prisoner you earned greater honor and, in most cases, went willingly to the sacrificial stone knowing that your soul would enter The Paradise of the Sun. Compare this holy practice, if you will, with the "wars" of the bleached faces. Thousands are slaughtered in meaningless, unholy deaths. Victims are dispatched into hell without benefit of holy purpose or the blessing of their God. The victim's blood is spilled, unconsecrated and meaningless—a gift to no one. This is truly filth, the real cruelty and violence, and it is committed by the bleached faces on behalf of their "Redeemer," whom they sacrifice and re-sacrifice daily in ritual enactment.

The bleached ones speak of their "Redeemer" as the "Ultimate Sacrifice." They say that no more sacrifices are needed—no one else is as perfect or as pure a sacrifice as He is. Perhaps, but it seems filthy to me. In The One Universe it was considered hubris for the people to sacrifice one god to another god. These were matters left to the gods themselves. The bleached ones have a filthy, weak, and inconsistent ideology. They have replaced the piety and beauty of The One Universe with ignorance and filth.

Juan Insults Marco's Woman

Friday Morning, July 4, 1984, 9:00 A.M. Mexico City

The precinct house hummed with activity. David squirmed in his chair, barely able sit still. Though early in the morning, yesterday's acrimony and discontent had yielded to a simmering excitement. The vibes were more positive. David's discoveries at Tacuba and Luis' new theory of Raúl's murder imbued everyone with hope. The captain had delivered the autopsy report to Lobo's secretary and requested that he call upon arrival. Tony was bringing the long-delayed transcription of the phone logs.

Professor Wolf, his taste for discovery whetted, could not focus on the investigation. The discovery at Tacuba had become his immediate concern. He had notified the policía to place armed guards at the site to prevent looting, then checked in with the Anthropology Department. Linda sulked in a chair, upset that Luis refused to release Juan and Marco, even though he agreed they might be innocent.

295

Tony arrived with the phone logs and informed everyone that Juan and Marco would finish eating and bathing soon. A cursory glance at the Vicario house phone logs brought groans of despair. It would take a month to trace the numbers without a computer, if such a program even existed at this point. Computers promised a lot, but had delivered very little that was useful as far as Luis was concerned. Computers the future? Luis doubted it. The Vicario house had four phones and the calls came and went to residences all over the city and country. The minister must have been on the phone all the time he was at home. At first glance, the museum phone logs seemed less daunting and showed promise of being easier to identify anomalies within patterns. Most of the numbers were identified as vendors of goods and services and others as calls to Raúl's mother's home, where he lived. Late night calls to the Vicario home were immediately identified, and several of the numbers had university prefixes.

"If I were to flag anything, it would be these," Tony pointed. "The prefix identifies them as being a residence close to the museum. If it's okay with you, Paulo and I will start checking some of these. I got some addresses from the phone company."

"Go ahead," encouraged Luis, "and start with that number near the museum. I'm curious. Do we have a museum employee that lives close by?"

Juan and Marco traipsed in looking disgruntled. The swelling in Juan's face had diminished considerably, but had turned dark. One eye had swollen shut. The other had red streaks and lay inset within a swollen, black-purple hematoma. Marco, completely ambulatory now, moved around with ease and made sarcastic comments concerning jail hospitality.

"Good news and bad news, guys," said the professor, anxious to relate his discovery to someone who would appreciate it. But before he began, Linda, who had been eyeing the new arrivals, interrupted.

"What's going on? You two been arguing again?"

Neither spoke for a moment then Juan said, "It's not important. He's finally agreed that I'm right."

"Drop it Juan! Do I need to ask for a cell transfer?" Marco's hands clenched into fists. "You haven't exactly made a lot of bright decisions yourself lately."

"What's this all about?" demanded David. "Aren't you in bad enough shape without arguing among yourselves? Come on, spit it out!"

Marco looked askance at Juan, who returned the look. Juan said, "Aw…it's my fault…I guess. I called his girlfriend a puta." He frowned, contorting his swollen face. "I've never liked her. When I worked at the museum she was sleeping with the boss. She used to try and get me into bed even though she was having an affair with Raúl. If Marco hadn't gone chasing her skirt, we'd both have an alibi."

Tony and Luis's eyes joined. Tony said, "Amparo Ocampo didn't check in yesterday. I sent Pedro to look for her. He's at the Apollo now."

Luis held up his hand. "Degas…are you saying that Amparo was having an affair with Raúl Cordoba and Hector Vicario at the same time, while continuing to make sexual overtures to you?"

"I didn't know about Vicario, but everyone at the museum knew she and Raúl had a thing going. It wouldn't surprise me, though. The woman has no boundaries. Anyone who'd go out with Marco would have to be a blind social worker or on a

297

mission of mercy!" he joked, trying to assuage the hurt in Marco's eyes.

Luis stared through the plate glass and into the Central Investigation Room. Cheating on her sugar daddy and having a fling on the side with her boss? All the while chasing Juan Degas and trying to get him between the sheets? Wait a minute, Luis berated himself, realizing he might have messed up again. He thought it through. She's a snake, he decided, a duplistic two-timing puta. Had she played one against the other? Were men playthings and toys? Did she envision herself as the puppeteer? If so, what was her motive? Why would she risk everything to have an affair with an effeminate reptile like Raúl?

"Tony...have Pedro call me as soon as he returns. Our Little Miss Innocent has some explaining to do. Arrest her. She's playing us for fools." He looked again at Degas and Gonzalez, then said, "Okay, this is the new plan. Tony instead of the apartment, call the Señorita Vicario and make arrangements with **Tactical** to get us into that vault. I don't care what it takes. Find out where Vicario bought the locks and have them open it. Knock the damn door down if you have to. She can't stonewall us any longer. We must get in for a look. Our motive may be in there waiting."

To David, he said, "Gringo, you and I will stop by that apartment near the museum, then meet Tony at the Vicario home. That vault is full of archaeological pieces and your expertise will be invaluable. Agreed?"

"I'd love to," said the professor.

"Young lady...can you entertain our guests until we return?" asked Luis.

"You couldn't make me leave," she insisted, her hand resting on her abdomen.

298

"Tony…get someone to watch these guys, and radio Pedro about Amparo Ocampo. See you at Vicario's." He headed for the door with David in tow.

"Hey, professor!" called Juan, "what's the good news?"

David, with a munificent smile, said, "Thought you'd never ask. I've discovered Moctezuma's gold!"

"Yeah? Well…that's great…I guess," said Juan, unbelieving and disappointed at the absence of good news. "I thought it might be something like that."

As Luis and the professor strode down the dark hall they heard an exclamation from the office, "You're kidding?!! Really?"

Amparo Plans To Leave

Friday, July 4, 1984, 10:00 A.M., Mexico City

Amparo parked her blue VW bug and walked the final block to El Mercado de Coyohuacan. The outdoor market, covering four square blocks, had virtually everything imaginable; vendors, jewelers, leather works of every kind, shoes, sandals, blankets, pottery, curios, food, and more. The stalls were arranged haphazardly and one couldn't move too quickly for fear of hitting one's head on hanging sandals or bumping into onyx chess sets. Its odor was unmistakable; refuse, leather, cooking food, rotting meat, and diesel exhaust presented themselves as one.

She stopped to purchase a ball of sisal rope and heavy strapping tape. From there she threaded a crowded aisle, looking for the joyeria, the jewelry shop she saw on her last visit. She paused in front of six plucked chickens that hung from a line above her head and inquired from the butcher the location of the jeweler. The butcher's wife, meanwhile, soaked paper-thin strips of beef in lime and salt, then hung them to dry over yellow polyester twine amid swarms of black flies.

300

The head of the cow from which the meat had come sat on a spike and stared balefully through black eyes. Potential customers, of course, want to see for themselves the source of their purchase. Amparo listened carefully, thanked the butcher, then crossed to the other side of the market. She asked instructions twice more before finding the jeweler. She was loathe to part with the gold necklace, a gift from Hector, but the money saved from his occasional gifts had long since disappeared on frivolous shopping sprees.

Amparo had decided to leave town with her new friend. They would go first to Chihuahua to visit her sister, then on to Nogales to make arrangements to enter the United States. She had grown weary of being used and abused by men and her new friend had experienced much the same horror as she. Bonding immediately, they had developed an intense friendship in only a few days and decided to leave Mexico City together. Her friend had valuable connections in Nogales and Amparo had a sister whom she hadn't seen in eight years.

She finished haggling with the jeweler, who gave her a quarter of what the necklace was worth. It would do for now. She opened her purse to place the money in her wallet, moving aside a .32 automatic pistol in order to do so. The pistol sparked a memory and she repressed a twinge of guilt as the recollection of her last boyfriend, lying dead in a scarlet pool of blood, soaking soft the hard-packed soil of the Chihuahua desert came to mind. Her boyfriend of one month, Gregorio, had beaten her senseless again after an imagined infidelity. It had occurred one time too many and when he stopped at a Pemex for gasoline, she had taken his pistol from under the seat and forced him out of the car and onto a lonely stretch of desert road in Zacatecas. Tearful, angry beyond control and half out of her mind, she shot him like the rabid dog he was.

No one saw the deed. Trembling and fearful with the enormity of the act, she turned the car north, leaving Gregorio to a merciless desert and its scavengers. She drove to El Paso and boarded a southbound bus and returned to her place of birth, Mexico City. In a country with few computers and a city of twenty million, no one ever questioned or connected her with the crime. It became just one more item on a long list of unresolved and shameful, guilt-ensconced acts which she pushed into the recesses of her memory to fester and rot.

But the time had come to hire a truck and driver to transport the six boxes she refused to ship on the train. The train wasn't safe. Things were easily stolen, and these valuable crates and boxes were her future - all she had to show of her life in Mexico City. They also bulged with priceless stolen artifacts from the Tacuba site; each worth a fortune many times over.

Seeing the gun brought to mind her promise to herself and her new friend, Lupe. No more men. They were all ass-holes; brutal, selfish, insensitive pigs incapable of love. Men were from another planet. Her new companion had suffered the same misogyny time and again— physical and emotional abuse, hatred and spiritual neglect. Amparo was finished being a sperm receptacle and mother/whore to crippled, inadequate men.

Hector and Raúl got what they deserved. Amparo didn't believe in hell, but if it did exist, she hoped they both roasted and suffered plenty for what they had done to her. They were just like her father—mean, abusive cretins.

Lupe's Colombian lover, Cholo, had inexplicably deserted her and his beautiful white stucco on Calle Oso, but not before beating her until her face had swollen and her arms turned black and green with bruises earned in her defense. The bruises would heal. The hurt and betrayal were invisible, but permanently indelible, forever carved into the psyche of a fragile personality.

She knew Lupe from when Hector used her to deliver messages to Cholo. Her attraction to Lupe had been immediate, and their relationship had grown stronger the last three days as they shared their stories and aspirations in this apartment near the museum. Amparo had found her first true female friend and would allow nothing to interfere with her plans to take this treasure north and cash in on a new life. Soon they would never want for anything again.

Thirty minutes later, emboldened with her plan and anxious to execute it, she pulled into the parking lot of the apartment complex. It felt great to be leaving! The truck and loaders would arrive within the hour and she needed to finish tying the boxes and firming up the sides with strapping tape. Small sturdy crates already held the heavy pieces and were nailed shut and ready to go. She opened the door of Raúl's plush apartment, and called out.

"Lupe! Lupe, I'm back, dear. Come and help me finish with these boxes. The movers will arrive soon and they must be sealed or there'll be trouble."

Amparo dropped the purchased goods onto the couch and went into the kitchen seeking her new friend. She thought it peculiar that Lupe didn't answer. Amparo had told her that she would be gone about an hour. The boxes sat unattended and unpacked, and the room was strewn with pieces of gold and silver jewelry. Priceless artifacts stolen from the Tacuba excavation lay everywhere in disarray.

She considered the missing Lupe a moment, then decided to go to the bathroom. She retrieved her purse, and upon turning around, found Lupe standing in the bedroom doorway.

"Amparo, some men are here to see you," said Lupe, her voice tremulous with emotion, "and one of them is a policía."

Captain Alvarado stepped into the room from behind Lupe, his hand gun cocked and pointed at Amparo. David stepped out of the bathroom at his side.

"You're under arrest for conspiracy to murder and for theft and conspiracy to sell pre-Colombian antiquities. Drop that purse and get down on the floor."

Amparo quickly moved and hid behind one of the crates, withdrew her pistol and fired at Luis, who'd shoved Lupe to the side. Amparo's pistol barked loudly three times, striking Lupe in the head and Captain Alvarado in the shoulder and leg. He groaned, rolled off the fallen Lupe and onto his stomach, and returned fire.

A long, mournful wail rose from behind the crate as Amparo snapped, realizing she'd shot her only friend. She screamed and hurled insults, reacting like a cornered scorpion as rage and fear drove her into a familiar abyss of insanity. Her childhood friends, clamoring rapacious demons, welcomed her home. An intimate darkness cloaked her as she stepped into her personal hell, oblivious to reason and purpose, a martyr to her father's sins.

A hail of bullets popped and splintered the apartment as Luis kept her pinned behind a crate. The professor dove into the bedroom and looked frantically for a weapon or mode of escape. In his first gun battle without a gun, a quick terror seized him like the terrible jaws of a crocodile. His brain vibrated with adrenaline-induced responses that insisted he run or fight. Frantic, he sighted the balcony door and quickly opened it while the gun battle raged inside. Pop! Pop! A moan from Lupe and a wet gurgle as she choked. A shout from Luis.

From the balcony, policía cars sped into the parking lot, responding to their hurried radio transmission for help. Tony jumped from a car with his Colt .45 automatic in hand and sprinted up the sidewalk.

"Third floor…apartment 312!" screamed David from the balcony. The big detective waved acknowledgement with his gun and hit the stairs, taking them two at a time, until he reached the top floor gasping for air. He quickly checked the room numbers, heard two more shots, and charged to the end of the hall. He fired a shot into the door lock and kicked it wide. He stood with the gun gripped in both hands pointed directly at Amparo's back.

"Freeze bitch, or you're dead!" he yelled at the terrified woman who reluctantly dropped her gun onto the floor.

"Please…daddy," cried the tortured young woman. She gave the confused detective a wan smile. "Don't hurt me, daddy. We can do it if you want. You don't need a gun to do it with me."

"What…the…?" Confused, Tony's mouth hung slack, then he quickly recovered. "You crazy bitch. Down on the floor before I put you in the ground with your mother Malinche!"

Juan And Linda Drink Champagne

Saturday, November 5, 1984, Presidential Palace (Three Months
Later)

Clinking champagne glasses and joyous laughter contested
with the upbeat rhythms of the mariachi band inside the
presidential residence of El Pino. Dark-suited secret service
agents patrolled the outer walls of the two-acre backyard while
others mixed with the guests. Linda Maria and Juan were
celebrating their wedding reception at the home of El
Presidente and his wife, Concepcion. Well-dressed children
scurried back and forth across the spacious green Bermuda,
playing chase games and energizing the palatial back-yard.
Juan and Linda, champagne glasses in hand, stood in the shade
of a long row of bald cyprus, accepting the felicitations of
wedding guests.

It was a celebration of Mexico and a gathering of winners.
Feature writers for the city newspapers had trumpeted their
adventures shamelessly, making them overnight heroes. Juan

and Marco's suffering, the murders of prominent citizens, Moctezuma's gold, the attempted theft of priceless antiquities, and the climactic shoot-out at the Coyohuacan apartment were a writer's dream come true.

Captain Alvarado, limping but sporting a new white suit, earnestly engaged El Presidente and Marco in conversation about vintage automobiles.

Linda Maria's father, Mario, reveled in attention, gloriously drunk and happy as a pig in a wallow of excrement. He fully approved of Juan's friends and always knew the boy would make it big someday. His son-in-law's promotion to the Directorship of the National Museum of Anthropology made his chest swell with pride, and he alternately cried and laughed with happiness.

Concepcion steered the professor toward the mansion and into the charge of a beautiful, rich, 55-year-old widow who wanted the whole story. She sat on the edge of her chair, rapt, punctuating his narrative with appropriate sounds of incredulity, sympathy, and laughter. David hadn't felt this comfortable in the presence of a mature woman in twenty years, and he began to wax eloquent in his rendition.

"...and so...then we knew Raúl had found the site of the Conquistadors' massacre. Earlier, he'd removed a gold statue of the Aztec goddess Tlazolteotl, also known as Filth Eater, and made the mistake of telling Hector Vicario. Hector, of course, wanted it, but didn't know that it was made of gold. Raúl realized that Hector would want everything and he panicked. Amparo, Hector's mistress, was planted at the museum by Vicario to spy on Raúl, but she immediately began having an affair with Raúl. They met for trysts during the day at a nearby apartment and Amparo slept with Vicario at night.

307

Intriguing woman, wouldn't you agree?" He took a sip of his champagne.

"But how did each kill the other, without the other suspecting?" she asked, placing her hand on his knee for just an instant, then removing it. "Amparo forced the issue by bringing Hector a copy of Juan's report. Juan had written it a year ago, but Vicario knew nothing of it. It scared him to death, and he blamed Cordoba for not telling him. So…he hired a terrorist to kill Raúl with a bomb. In the meantime, Amparo and Raúl were robbing the Tacuba excavation of all the gold they could find, which was a lot. We've uncovered nearly a metric ton!" He smiled radiantly, flashing his pearly teeth at the widow. "She encouraged Raúl to kill Hector, before Vicario killed the museum director, then left for the U.S.A. with Marco Gonzalez. This implicated both Marco and Juan as having a motive, and left them no alibi."

"How fascinating! Tell me David, could we go for a short walk in the yard?" She smiled and leaned towards him, her hand resting lightly on his knee. "I could use another glass of champagne and some air."

"Of course!" he volunteered, offering his arm. They strolled to the champagne fountain for a refill, then walked in the shade of the west wall. The professor felt alive and vibrant in the company of Alexandra, and old familiar behaviors, long discarded from lack of use, reasserted themselves. He walked with a spring in his step, occasionally glancing at the refined, stylish Spaniard accompanying him. Her shapely profile caught his attention in a way no woman had for many years.

"Did they ever identify the poison used to kill Hector Vicario?" She stopped to sip from her glass, still curious about the story.

"He was killed by a derivative of curare, a neurotoxin extracted from the skin of poison-arrow frogs found in the Amazon. Amparo says that Raúl stole them from the National Zoo across the street from the museum. He took them to a witch in Puebla who showed him how to extract the poison with urine and lye."

"Yech." Her nose wrinkled. "What ever happened to that gold statue? I read somewhere that a fake statue was used to kill the minister."

"Don't know, but according to one witness it stood 20 centimeters tall and weighed over six kilos. My theory is that it was likely a family heirloom, the Filth Eater used by Moctezuma himself. It may have been in his family for generations. Who knows?"

"David, you're a fascinating man, so interesting! It must be wonderful to work with such intriguing things." She leaned against him as they walked beneath the protective shadows of El Pino's walls. After a few more steps she suddenly changed the subject.

"David...do you dance?"

Alarmed, he said, "Oh no! I haven't danced in over twenty years. I'm sure I've forgotten how."

"Nonsense!" replied the elegant lady at his elbow. Taking his arm, she guided him toward the house and the Mariachi band. "It's like making love...once you begin, you never forget."

Filth Eater

There are many among the bleached souls who employ their religion as a tool of deceit. The Spaniards were such a people. Their priests routinely destroyed places in The One Universe that had special religious significance. New buildings were erected, some of them beautiful and grandiose, but always upon a site deemed holy to the gods. This was filthy — to surreptitiously place profane structures and ideas upon the holy spots of The One Universe. The confusion resulting from this filthy act is still apparent today — five-hundred years — after the coming of the Bleached Ones.

The peasants of The One Universe's many villages enact religious rites that are neither Christian nor Aztec. They are a fusion, a synthesis of belief systems that are filthy because the new system is impure. This synthesis is a lie.

Four-hundred years of slavery and five-hundred years of poverty changed the inhabitants of The One Universe into an estranged people. They now profess to having been born filthy like the Christians, but their Creole religious rites show that they pine for the meaning and ritual of the old gods. But, I fear it is too late. Though unaware of it, the people of The One Universe engage in filth daily. They have become slaves to the religion of their Christian Filth Eater and mindless adherents to dogma unrelated to his teachings. Those who are not believers have no alternate belief system and no conscience. Perhaps it's true? Maybe the bleached ones were born filthy? If so, my services are surely needed.

Epilogue

Saturday, September 30, 1984, Puebla Highlands Three Months Later

Eighty miles to the southwest, high in the mountains of Puebla State, a small boy stood smoking tobacco to ward off evil spirits and demonstrate his respect for the shamaness. He hated tobacco and it made him ill, but it paled in comparison to the apprehension he felt at being here at the witch's house. Her home sat apart from the village, comfortably nestled between a small arroyo and a narrow percolating stream of water that meandered from the highlands into the fertile green valleys below. The snow-capped peaks of the volcanoes Popocatepetl and Iztacciutatl, primordial lovers in the earliest lore of the Indians, loomed huge and crystal clear in the late afternoon sun.

"Go home, little one! I know your grandmother. Tell your father I'll come after the priest is finished."

The frightened ten-year-old ran without stopping until he reached the other side of town and entered a small house. Its white exterior was stained and dirty and the stucco distempered and cracked and fallen onto the sidewalk. Dimly lit, but immaculately clean, the home's furnishings of wicker and pine identified the inhabitants as poor. Pictures of the Virgin of Guadeloupe were placed in each room and candles were lit to provide light. The home had no bathroom, running water, or electricity.

A Catholic priest, his back bent in concentration, sat on a stool next to a dying elderly woman, hearing her last confession. The priest had known her for many years and knew her to be a good person, yet she seemed troubled by things she'd done seventy years ago as a young girl. He listened politely to her short list of venial sins, then gave her absolution. They prayed together then he patted her arm and left the small, dark room.

The family thanked him for coming and brought a cup of strong black coffee, brewed fresh and stout. They conversed about the tragedy of old age, the beauty of God's promise of another life, and then he rose to take his leave.

The priest, stooped with arthritis, slowly crossed the cobblestone street, and with great effort, lifted himself over the steep curb. He walked past rows of doors, each an entry to a separate household. The connected homes, a fortress block of stucco, were virtually indistinguishable, yet he knew who lived in each and everything about the inhabitants. One could not shepherd a flock without knowing the sheep.

***

Doña Lenora, the shamaness, slowly made her way across town. The sick woman was a very good friend of her mother's, and urgency drove Dona Lenora to arrive before the old

313

woman died. Her mother, a shamaness in the old tradition, had taught her everything she knew of the old gods and spirits. Dona Lenora had taken on the onerous, thankless job of healer and intermediary to the old gods.

She was Catholic, or tried to be, but one couldn't ignore the old gods and spirits. The villagers frequently called upon her to perform an old ritual, undertake a healing, or guide a ceremony. The old priest barely tolerated her activities and sometimes cursed and reviled her, but she didn't care. The town's people trusted and respected her and she valued this more than anything.

Dona Lenora's grandmother was one of the few survivors in the *War of The Witches* that took place in the late 1800's in Puebla State. Most of the witches died violent deaths in a feud whose beginning and cause was long forgotten. She remembered well the stories of her mother, and had become a serious student of the old healing arts and rituals before her first communion at age seven.

Today she was urgently needed and had not hesitated to respond to the call for help. She tightened the colorful rebozo scarf around her neck and shoulders to protect against the chill of the high altitude cold. Her basket was heavily laden and clumsy with weight. As she turned the corner, she bumped into and nearly flattened the old priest making his way back to the church.

"Ahhg! It's you! What evil are you perpetrating this dark day?"

"Excuse me, padre. I was on my way to perform an errand," she replied, moving to avoid a confrontation.

"An errand you say? That's a lie! I know where you're going! What do you have in the basket? More of your trash for the black arts? Take heed, woman! Satan is preparing a bed for you

314

from which you will never escape!" he threatened, shaking a fist.

"Goodbye, padre. I'm in a hurry." She ignored his threats and walked on, leaving him to fume and rant at her retreating figure.

The family was waiting, and quickly ushered Dona Lenora into the back bedroom and left her alone with the dying woman.

"Thank you for coming, old friend," whispered the small, frail, raisin-faced woman on the bed. "I have much to say...some of which I've never told anyone."

"I understand. That's why we're here," said the shamaness as she extracted a beautifully burnished gold statue of Tlazolteotl giving birth to the Corn god, Centeotl.

When approached by the bald-headed bureaucrat with the soft hands, Dona Lenora had driven a hard bargain. He had brought the gold Tlazolteotl to her under the pretense of academic research, seeking her esoteric knowledge of poisons and animals. But she knew him to be a liar and up to no good purpose, and immediately upon seeing the gold Filth Eater had recognized it for what it was: an ancient, sacred treasure of the Great Ones, the Aztecs. She insisted on a trade, wanting to save it from the certain corruption it would endure at his hands. A deal was struck—her knowledge and a cheap, green onyx imitation of the Filth Eater in trade for the gold one. Desperate for her assistance, he had capitulated.

But now, in the flickering shadows, the only light came from candles and the only sound the labored breathing of the old woman. Dona Lenora held the goddess in her lap, craddling it like a child. Closing her eyes and opening herself as a vessel through which the spiritual mysteries flow, she said, "You may begin, señora. The Filth Eater is here to eat the sins of your long life."

Fin

www.ingramcontent.com/pod-product-compliance
Lightning Source LLC
Chambersburg PA
CBHW071105250626
47159CB00002B/603